PROMISES

EILEEN DONOVAN

WALDORF PUBLISHING

Published by Waldorf Publishing
2140 Hall Johnson Road
#102-345
Grapevine, Texas 76051
www.WaldorfPublishing.com

Promises

ISBN: 978-1-64316-629-2
Library of Congress Control Number: 2018943865

Copyright © 2019

For Donald, my eternal muse.

Not all victims of war lie on the battlefield.

The promise given was a necessity of the past: the word broken is a necessity of the present.

Niccolo Machiavelli

Chapter 1

"Farming or fishing?" The matron's hand waited to grab the right stamp. "Come on, come on! We don't have all day for you to decide." Her bulldog face glared at Colin and me from behind the heavy metal desk.

She terrifies me so much I can't even answer her. This is nothing like the grand adventure I thought it would be.

"Well?" she barked.

"I like fishing, Lizzie," Colin's tiny voice whispered. He squeezed my hand so tightly it hurt. I looked down into my little brother's eyes and saw fear and confusion. I wanted to grab him and run back home to Mum.

"Fishing it is," the matron said, and stamped our papers with a force that shook the desk and made us jump. "Next!"

Another matron attached a baggage tag to our collars: "Children's Overseas Reception Board (CORB)" with our names, a number (mine was #158, Colin's was #159), and our destination – Halifax, Nova Scotia. A different matron herded us to long wooden benches in the corner of the cavernous room. The ceiling must have been three stories high and the walls were dirty gray concrete. One wall was missing. The open space led directly to the docks and the sea. Workers and seamen roared orders to get the ships loaded while the squawking gulls circled above looking for scraps of food.

"Girls to the left, boys to the right."

"No!" Colin screeched. "Don't leave me, Lizzie. I'm scared."

Me too. Everyone shivered from both fear and the biting wind that tore through the room. Only the matrons, with their warm woolen shawls, seemed immune as they patrolled the aisles alongside the benches.

"It's okay, Colin. Soon we'll be on the boat, together again, and out in the warm sunshine," I said wrapping my arm around his shoulders and pulling him close. "Here, don't forget your gas mask."

"Do I have to? I hate that thing. It stinks."

"I know, but you won't have to wear it much longer. Soon we'll be away from here."

I hated the gas masks too. They were made of rubber and covered your whole face. An air filter hung down from the bottom like an elephant's trunk. The plastic eye shields misted over in hot weather so you could hardly see through them. Each one came with its own cardboard case and string, so you could carry it over your shoulder wherever you went.

"Let's go," the matron said. "I don't have time for your nonsense or crying. And, you should have been carrying your own mask. What would you do if your sister was separated from you? Now take a seat and be quiet or you'll answer to that man."

I looked where she pointed. A giant of a man sat on a tall stool placed behind a podium that stood in front of the benches. He smacked his switch against the palm of his hand and stared. His dark beady eyes burrowed right through me. I had seen that look before from teachers and headmasters. I knew there would be no warning, only the swish of his switch on my back. I gave Colin's shoulder a quick shove, sat down, and folded my hands in my lap. He stared at me in horror. I had never pushed him away before. *I think I'm going to be sick.*

After I settled on the rough wooden bench, I stole a quick glance across the aisle at Colin. He sat rubbing his palms up and down his thighs, a habit he had when he was scared. I had promised Mum I would never leave him alone, would always protect him. Now in the first hour after arriving at the departure dock, I had left him alone. *How can I watch out for him if he's not sitting next to me?* My stomach churned. *I know I'm going to be sick any minute.* I raised my hand to ask to be excused, and just as quickly pulled it back down. *If I turn sick, they won't let me go on the ship. Then Colin will really be alone.* I took a deep breath and swallowed hard. I had to make sure Colin understood I would never leave him. We all have to be brave now, just as brave as our boys fighting Jerry. I glanced at Colin again and smiled reassuringly. An older boy, seated next to him, held his hand for a minute. I nodded my thanks to him. Colin looked up at him, turned and gave me a weak smile. *We'll make it through this.*

I looked around the room. A line of children stretched out the door. *How many more are there?* There were already about a hundred boys and girls bunched together on the benches. Everyone looked frightened and worn out. I was tired and hungry. My feet were numb from the cold concrete floor, and my body ached from sitting still. There was also the constant fear of one of the matrons slapping me for some imaginary wrongdoing. One of the boys had already been slapped for whispering. At least that's what the matron said he did. Or worse yet, the ogre in charge of the room might come down from his high stool and lash me for disobedience. I had seen it happen in school. Was it my turn now?

I forced myself to think of other things. The familiar scent of the salty sea wafted through the opening along with the stench of the rotting garbage on the docks and in the harbor's waters. I could hear the waterfront rats scurrying around the corners of the room, always prowling for something to eat. The hard, rough wooden bench was making my bum numb. I wondered how many other children had waited on them and if they'd been as nervous as I was at that moment.

I stared at the ceiling and tried to imagine what Canada would be like. What a glorious adventure I had hoped this would be. I crossed my fingers and prayed I was right.

Chapter 2

After hours of waiting in the dockside warehouse, a Navy officer came in and talked to the ogre at the front of the room.

"There'll be no sailing today. Too many U-boats in the area to ship out safely."

"What are we supposed to do with all these children?"

"We made arrangements with a school and a factory down the road to house them for the night. It's the best we could do. With luck, we'll sail tomorrow."

"Thank you, Lieutenant. Matron, let's get the children lined up and over to the school."

"Yes, sir. Children, listen up. The matrons will line you up in twos by rows. Be quick now, and no talking."

Margaret became my partner on the walk over from the docks, but I didn't know her name until later that day. She would soon become my best friend. When we got there, we were led to a large gymnasium-like room. Its walls were a dull light green color, and the wooden floor was scratched and worn from years of use. The smell of sweat filled the room. It was just as cold as the warehouse, but at least there were no open doors to the windy harbor. There was a pile of long white cotton sacks about three feet wide and six feet long lined up against the wall.

"What are those?" I asked the matron.

"They're your beds. You're going to fill them up with the straw that's stored in the trash bins, so you have something comfortable to sleep on tonight."

It was hard work, but we finally finished. The older girls had to work extra hard and help the little ones. When we were all done, the beds still didn't look like they would be very comfortable. And they weren't. At last, we were given a cup of weak tea and a slice of bread with wartime "butter." Ever since rationing began, we made "butter" from a large brick of white margarine that came with a packet of yellow dye. If you stirred the dye into the margarine for a long time, it started to look a little like butter. But no matter how hard you stirred, the color was always streaky. It never tasted like butter, either. No one liked it, but as Mum always said, "Everyone has to do their part for the war." There were even pictures at the cinema of King George stirring a big bowl of margarine for his family. "If it's good enough for the King and Queen, it's certainly good enough for me" became our favorite saying whenever we had bread and butter.

"Girls, you may talk quietly while you have your tea," the matron said.

"What's your name? I'm Lizzie."

"I'm Margaret."

Margaret and I found a spot on the floor where we could sit, lean back against the wall, and take our time eating. *We probably won't eat until we get on the ship tomorrow. If we get on the ship tomorrow. Might as well enjoy this meal.* I looked over at my new friend for a minute and surprised myself when I blurted out, "I like your red hair, and it's so curly. Not like my plain straight brown hair. I always wished I had curly hair."

"You wouldn't if you did. It takes Mum forever to braid it. And it's so hard to brush. Your hair is beautiful. It's so shiny. I always wanted straight hair, but I guess we're stuck with what we have."

We sat silently for another minute. "I wonder if we'll really leave tomorrow," Margaret said. Then a few minutes later, she asked, "Where did you come from?"

"Right here, in Liverpool."

"I'm from Manchester and I'm thirteen."

"So am I! Are you excited about going to Canada? I can't wait to see everything."

"Do you think we'll see lots of cowboys and Indians?" Margaret asked. "Do you think they'll be waiting for us at the docks when we land?"

"I hope so. The man from CORB who came to our house told us Canada is full of them. Colin, he's my brother, wants to be a cowboy someday and learn to ride a horse. I wouldn't mind learning how to ride either, but I don't think I want to be a cowgirl. Do you, Margaret?"

"Oh no! I can't imagine being a cowgirl. Besides, we're only going to be there for a few months. My Mum said she knows our boys will squash Jerry and put an end to this silly war."

"Of course, they will. And they'll be quick about it for sure. But I do hope we get to see at least some Indians, and cowboys of course. And I would like to see the mountains. The CORB man showed me some pictures. They had snow on the tops even in summer!"

"I wonder what the people will be like. Are you scared, Lizzie? Do you think they'll like us?"

Before I could answer, the head matron flicked the lights. "Time for bed! All talking stops now! Make sure you have your gas masks next to you. Say your prayers girls and get to sleep. Tomorrow will be a long day."

She gave us a few minutes to settle down, then shut off the lights. The room was plunged into inky darkness. The tiny windows at the ceiling line had blackout curtains, so not a whisper of moonlight entered the cave-like room. I was still hungry after our meal; but since we never had much to eat at home anyway, I had grown used to the feeling. I worried about Colin though. I hoped the older boy from the warehouse was keeping an eye on him.

At the far end of the room, one matron sat behind an old wooden desk with a small lamp burning. She took out a book to read as she pulled her shawl tighter across her shoulders to ward off the damp chill. Muffled sobs and whimpering filled the room. I bit my lower lip and refused to cry. I had to be brave and somehow send that strength to Colin. Margaret reached out and squeezed my hand. I squeezed back; glad I had a friend. The thin coarse blanket didn't provide much warmth so we huddled together, and I finally fell asleep dreaming of Canada.

Chapter 3

My eyes flew open at the sound of the siren – an air raid! "Colin!" I cried out. I realized that Colin wasn't there. I was in a mammoth hall with dozens of other scared girls. A thousand thoughts ran through my mind. *Where can we go? What should we do? Is Colin all right? I need to get to him, to protect him.*

Bloody Jerry! If only I were a man, I'd go over there and wallop all those Nazis.

Suddenly, the lights came on. The head matron stood at the side of the desk. "Girls, get your gas masks and line up. We're going to the shelter. No dawdling, be quick about it, no running, and no talking. Let's conduct ourselves as ladies, please."

Margaret and I grabbed our gas masks and each other's hands and walked toward the door. We filed out two by two and started down the street to the shelter. I turned and looked around, but couldn't see Colin, or any boys at all. I started to panic. I gasped for air. *I have to find Colin! He's too little to be on his own. Where is he?* My heart was beating so fast and loud I thought it would break through my chest. I pulled my hand away from Margaret's and ran ahead to the matron.

"My brother, my brother, I've got to find him! I promised Mum I'd look out for him! I've got to keep him safe!"

The matron glared down at me. Even in my panicked state, I could see the disgust she felt for me. Like so many people, she looked at us seavacuees, which is what we were called, as gutter trash. "Get back in line," she snarled. "I can't worry about one little boy when I have all these girls to see safely to the shelter. Where is your partner?"

She grabbed my arm so hard I was sure her fingers would go right through to my bone. She marched me down the line until we came to Margaret.

"Is this your partner?"

I nodded. I knew if I opened my mouth to speak, the only sound would be a piercing scream of frustration.

"You!" the matron said pointing at Margaret, "Make sure she has no more outbursts like this again or you'll both get a lashing." She turned and went back to lead our sorry group along to the shelter.

I couldn't look at Margaret. Not only had I deserted Colin, now I had gotten my new friend in trouble. A lashing! Even my strictest teachers never did that. It was only because Margaret held my hand in a death grip that I made it to the shelter. My constant flow of tears prevented me from seeing anything. The world around me was a blur of black shapes, almost as black as the thoughts of my failures on this, my first day away from Mum.

Chapter 4

The first sound of an air raid was always the low thunderous drone of the planes. Then the anti-aircraft guns would start firing. The noise filled the room, almost blocking out the screeching descent of the bombs – but not quite. Margaret and I sat arm in arm on the hard, concrete floor and pressed our backs against the cold stone wall. Besides the girls we came with, there were dozens of other people crammed into the shelter, from crying babies to withered old men and women too crippled with arthritis to sit on the floor. Instead, they leaned against the walls, eyes closed, lips moving in silent prayer. Every time the shelter door opened, I hoped Colin would come running down the steps. *Where was he? How was he managing during this raid? We had gone through them before, but always together – and with Mum. At least I had Margaret to hold onto. Did Colin have a friend tonight?*

BOOM! BOOM!

The building shook. Plaster dust sprinkled down from the ceiling and coated everyone in white. We looked like an army of ghosts gathered in our gloomy gravesite. People's tears traced down their cheeks. More bombs fell. Someone grabbed my arm. I could hear sirens from the fire brigades and ambulances. Another bomb fell. The building shook. Margaret and I held on tight to each other. The smell of sweat crept through the shelter as the bombing continued. I thought it would never stop. The basement refuge became muggy. The walls seemed to creep in closer and closer. Fear rose in waves.

"The Lord is my shepherd…"

"Hail Mary, full of grace…"

"Our Father, who art in heaven…"

Whispered prayers competed with the sound of bombs landing on the city surviving above our ceiling. At least I hoped Liverpool survived this onslaught. I couldn't allow myself to think of what would happen if the city was wiped out by this barrage. *Where would we go if our ship was destroyed? What would happen to all the people huddled here? Would this become our grave? Where was Colin? Would I see him tomorrow?*

Suddenly, silence. We all waited, hoping it was over for tonight. Finally, the all clear signal sounded. Everyone let out a sigh of relief. I felt air push out of my chest. I didn't even realize I had been holding my breath. The Air Raid Warden's face and tin hat peeped through the door and said, "All clear, folks. Our boys chased Jerry back where he belongs."

A rousing cheer rose from everyone in the shelter.

"Anyone hurt?" the warden asked. Everyone looked around to see if anyone was injured, maybe unable to speak for themselves.

"All seems fine here," a man shouted.

"Yes, we're good. Just could use a little fresh air and definitely a cup of tea," said a woman.

I could hear people mumbling their agreement and some nervous laughter.

"Cup of tea, indeed!" another woman said. "I myself could go for a decent glass of brandy!"

Lots of loud laughter and hearty agreement followed that remark.

"All right, girls. Let's get up and back to the school," the matron said.

"If it's still there." I heard a man say under his breath.

The matron shot the man a scathing stare and turned

back to us. "Come along, no need to dawdle. Dust yourselves and your partner off. We don't want to bring all that plaster dust with us."

We began vigorously pounding each other, and huge clouds of dust rose from our efforts. Everyone started choking and coughing.

"Girls! Stop immediately! Dust yourselves off outside. Honestly! You should have more sense than to do that in this enclosed space. Now line up as best you can."

"You'd think the matron would have more sense before she started issuing orders. Poor little orphans were just trying to obey her instructions," an old woman said.

I wanted to spin around and tell her I was not an orphan, but the matron was shuffling us up the stairs. However, the line froze when the leaders reached the street.

"What is the problem?" the matron yelled up the stairs.

"Sorry, ma'am," another matron answered. "I just... the destruction...so vast.... I'm...I'm all right now. Come on girls, let's keep moving. There are lots of people behind us who want to get home."

Margaret and I made our way up and out of our refuge and stared all around us. The air was clouded with dust from the bombed-out buildings, and the smell of fire was everywhere. Fire brigade and ambulance sirens pierced the night and muffled the wails of the people of Liverpool. There was rubble all around. Even in the darkness, we could see the buildings we had passed on our way to the shelter were destroyed. One or two crumbling walls now stood where before there had been a busy factory. People wandered around the street in a daze, eyes glazed over, muttering, and crying. Rows of houses were gone, leaving only broken bits and pieces of their owners' belongings scattered among the bricks. As we walked back to the school, the cries and screams grew louder. More and more people surfaced from their underground sanctuaries to find they had no home to go to, no possessions left. Even the head matron was shocked into silence.

We walked in a daze not knowing what we would find around each corner. When we spotted the school, Margaret and I gave each other a little hug. Somehow, amidst all the destruction, it still stood untouched. Everyone sighed with relief. We had a place to spend the rest of the night, although I was sure I wouldn't sleep. How could I when I didn't know if Colin was safe?

I woke to the clanging of a bell.

"All right girls, settle down," the matron shouted over our chattering. "We'll take turns eating and washing up before we leave for the docks. This first row will begin the washing up, just faces and hands today I'm afraid. Second row, go with the matron at the door for your tea and toast. Everyone needs to move swiftly. We don't want to keep the boat waiting for us."

"Do you think that means we'll sail today?" I asked Margaret.

"It sounds like it to me."

"Oh, I do hope so. Maybe then, I can see Colin."

I pushed my way to the front of the line. "Matron, have you heard any news about the boys? I'm worried about my little brother, Colin. Is he all right? When will I see him?"

"Get back in line. I have enough to worry about, taking care of you girls without checking up on other people's charges. You're becoming quite a nuisance."

I dragged myself back to Margaret's side. Everyone was staring at me. I wanted to scream at all of them,

"I'm worried about my brother. Aren't any of you worried about someone?"

Margaret put her arm around me. "I'm sure he's fine, Lizzie. Didn't you tell me there was an older boy looking out for him?"

"At the warehouse, yes. I hope he stayed with him through the night."

"They must have matrons taking care of them too, Lizzie. He probably thought the whole thing was a jolly good lark."

I nodded and remembered all the silly pranks Colin played on me that usually got me into trouble with Mum, and how he loved to play war games with his mates. *Margaret's probably right. I'll bet he spent the whole night imagining himself in a Spitfire battling with Jerry and downing each one he spotted.*

"It's our row's turn, Lizzie," Margaret said waking me from my daydream.

We filed into the school's washroom and did a bird-bath wash up, as my Mum always called it. We went straight to the lunchroom to get our "buttered" toast and tea. In no time at all, everyone had washed, eaten breakfast, and lined up for our walk back to the docks – a walk that seared itself into my memory forever.

Chapter 5

Fire Brigade hoses snaked across the streets. One occasionally slithered out to attack and devour the fires still consuming Liverpool.

"Mind your step, girls," a Civil Defense worker shouted. "Don't want to trip on the hose."

I looked to see who said that. Some of my friends' dads had joined the Civil Defense or the Home Guard if they weren't able to be in the army. Maybe he was one of them. Maybe he had seen Colin. Maybe he had some news about Mum. But he had already turned and gone back to searching through the rubble for survivors.

Vans drove up and down the streets announcing meetings for the homeless. Their loudspeakers blared out instructions we had heard every day since the bombing started:

"When the air raid signal sounds, get to a shelter as quickly as possible! Keep diffusers on torches and pointed down at all times! Do not touch any unexploded incendiary bombs or parachute mines! Call the Fire Brigade if one of these is in your yard!"

Other vans with Women's Voluntary Service members roamed the streets giving first aid demonstrations. Everyone needed to know what to do for injuries because ambulances were often delayed for hours. Our group of girls walked around huge craters created by last night's raid. On some streets, one home was destroyed while the rest of the street was untouched. Some homes had a wall completely blown away. You could see the family inside picking through the rubble for whatever they could rescue. Other families went on with their lives as if there was nothing strange about living in a house with three walls. I had seen other streets that looked the same in my neighborhood. It wasn't a shock to me anymore.

"Over here, men. This was an air raid shelter," someone shouted. "There's bound to be some survivors here." *Please don't let that be the shelter Colin was in.*

Men in tin hats climbed over the pile of debris to begin the search. Boys and girls scurried from one bombed out building to another searching for shrapnel – a favorite souvenir. Colin and I went on scavenger hunts just like these, every morning after a night of Jerry bombings. I still kept a piece in my pocket for luck and had given one to Colin with part of a German word on it. Those were especially prized. A group of us had formed The Jerry Spotters Club. We built a fort out of wood scraps and cardboard where we could meet and watch for Nazi planes. We posted pictures of their planes and ours on the walls. We also had a collection of plane pieces, shrapnel, bits of bombs, or anything we could rescue from the nightly raids. As Jerry Spotters, we played our part in supporting our parents, especially if one was off fighting or had died.

The Nazis had been bombing us for a while now, so this morning's results weren't a real surprise. Even before Jerry started bombing here, I had seen newsreels at the cinema of the war's destruction. They were shown at every performance, even the children's shows. Of course, when Liverpool was attacked, it changed everything. Now, walking past the results of the raid, knowing I was leaving the city, my home, I wondered what it would look like when I returned. *Would the whole city be a pile of broken bits of brick? Would there be any houses left? Would I ever be able to live in Liverpool again? I hated what was happening. I hated this war. I hated*

Jerry.

Someone started singing and we all joined in:

"Whistle while you work!
Mussolini is a twerp!
Hitler's barmy
So's his army
Whistle while you work!"

"God speed, children. You'll soon be home again!" a worker shouted from a pile of rubble. Lines of children walking towards the docks headed for evacuation had become normal. So had bombed-out houses and friends disappearing. Some moved because they didn't have a house to live in anymore. Others moved to a relative's home in the country for safety.

Ahead of us, soldiers with bayonets on their rifles marched a column of men, and some women, down the street. They all carried suitcases and held their coats over their arms. I recognized some of them and wondered what they could have done. I saw Mr. Schmidt, our butcher. He was one of the nicest men I ever knew. Before the war, whenever Colin and I went to his butcher shop for Mum, he would give us each a thick slice of ham – for free! Mr. Giordano was in the line too. He had the best bakery in the neighborhood. *Why were the soldiers arresting these people? What had they done?*

I yelled to them, "Mr. Schmidt, Mr. Giordano, where are you going? What's happening? Who's taking care of your shop?"

"Lizzie, stop!" Margaret hissed. "If the matron realizes it's you yelling we'll both be in trouble."

"I don't care. Where are the soldiers taking them?

This isn't right, Margaret. They're my neighbors." *Who else will the soldiers take away? Will they arrest Mum because she talks to them and buys things from their stores? I don't understand this. It makes no sense.*

Mr. Schmidt looked over at me and dropped his head onto his chest. His feet dragged across the cobblestones as the line plodded forward.

I started to run over to him to find out where the soldiers were taking him.

"No," Margaret said, grabbing my arm. "Come on, Lizzie. You can't do anything to help them. There's no sense in getting into trouble over them. They're Germans, or Italians. We're at war with them. The soldiers have to take them away. They started doing the same thing in Manchester before I left."

"But they're nice people, Margaret. They're not like the Nazis or Mussolini's army. They're from here, from Liverpool."

"I bet they weren't born here. They could be spies. That's why our soldiers have to take them away."

"That's not right. They can't be spies. I've known them since I was a little girl."

Margaret grabbed my arm and dragged me along to catch up with the other girls. I kept looking back over my shoulder to see where they were going. But the column turned a corner. Would I ever see them again? I'll never forget the look in Mr. Schmidt's eyes or the way he walked, bent over and staring at the ground. This wasn't normal or something that we would "get through" anymore. This was what war was really about, and it was horrible and ugly.

Chapter 6

Even though it wasn't very far, it seemed like the longest walk I had ever taken. When we arrived at the docks once again, we were marched into the immense waiting room and told to sit on the benches. The boys were already there. I searched the rows looking for Colin. *There! There he is!* He lifted his hand and gave a quick wave before scratching his ear. I could finally breathe easily. I smiled, touched my fingertips to my lips, and sent him a little kiss.

"Move along, girls," the matron ordered. "We must hurry if we plan on boarding the ship today."

We quickly settled on the benches. The ogre from yesterday walked in and rang a bell for silence. No one was talking anyway, but I guess he thought it would get our attention.

"Boys and girls, you will be boarding the S.S. *Oronsay* today and sailing for Canada. The ladies and gentlemen standing next to me will be your escorts on this voyage. Think of them as you would your parents or teachers. Respect them and obey them. They will answer any questions you have about the journey, and your final destination, once the ship is out at sea. Until then, do not pester them with silly matters. Once on board, go to your assigned rooms and wait for further instructions from your escort. Now stay silent and listen for your name to be called for boarding."

Margaret grabbed my hand. We looked at each other and crossed our fingers. I hoped we would share a room on the ship. The first group of names – I counted twenty – was called and they hurried to the front of the room.

The next group of twenty, and the next. I heard,

"Colin Gunn." *Colin's been called. Now I* have *to be called. What will I do if they've lost my name?*

"Margaret White," the ogre boomed out. She gave my hand a final squeeze and hurried up the aisle.

"All right, that's this group," I heard a matron say. My hopes to stay with Margaret burst like a popped balloon. I looked at the group and silently counted them.

"Wait!" I shouted and started up the aisle. "That's only nineteen. There should be one more." *I have to be in this group. Colin's been called. Margaret's been called. Oh please, please, call my name.*

The matron turned and stared at me. Her face was bright red, and the look in her eyes nailed my feet to the floor.

"Quickly count heads – again," she said. "There should be twenty."

"We're one short."

"Oh, for heaven's sake. We'll never get done if we can't even count to twenty on the list, Mr. Phillips," the matron snarled.

"Quite right, quite right, Miss Vaughn," the ogre mumbled. "Ah yes, my mistake. Elizabeth Gunn, come forward quickly!"

I flew up the rest of the aisle. I was in the same group as Margaret. We were still together! Margaret's grin was the biggest I've ever seen. She grabbed my hand as soon as I reached the front of the room. Everything was going to be all right after all. I would be on the ship in a few minutes, back with Colin. Hand in hand, Margaret and I walked out of the warehouse and headed for the gangplank.

Chapter 7

Outside, rows of people pressed against the barri-
cades. Dozens of children hugged their parents goodbye
and joined our group. I didn't realize there would be
others sailing with us. One boy's mum kept pulling him
back from the departure gate for another hug.

"Margaret, look! That mum reminds me of an octopus. Every time that boy gets one tentacle off him another one shoots out and catches him again."

Margaret and I started giggling. The boy's face was
bright red. Everyone was watching to see who would
win, the octopus or the seavacuee. Finally, one of the
CORB men went over and spoke to the woman who
switched her hold from her son to him. The boy ran up
the gangplank and looked back to see his mum hanging
on to his rescuer and sobbing.

"Don't worry, Mum," he yelled down from the
ship's deck. "I'll be back before you can miss me."

She started frantically waving her handkerchief,
which gave the CORB man a chance to escape her hold.
By this time, we were all laughing uncontrollably. The
boy pulled his cap far down on his forehead and headed
for the stairs trying to melt into the crowd.

I turned and looked at our ship for the first time. It
was gigantic! Even though I grew up in Liverpool and
saw ships at the docks every day, I had never been this
close to one. I couldn't imagine how it stayed afloat.
Something this massive should definitely sink. I thought
back to all the little wooden ships we built and "sent out
to sea," or the sailboats we raced on windy days. Everyone knew one extra bit of wood, or decoration, would
capsize the boat and all your work would sink to the bot-

tom like a rock

How could this ship, with all its passengers possibly stay above the water long enough to cross the entire Atlantic Ocean all the way to Canada? I wanted this great adventure, but now I'm terrified. I won't sleep for the entire voyage. Not until I can put my feet back on land. Why did I ever agree to this? And where is Colin? I promised this would be great fun. If we both die at sea, Mum will be all alone. Why do I always want to try something new, travel to faraway places, see what's in the next town? Why can't I be happy where I am, like Mum has always told me I should be? And where is Colin?

"Lizzie, look," Margaret said pointing up to the ship's railing, "there's a little blond-haired boy yelling down to you."

"Lizzie! Lizzie! Come on up! Hurry! It's wonderful. You can see all of Liverpool from here."

I looked up to see Colin waving his hat at me. He looked as happy as he did when Father Christmas brought him a bicycle last year. I forgot all my worries and fears. We were together again. Everything would be as wonderful as I dreamed it would be. What stories we would have to tell Mum when we got back.

"That's my brother, Colin," I told Margaret. "What are we waiting for? Let's go! Off to Canada it is for us!"

We laced our arms together and walked up the gangplank. On deck, our escort gave us our room numbers.

"Margaret, you're in Room 314. Elizabeth, you're also in Room 314," our escort said. "Go down the staircase and find your room. Then come back to wave goodbye to everyone who came to see us off."

"Oh, Lizzie, I'm so glad we're in the same room. I was starting to get a little nervous about this trip. But as long as we can stay together, I know everything will be wonderful."

"It will, Margaret. This will be the adventure I've dreamed about, I'm sure. Now, let's find our room and go find Colin. I wonder if his room is near ours. I hope so. Sometimes he gets nightmares and I wouldn't want to be too far away if that happens. Would you mind if he sometimes shared our room?"

"Of course not. I have a little cousin who gets nightmares too and whenever I stay at their house, she climbs into bed with me to feel safe. I guess it's just something you grow out of when you get older."

"It must be. My Mum never gets them, and neither do any of my Aunties. I guess the goblins only visit the little ones. Now that we're all grown up, they know they could never frighten us."

"They'd better not try," Margaret said punching a fist into the air.

We both ran down the stairs laughing and throwing punches at the ship's ghosts.

"Here we are, Room 314."

I opened the door to the most beautiful room I had ever seen. There were two bunk beds with gleaming wooden posts. Bright red plaid bedspreads covered them, and soft white blankets lay at the foot of each one. At each end of the room, two wooden wardrobes with mirrors stood waiting for our clothes, and two desks sat next to them, each with a green leather top. Lamps on the walls next to the beds and above the desks would give us all the light we needed at night to write or read.

"Margaret, it's the prettiest room I've ever been in," I said flopping down on the lower bunk. "Can this bed be mine?"

"All right. I don't mind which one I have. Look at this wardrobe, Lizzie. I'm sure we don't have enough clothes to fill it. This is the dreamiest room on the whole ship, I'm sure. I don't think I'll ever want to leave here."

Margaret was right about the wardrobe. Before we left, the CORB man gave Mum a list of clothes we could bring with us:

Two changes of underwear
A nightdress or pajamas
A change of socks and/or stockings
A spare pair of shoes
A bar of soap, toothbrush, toothpaste
A comb and brush
Handkerchiefs
A warm coat and jumper

Each wardrobe could hold at least three of everything on my list. And there were four wardrobes in the room!

"Hello," a little voice said from behind us.

Margaret and I turned to see two little wide-eyed girls with blond curls staring up at us. The smaller one carried a toy cloth lamb that had been white at one time. However, now it was a mottled gray with patches of white. One eye was missing and the tail looked like it had been a dog's favorite toy for a while. Although the older one stood tall and looked straight up at us with confidence, her trembling lip told a different story.

"Is this Room 314?" she asked.

"Yes, it is," I said. "Who are you?"

"My name's Mary and this is my sister, Jean."

"Well, Mary and Jean welcome to your new

home, for the next few days anyway," I said.

Tears began to fall down Jean's cheeks, and soft whimpers filled the room. Mary wrapped her arms around her little sister and in between quiet sobs said, "It'll be all right, Jean. You'll see. Remember, Mummy and Daddy told us we have to be brave little soldiers, just like Daddy has to be. It will only be for a little while, then we'll be back on a big ship like this one sailing home."

Margaret and I looked at each other and knew that, in addition to Colin, we would have two other younger ones to keep safe from nighttime spooks and goblins.

"Mary, Jean, Margaret, I think we should go up on deck to wave goodbye to all the nice people who came here to see us off. What do you say to that?"

"You're right, Lizzie. Okay, girls?"

Jean and Mary both nodded their heads so hard, their blond curls danced in front of their faces. Margaret and I laughed, grabbed them by their hands and headed for the upper deck. As soon as we got up where everyone was gathered, I looked for Colin.

"Over here, Lizzie."

I almost didn't hear him. Sailors were shouting orders to each other, longshoremen were getting the ship ready to leave port, and dozens of people were screaming.

"Farewell!"

"Bon voyage!"

"Safe trip!"

"Don't forget to write!"

Most of the children on board were sobbing and calling out for their mums. I looked around, hoping that maybe Mum had come to say goodbye, but I knew she was already working at Hornby Castle. *Maybe she asked for time off. I know she'd be here if it was at all possible.*

"Lizzie, Lizzie, look up."

I saw Colin standing on the railing, holding on to a post, waving his cap at me, his blond hair blowing in the wind.

"Colin! Get down from there before you fall right into the harbor. We must be thirty feet above the water. Do you want to drown before we even set sail?"

I imagined him landing in that filthy water. The dead fish and rotting garbage floating there smelled worse than the dead mouse Mum found behind the cooker. *If that happens, I'll never get the smell out of his clothes – assuming he doesn't die from the fall.*

I raced over to pull him down completely forgetting about my new young charges.

Colin was the daredevil of the family. If there was a tree nearby, he would climb it. If there wasn't, he would find something else to scramble up, or under, or through. Totally fearless, he never backed down from any challenge or dare. Of course, that encouraged every boy in the neighborhood to think of more and more dangerous tests of his bravery. More than once, Mum spent her afternoons in the emergency at Bootle Hospital waiting to hear what Colin had broken, sprained, or gotten stitched.

"Come on, Lizzie. Climb up. It's amazing up here."

I knew I'd never get him down, so I decided, just this once, to join him.

"That's it, Lizzie. Step on the rails, just like you're climbing a ladder. Hurry up though before one of the sailors makes us get down again."

"What? You've already been told to get down? And you climbed up again?"

"Oh, come on, Lizzie. We'll never see Liverpool

like this again."

He was right and I knew it. So, I climbed up next to him. It was exciting being this high up. The wind blew through my hair and brought with it the salty smell of the ocean. The rotting odors and cacophony of the docks faded away as I looked out at the rooftops of Liverpool and the sea of well-wishers on the pier below. I held on tight with one hand and waved to them. *I can't believe it! We're really leaving England!*

The ship began to inch away from the dock. Someone started singing, "Wish Me Luck as You Wave Me Goodbye," and soon everyone joined in.

"Cheerio, here I go, on my way" we all sang laughing and waving while we pulled further away from home.

"Not a tear, but a cheer, make it gay
Give me a smile I can keep all the while
In my heart while I'm away
'Til we meet once again, you and I
Wish me luck as you wave me goodbye."

The loud voices became a whisper as we sang the final line with tear-filled eyes: "Goodbye everybody, I'll do my best for ye."

Chapter 8

As Colin and I climbed down from our perch, I turned so he wouldn't see me brush away my tears. Even with Colin and Margaret standing next to me, I had never felt so alone. *Will I ever see Mum again?*

"Hi Colin, I'm Margaret, and this is Mary and Jean. We're all bunking together."

"Hi everyone, why didn't you climb up on the railing? We could see all Liverpool from up there, couldn't we Lizzie?"

As usual, Colin didn't wait for anyone to answer him but immediately rushed onto his next topic. "You have to come see my room, Lizzie. It's wonderful! I'm going to sleep on the top bunk and Jim, my roommate, is going to sleep on the bottom. He seems really nice. Oh, look Lizzie, that's him over there. He has a dark brown cap. Can you see him, Lizzie?"

"Colin! Slow down and take a breath!"

I looked where Colin pointed and saw a tall boy I remembered from the warehouse loading area. He seemed a little older than Colin, closer to my age. *Maybe Colin won't be visiting during the night to have me chase away the midnight goblins.*

"Come on, Lizzie, I want you to meet Jim and I want to show you my room. After that, you can show me your room. I bet your room isn't as wonderful as mine."

Margaret and I laughed at Colin's excitement about his new room. You would think it was really his, not just one of many on the ship. Colin grabbed my hand and began pulling me towards the stairs.

"Margaret, Mary, Jean you don't want to miss seeing his wonderful room, do you?" I asked. "Then we can all explore the ship. Unless of course, Colin, you've already done that?"

Colin's face turned a little red, and he mumbled, "No, I was waiting to do that with you, Lizzie. Is that okay? Can Jim come too?"

"That's exactly what I had planned too, Colin. Let's start with your room and see how close it is to mine. That way we can plan to visit each other when we're not busy exploring the rest of the ship."

We walked down two flights of stairs to Colin's room. The boys and girls were still separated – boys on the starboard side, girls on the port side. I was upset that I couldn't have the room next to Colin's, but at least I would be able to be with him during the day. All the cabins opened onto a long hallway that had a common bathroom at the end.

"Here's my room, Lizzie," Colin said opening the door.

It's exactly the same as mine. It even has the same furniture and plaid bedspread.

I must have looked surprised because Colin started jumping up and down, waving his arms, and yelling, "Isn't it wonderful? I bet there's no other room like this on the whole ship."

His eyes gleamed, and the enthusiasm that shimmered off him wrapped around all of us like a warm cloak.

"Colin, you might be exaggerating a little," Jim said. "I think we all have cabins that are pretty much the same."

"I don't know about that Jim. I'm sure this is the very best one on board."

A loud clanking noise startled us into silence. Mary

and Jean made tinny shrieking noises and grabbed hold of each other.

"Is the boat falling apart, Mary?" Jean asked, her eyes opening wide in fear while tears started falling down her cheeks. "Are we going to drown, Mary? I don't want to drown before we even begin our holiday."

Mary looked at us for some sign that we were safe, that the ship wasn't sinking, that our holiday at sea, and in Canada, would be as wonderful as everyone promised.

"Don't worry girls," Colin said, sounding very grown up. "No one's going to drown. Jim and I wouldn't let that happen, would we? We'll keep you safe all the way to Canada."

"Right you are, Colin," Jim said placing his arm around Colin's shoulder. "Just come to us whenever you feel afraid. We're like the men of the house now."

In a matter of minutes, Jim and Colin had become heroes to the two little girls. And I watched my little brother grow up right in front of me. I was incredibly proud of him.

Seconds later, the whine of the ship's propellers and the smell of hot oil and steam broke through the moment of idol worship, and Colin's face blanched.

"Hold on tight everyone! Here we go!" I said reaching for Colin with one arm and Margaret with the other. We all huddled together as the ship pulled away from the tugboats and began to make its way to the convoy sailing across the Atlantic. I was excited, but scared and nervous all at the same time. I knew Colin wasn't really ready to be a grown-up yet, and I would always need to be there for him, to protect him and keep him safe. I looked over his head at Margaret and saw all the same fears and hopes in her eyes that I felt. Both little girls held onto her, and Jim had his arms wrapped around both of us. We had become our own little family, and I knew we would be able to rely on each other for anything we needed.

Chapter 9

"Ladies and gentlemen, boys and girls, this is your Captain speaking," a voice boomed from the loudspeakers. "My name is Capt. Stuart and I hope to meet all of you before our voyage ends. For your safety, I must insist that everyone wear their life belts at all times. We will be traveling through waters where there has been some U-boat activity. I do not anticipate any problems since we are escorted by his Royal Majesty's Navy, but I would rather we are all prepared for any situation that may arise. Your deck stewards will be able to answer any questions you have, and they will also be distributing the lifeboat drill schedules. Again, this is only a safety precaution. I've made the voyage numerous times without incidents, and I'm quite sure this trip will be a most pleasant experience for all. Now, this part of my message is for all the boys and girls on board ship, so listen carefully children. To get our voyage started correctly, we must have a festive celebration. Therefore, I want all of you to meet me in the dining room for an ice cream social. Just follow the signs posted in the hallways. Parents, guardians, and escorts are welcome to enjoy tea in the lounge. Good day to all."

"Ice cream," we shouted.

"Lizzie, this is going to be the best adventure ever," Colin said. "Even better than I dreamed. Imagine, ice cream. And it's not even a holiday, or birthday, or anything."

We rushed out the door and started down the hallway toward the stairs with hundreds of other excited boys and girls. I thought someone would be trampled as we headed for the feast. Somehow, in the rush of everyone struggling to reach the dining hall, we managed to stay together. I was glad since the hall was immense. It was also the most beautiful room I had ever been in. Three crystal chandeliers hung along the length of the room. The sunlight that came through dozens of windows made them sparkle like Christmas lights. White linen covered each round table and jacketed stewards stood around the room waiting to help us. Thick red patterned carpeting dulled the noise of our shoes.

"This is like a room right out of Buckingham Palace," I said.

"It is, isn't it?" Margaret said.

"The line starts over there, Lizzie," Colin said, pushing his way through the crowd.

For a minute, I lost sight of him and panicked before I spotted him bobbing up and down to see how far away he was from the ice cream servers. *Calm down, we're on the ship now. Colin can't get lost. He's safe. I wonder if I'll ever be able to really believe that.*

"Come on," Margaret said, "we don't want them to run out before we get any."

We worked our way over to the side of the room where the ship's stewards had formed everyone into a line. When we reached the servers, they offered us a choice of vanilla or chocolate, or both. We could have a scoop of each flavor, and there was chocolate sauce to ladle on top. After the rationing at home, this was a real treat.

"I bet even Princess Elizabeth and Princess Margaret don't get desserts like this," Jim said. "What do you think, girls?"

Mary and Jean looked at him in wide-eyed amazement. "Really, Jim? Even the Princesses don't get ice cream?"

"Not with the rations they don't. Now let's find a table and enjoy it."

"Lizzie, Lizzie, over here. I've got a table big enough for all of us."

I spotted Colin standing on a chair, waving furiously at us.

"Colin! Get down from there immediately!" I shouted, pushing through the crowd to reach him. "Mum would be so ashamed of you standing on a dining room chair like that. What were you thinking?"

Colin's look of excited triumph turned into one of shame and embarrassment.

"Sorry, Lizzie," he mumbled. "I thought you'd be happy I found us a place to sit together."

I felt horrible. The ice cream treat now made my stomach turn.

"Colin, I'm sorry. I shouldn't have yelled at you. It's wonderful that you found this table for us. Everyone, aren't we lucky that Colin saved us a place to eat together?" I said turning to the rest of our group.

They all agreed that Colin was the hero of the ice cream stampede. I was even able to swallow a few mouthfuls before I gave the rest to Colin.

Once everyone had their fill, Captain Stuart asked for our attention.

"I hope you enjoyed our surprise welcome, children," he said.

A loud cheer rose from the hall.

"Good, good. Since we are all gathered here, I want to introduce your escorts. Of course, some of you are traveling with your parents or guardians, and you don't need any introductions to them, I'm sure."

Giggles sounded all around us. "Imagine being introduced to your own Mum," Colin said.

"But some of you are here without parents, so please pay attention. Your escorts are here to see to your safety, education, and any needs you have while on board the *Oronsay*. They are also in charge of disciplining any children who don't behave. You must realize we have to obey the rules of the ship so everyone has a safe and happy voyage to Canada. Now, if the escorts will please join me on stage, I will make the introductions."

There were six escorts in all. Miss Julia Hughes was assigned to our hallway for the girls, and Father Brown was escort for Colin's and Jim's hall.

"Children," Captain Stuart said, "please go to the section of the dining hall where your escorts are waiting. They will have some information for you. Children who are traveling with relatives may leave and join your families."

My eyes followed Miss Hughes as she walked across the room to a far corner. When she sat down, we scrambled over to her table. I wanted to memorize everything about her. She was about twenty-five years old, the same age as Auntie Cecelia. She had a pleasant face and short brown hair, cut like one of the movie stars I had seen at the cinema. She sat quietly, hands folded on the table waiting for all of us to settle down.

"Right girls, it looks like we're all here. I'll just call your names to see who's who, all right?"

We all nodded. I had never had a teacher ask my permission to do anything. They did whatever they wanted whenever they wanted. I liked her already. This was going to be a great adventure.

After roll call, she said we could call her Miss Julia.

Since we would be living together for the voyage, she wanted us to think of her as a big sister, not a parent or teacher. We would have classes with her, or one of the other escorts, in the mornings, and have games, music, or art instruction in the afternoons. She also reminded us that we had to keep our life belts on at all times. When we went to sleep at night, our life belts and coats had to be placed at the foot of the bed. I was glad we didn't have to sleep in them. They were heavy and uncomfortable. *Guess we traded in our gas masks for life belts.*

While Miss Julia talked, I watched the stewards clean up our ice cream dishes, which were now sliding around the tables. The ship rocked back and forth more violently now than when we pulled away from the dock. Ice cream rolled around in my stomach like the dishes on the tables. *Maybe if I look out the window at the sea, I'll feel better.* But seeing the horizon line bob up and down made me feel worse. I looked around. Everyone seemed a little pale and sick looking.

"Girls, I think we should all go back to our rooms now and settle in." Miss Julia stood up and grabbed the table's edge. Her face turned a gray color and she staggered from table to table towards the hall. She looked like Mr. Wells walking home after an afternoon at the pub. Soon we were all following her, stumbling from table to table. I felt miserable and knew I was going to be sick. I had to get out of the room. I couldn't throw up on the carpet. Somehow, I got outside. I reached the railing and got sicker than I had ever been. There were people all around me throwing up. Puddles of vomit covered the deck. All I wanted to do was lie down. I wanted Mum to put a cold cloth on my head and tell me I would feel better. But that wasn't going to happen. Mum was far away now, and I was going even further away from her every minute. *I don't want to be on this great adventure anymore. I want to go home. I miss Mum.* I started crying and didn't think I would ever stop.

Chapter 10

After three days of near-death seasickness, I was able to eat a little. Tomorrow, we would start classes. The escorts were also feeling better and ready to make up for the lost days. Our days of doing whatever we wanted were gone. Instead, we now had a routine that was posted in the playroom:

DAILY SCHEDULE
6:30 – Rise, wash, and dress
7:00 – Run or exercise on deck (if it wasn't raining)
7:30 – Breakfast
8:00 – School lessons
10:00 – Prayers and snack
10:30 – School lessons
12:00 – Lunch
1:00 – Games/art/music
2:30 – Free time
5:30 – Dinner
8:00 – Hot gruel
8:15 – Lights out/bed check

As much as our escorts tried to stay on schedule, the Captain called three or four lifeboat drills a day, breaking into our lessons. The first few days, I thought I would die before I reached my station. I don't ever want to be that sick again. When the ship's siren sounded, everyone went to their muster station. We followed the hall and staircase arrows for directions to our places on deck. The crew made sure we knew where they were from the very first day on board. As soon as we got to our assigned spots, the escorts took roll call and brought us to our lifeboat station. Sometimes, we would practice climbing into the boats and finding a seat. That was the difficult part. Water and mud swished back and forth along the boat's bottom. The first ones in the boats always slipped and fell on the slimy deck. Then the ones behind them would fall on top. By the time we filled the boat, there were lots of bruises, cuts, and muddy clothes and faces. One after another, girls started throwing up again. Now we would have to muck through mud, water, and vomit on the boat's bottom to get out.

Colin told me he and his mates, the ones who weren't sick, played in these boats all the time. The escorts and crew didn't know it of course, but the lifeboats were their favorite hiding places. I couldn't imagine playing in them with all the mud at the bottom. Now with puke splattered all over, I was sure the boats would be abandoned.

"Looks like the sailors will have quite a bit of cleaning up to do after the drills today." I heard one man from first-class say.

"Won't want that job," another man said.

"Really, must we talk about it," a woman in a fur coat said holding a handkerchief over her mouth. "Reginald, I need to get back to our cabin. This is all too much for me."

"I think I need to get back to our cabin, too," Margaret said.

I agreed, and we asked Miss Julia if we could go below. She just nodded and leaned over the railing, throwing up again.

Colin and his mates kept exploring the ship and finding every nook or closet to use as a hiding spot. But I never heard him mention the lifeboats again. Every night while I was sick, Colin would come and tell me about his day's adventures.

"Lizzie, this ship is a floating palace. I can't wait to show you everything."

"Colin, promise me you'll stay out of trouble until I can watch out for you."

"I don't need you to watch out for me. My mates and I are just having fun. We're not hurting anyone."

"I should hope not! Now, I'll try to stay awake while you tell me about your day."

"Today, one of the sailors taught us how to make a lasso. We practice roping the deck chairs. Since almost everybody is sick, there're plenty of empty chairs on deck. He told us there are contests called rodeos in Canada where cowboys ride bulls, and wild horses, and rope cattle with lassos. He said he even tried to do it once, but he wasn't good enough to win. I'm going to practice every day. When we reach Canada, I'll be the best roper on board.

"I'm pretty sure I'm going to be a cowboy once we get there. I can't practice riding bulls or wild horses, but it can't be much worse than learning how to walk on the ship, the way it goes up and down and up and down and…"

"Colin, stop!" Just thinking about it made me dizzy and sick feeling. "What else did you do today?"

"We explored all the shops. Lizzie, did you know there are shops here?"

I shook my head. The only parts of the ship I had seen were my cabin, the dining hall, and the toilet. The only time I went on deck was when I dragged myself up there for lifeboat drills.

"They're amazing. There are shops with clothes and

jewels. There's a chemist with everything in it just like at home. There's even a newsagent. But best of all is the sweets shop. You should see it, Lizzie. There's all kinds of sweets. Those Mars bars sure looked good."

"Colin, I think I'd like to sleep now. Come see me tomorrow and tell me some more."

"All right, Lizzie. I should probably get back to my cabin anyway. It'll be lights out soon."

Colin bolted out the door, and I tried desperately not to throw up again. I had to think of something besides the sweet sticky Mars bar, or I'd spend another night in the toilet.

Now that I was feeling better, I watched the sun sink below the ocean's horizon, and the sky turned brilliant oranges, pinks, blues, and purples. I regretted my days below deck. The salty sea air reminded me of home. Colin stood next to me and leaned over the railing hoping to see some of the fish he swore swam alongside us every day. *He really is an amazing little brother.*

"Lizzie, are you scared?" he asked still staring into the water.

I'm terrified. I remembered my first day on the ship and how much I still missed Mum. "A little," I said. I couldn't let Colin know how I really felt. I was supposed to be the big sister, his protector, his role model. "But remember all the pictures the CORB man showed us, and what he told us about Canada?"

"I know. It sounded so exciting. He promised we'd see real cowboys and Indians there, not like the ones in the cinema. He even said I could learn to ride a horse. I'd like that. But right now, I'd rather be home with Mum. Don't you miss her, Lizzie?"

"Of course, but she moved to the Castle, remember?

We couldn't live there with her, and we couldn't stay in Liverpool by ourselves. And I don't know if I want to go back there, not with Jerry dropping bombs every night. At least here on the ship we're safe, and I promised Mum I'd take care of you."

"I don't need protection! I'll be ten soon, almost old enough to go out and work. If we went back, Mum could come home and stay with us all the time."

I stroked the shrapnel piece that I kept in my pocket for luck, and thought about home and Mum. *I know she'll be all settled in now at Hornby Castle. I wonder what exactly a maid-of-all-work does, but Mum seemed excited about the position, so I guess she felt it was something she would like.*

"What do you think of that idea, Lizzie?" Colin asked, his eyes now focused on me instead of the sea.

"Sorry, Colin, I guess I was daydreaming. What was your idea?"

"To go back to Liverpool. I figure that when we land in Canada, there will be a lot of confusion and people running about, so we can hide somewhere and when the ship sails back to England, we'll pop out and surprise them."

"Stowaways? Oh, Colin, we can't do that! Remember the stories Uncle Joe told us about what happened to stowaways on his sea voyages? We'd be put in jail and fed nothing but bread and water. And Mum would be so angry with us. Maybe she wouldn't even want to leave Hornby. Maybe she never wants to see Liverpool again." *Maybe she doesn't want to see us again.* That thought sent an ice-cold chill through my whole body. *What if she was tired of taking care of us? What if she sent us away to get rid of us, not to protect us?*

"Lizzie, why are you crying?" Colin asked.

"I'm not. The wind is making my eyes water, that's all. Come on, let's go to the sweets shop. My treat!"

Chapter 11

Colin finished his sweet and ran off to find his friends. I decided to go for a walk around the deck. Miss Julia managed to get outside this morning, so I knew my freedom to roam would end soon. I was still thinking about my conversation with Colin and remembering home. I loved Liverpool. It was so exciting, so interesting. I wondered if all port cities were the same. Ships came and went all the time. Sailors from other countries always seemed to be in the streets. Sometimes, a group of us would surround one or two and get them to tell us about their homes. I imagined traveling to all of them. Whenever I could, I went to Bootle Library and read about all these faraway places. Maybe that's why I was so excited about this adventure. I guess I never thought about how much I would miss Mum and all my friends.

I popped the last bite of my sweet into my mouth and remembered William Ross, the greengrocers. Of course, the shop sold all kinds of fruits and vegetables. One day…

"Auntie Mae, that looks like chocolate in the window," I said. She and I were on our usual Tuesday afternoon shopping trip.

"It is, Lizzie. They started to sell Cadbury's here – chocolate bars with fruit and nuts."

"That's not right," I said. "Fruit stores are for fruit, and sweet shops are for chocolates. Why are they mixing things up?"

"Sometimes, change is a good thing," Auntie Mae said. "Maybe if you're exceptionally good this year, Father Christmas will bring you a Cadbury."

"Father Christmas! I have to wait all year! What if

they stop selling them? What if they run out? Can't we buy one now?"

Auntie Mae laughed. "I'm afraid they're a little too dear for me right now. But ask Father Christmas for one."

I couldn't imagine waiting nine long months for a sweet! I was sure someone else would buy it, and I'd never get to taste this new treat. The next day, I got all my friends together and brought them to the greengrocer's window.

"See, just like I told you. It's a sweet in the fruit shop."

We pushed our noses and hands up against the glass staring at this strange mixture of fruit and chocolate.

"What do you children think you're doing?" a voice boomed at us. "You've got fingerprints and smudges all over my clean window. Who's going to clean this?"

We jumped back and stared at Mr. Perkins, the store's manager. His face was as red as his radishes, and he stood with his fists clenched at his sides. Before he could say another word, we ran as fast as we could. I hoped he hadn't recognized me. If he told Mum, I'd be washing his windows for the rest of my life.

Naturally, after seeing this new miracle of sweets, my friends and I had to try it. We saved up whatever coins we could, managed to finally buy one, and split it up among us. It was quite a treat! Different-tasting than the sweets we were used to, but it was an instant favorite. I decided right then and there to ask Father Christmas for one of my very own. But that was before I found out I'd be sailing to Canada.

I thought about other things they might not have in Canada. They probably don't have a rag and bone man like old Mr. Wilson. It was always a treat when he pushed his handcart into our street blowing his bugle to announce his arrival. All the boys and girls would run to greet him like he was a celebrity. You never knew what he might have in his cart.

"Give you a farthing for this skate blade," one boy shouted.

"Bah! It's worth at least a thrup'nny bit," Mr. Wilson said.

They tossed amounts back and forth until both agreed to a price. In between the sales, his main business was collecting jam jars. The women on the street would give him their used ones, which he sold to Hartley's jam factory. In exchange, Mr. Wilson would announce all the news of neighboring towns since telephone service was sometimes interrupted, and the post was often slower than Mr. Wilson.

"Mr. Wilson, without you I don't think we'd have jam for tea," Mum said.

"Hope it never comes to that," he'd reply.

"Lizzie, there you are," Margaret called. "I've been looking all over for you. There's going to be a wrestling match this afternoon. Want to sign up? I have."

"Wrestling? I've never done that before."

"You've fought with boys, haven't you? It's just like that, only you can't throw any punches. You just sort of grab them, try to get them down on the ground, and hold them there for the count of three. It's great fun. You can watch today if you like and sign up for the next match."

"Well, if it's just a matter of knocking a boy down, I can do that. Where do I sign up?"

"Bob, from G Hall, has the list."

"Let's go find him."

Chapter 12

We found Bob, signed up, and went to the dining hall to strengthen ourselves for the upcoming battle. Cook must have heard about the afternoon's matches. Lunch was a thick Irish stew packed with lamb and potatoes, and there was plenty of bread to sop up the gravy. Dessert was a rich rice pudding.

"Margaret, I think we'd better take a walk around the deck after that meal. I'm so stuffed I could go right to my room and take a nap."

"Oh, no you don't. You signed up, and you're not going to leave me out there all alone. We have to cheer each other on."

We left the comfortable dining hall and went outside. The sea air slapped me fully awake. By now, I was pretty good at walking a fairly straight line, so I only bumped the railing a few times. *Will I ever be able to walk like the sailors? They act like the ship isn't rocking back and forth at all.* We walked around the deck a few times before Bob spotted us.

"Didn't you two sign up for the wrestling match?" he asked. "We're going to start soon." We followed Bob around to the other side of the ship where a mat was placed on the deck. I looked up and saw the first-class passengers leaning over the upper deck's railing to watch the show. My stomach started doing flip-flops. *Maybe this isn't such a great idea.*

"Listen up, here are the rules: no punching, no biting, no kicking. Anything else?" Bob looked around to see if anyone wanted to add something. "All right, let's begin. First match – Joel Burns and Tim Simpson."

Not me, thank goodness! I didn't realize how ner-

your I was until my shoulders slumped back into place
and my fists unclenched. I watched the match carefully
for tricks I could use. When one of the boys hit the mat,
a cheer went up from the audience. Two matches later,
Margaret stepped onto the mat.

"Hurrah, Margaret," the girls shouted.

She circled her opponent crouched down like a cat
looking for an opportunity to grab him. She struck and
at the same moment he stretched his leg to pull her foot
out from under her. Bam! Margaret hit the mat hard.
He jumped on top of her to pin her down but Margaret
wasn't giving in. She grabbed his arm and twisted it so
he had to roll off her. She jumped on his chest and held
him down. Match over!

Cheers and whistles rained down from the upper
deck. Everyone clapped as Margaret took a bow.

"You were wonderful!" I said. "How did you learn
to do that!"

"That was nothing I've been wrestling with my
three older brothers for years."

I stared at her in amazement. "I didn't know you had
three brothers."

"I don't talk about them because they're all in service overseas. I know it's silly, but I keep thinking if I
don't mention them, they'll be safe."

She looked out across the sea.

"Lizzie Gunn, Lizzie Gunn, second call. Are you
here?"

"She's probably scared."

"I bet she's hiding somewhere."

"I'm right here," I shouted. "I was congratulating
my friend, Margaret, on her win. Now, who's willing to
try to wrestle me down?"

*I hope I sound braver than I feel. Maybe my oppo-
nent will give up before the match starts.*

"I'm ready," one of the boys said.

We met in the center of the mat and shook hands.
That was the last friendly move made. I tried circling
around the mat. But he was too quick for me. He knocked
me down twice, but I was able to get away before he
could pin me. The third time I wasn't so lucky.

"The winner, Louie Finch," Bob shouted, hoisting
Louie's arm above his head.

Now the cheers and whistles sounded like the
bombs' whines.

"Cheer up, Lizzie," Margaret said. "This was your
first time. Now that you know what to do, you'll do better next time."

"Lizzie, Lizzie, you were wonderful!"

I turned around and saw Colin grinning up at me
like I was a hero or his favorite cinema cowboy.

"Colin, I lost the match."

"I know, but you went up against Louie Finch. He's
the biggest boy here. Everyone else was too scared to
wrestle with him, but you went right in there. You were
great!"

The other boys and girls were patting me on the
back.

"Good match."

"Proud of you."

"You'll get them next time."

Maybe I didn't do as badly as I thought, but I wasn't
sure I wanted to wrestle Louie again.

Chapter 13

"Lizzie, you're daydreaming again," Miss Julia said.

"Sorry, Miss Julia."

I tried to pay attention, but the further away we sailed, the more I thought of home and Mum. I wondered if she missed us, if she was sorry she sent us away. *Why couldn't she have figured out a way for us to stay together? Why couldn't we have moved in with Auntie Mae or Grannie? Wasn't there a cottage near the castle we could have let? Why didn't she talk to us before the CORB man came? Why did she even buy an Anderson shelter if she knew we weren't going to be there to use it?* I started to get angry. I remembered the day Uncle Bob and the neighbors built it.

"Helen, can you give me a hand out here?" Uncle Bob yelled from the garden.

"Coming, Bob. Be there in a tick," Mum said.

I watched out the window as they lifted the heavy corrugated iron roof into place. They bolted the steel plates at each end. Yesterday, Uncle Bob and our neighbors had dug a pit in the ground. As soon as the roof was attached to the sides, he promised that Colin and I could pile dirt on top. Jerry would never know where we were hiding.

I hated that shelter. It was damp and musty-smelling. But it was pretty roomy inside since the shelter was meant to hold six people and there were only three of us. Mum tried hard to make it comfortable. She put straw mattresses on top of benches she had made from old pieces of wood and bricks. But the cave-like structure still felt like a grave. Sometimes, neighbors would stay there with us. Even with their extra gas lamps, sweets, and made-up games, the dark gloom never left. The overwhelming noise from Jerry planes and exploding bombs bounced off the metal walls and roof. Dirt fell through tiny cracks, and I was always afraid the whole shelter would collapse.

One morning, after a night with lots of bombs falling, I asked Mum, "Can't we stay in the house? Do we have to go to the shelter?"

"Please, Mum," Colin said. "I don't want to be buried here in this crummy old shelter."

Mum kept folding the blankets we had brought with us and walked around the kitchen picking up anything that had fallen during the night. Colin and I watched her, waiting for an answer.

"All right, but as soon as the siren sounds, we'll all get under the dining room table. You children will have to bring your blankets and pillows with you. And keep your siren suits at the foot of your beds. I want you to put them on as soon as you hear the sirens. That way, at least you'll stay warm."

I didn't mind that too much. I rather liked my suit. It was a one-piece and bright blue. I could slip it on over my pajamas quickly. The inside was woolly and the outside had big buttons down the front and a hood to keep my head warm. We put them on every day when we came home from school just in case we had to run to a shelter. At least we would stay warm if we had to spend the night there.

"Hurrah!" Colin shouted. "Maybe I'll sleep in mine. That way I won't have to remember to put it on."

"Oh no," Mum said. "You toss around so much you'll have it in tatters before the week is up."

Colin's face turned pink and he mumbled something about it not being true, but Mum and I were laughing and couldn't quite hear him.

"Mum, you'd better wear your suit too," Colin said.

"Do you think so?" Mum asked winking at me. "I don't know if I'll need it."

"Yes, you do Mum, you do," Colin insisted. "What if we have to go to the shelter after all? What if our house gets bombed and we have to run for our lives? What if we have to stay away for days?"

His fears tumbled out, one question after another. Mum pulled both of us close to her. I don't know how long we stayed like that, but our shirts were wet from our tears when Mum let us go.

Chapter 14

"I'm as stuffed as a Christmas goose," Margaret said.

"You should be," I said. "Really, Margaret, Rice Krispies, and eggs, and bacon, and fried tomatoes!"

"I know, but they all looked so good. Besides, you're as bad. Didn't I see pancakes and kippers on your plate? And how many cups of coffee did you drink?"

"I did overdo the coffee a little, but they've never let us have it before and I wanted to try it. It's not bad if you put enough sugar and milk in it."

"Nothing's bad with enough sugar," Margaret said.

We both laughed. I wished I could box up some of the sugar and send it home to Mum. *I wonder if they have sugar at the Castle. Maybe they have a whole pantry full of sugar. Wouldn't that be amazing – a mountain of sugar for Cook to use every day.*

"Lizzie, Margaret, look!" Colin ran towards us pointing out to sea.

"It's an iceberg!" Margaret said. "I've seen photos of them, but I never thought I'd see one up close."

The sun bounced off the rough sides of the enormous block of ice blinding me for a minute. I don't think I've ever seen anything so majestic. It stood silently like a sentry supervising its section of the sea.

"It's magnificent," I whispered.

We stood watching it slowly slide away as we sailed west.

"Colin, is that the first one you've seen?" I asked.

"No, my mates and I saw one last night. There was just enough moonlight to pick it out."

"Moonlight! What were you doing on deck after

dark? What about bed check? What if you got caught?"

I realized I hadn't been checking on Colin that much. I didn't think he could get into too much trouble on the ship. After all, we had to stay on our deck. We were only allowed to go to the sweets shop on the upper deck once a day – morning or afternoon. With Colin's sweet tooth, I thought he would've spent his shipboard shilling long ago. When we came on board, each of us received a shilling and the Bible. Miss Julia offered to hold our money. When we wanted a sweet, she would give us the money and write it down in her notebook.

"What else have you been doing with your mates? I'm not sure I really want to know, but you'd better tell me."

"Oh Lizzie, this ship is simply wondrous. The lounges are so big and the chairs are the most comfortable ones I ever sat in."

Colin beamed at Margaret and me like he had been invited for tea at Buckingham Palace.

"What do you mean the chairs are so comfortable?" I asked slowly.

Colin blinked and looked away. "I mean, I guess they must be. After all, the passengers up in first class would demand them, wouldn't they? They must have lots of money. All the women wear fur coats and musicians play music for them in the afternoons before the gong."

"How do you know all this?" I asked. "We're not allowed on the upper decks."

Colin shuffled his feet and looked out to sea. "Lizzie, I think I see a whale."

"Don't try to distract me, Colin. How do you know what's going on in first class? Have you and your mates been sneaking around up there?"

"Only a couple of times," he said, suddenly very interested in a spot on his shoe. "But we make sure everyone's gone before we go in."

"How do you know everyone's gone?" Margaret asked.

"Like I said, we wait for the gong. Once that sounds, everyone leaves to get dressed for dinner. The musicians play until the room is empty, then they pack up and leave. That's when we go in."

Colin smiled in triumph, proud of how clever he was.

"Why don't you to come with me today? You'll see how easy it is to get upstairs and not be found out."

"Colin! How can you even think such a thing? You have to promise you'll never go there again."

"You know Lizzie, it might be fun," Margaret said. "Wouldn't you like to see what first class looks like? We'll probably never have another chance. Let's do it. Let's go with Colin and his mates. Come on Lizzie, it sounds like great fun."

Colin stared wide-eyed at Margaret, then turned to me nodding his head up and down.

"Yes, come on, Lizzie. It is great fun and just a little bit dangerous. It's a once-in-a-lifetime chance. What about it?" Colin asked.

I felt a tingle run up my spine. It did sound exciting. *But what if we got caught? What would they do to us? Would they send us back home? Would they lock us up?*

Colin and Margaret stood there begging me to join their pack of invaders. Eyes shining, Colin tugged at my sleeve while Margaret counted on her fingers all the reasons we should go. Their enthusiasm was contagious.

"All right, all right," I said. "Stop tugging at me, Colin. But we do this one time, and one time only, understood? Margaret? Colin?"

They both nodded their heads so violently I thought they would break off and fly away. Colin told us his plan – where to meet, what time, what to do if we saw someone. I began to think he was headed for a life of sneaking into forbidden places. *I'll have to keep a better watch on him for the rest of this voyage. Or plan on visiting him in the ship's jail.*

Chapter 15

The steward placed a plate of roast chicken, pota-toes, and green beans in front of me. One of my favorite meals. Mum only served it on holidays. *Was this a spe-cial day? Was this my last day of freedom before being caught raiding the upper decks? Would I be in jail to-night feasting on bread and water?*

"Lizzie, why aren't you eating? The chicken is deli-cious," Colin said, "even better than Mum's."

"My stomach's a little nervous."

"You'd better eat to settle it. Isn't that what Grannie always tells us?"

I smiled at Colin and watched as he attacked his meal. *He's right. I shouldn't go on our secret mission without a good meal in my stomach.* I took a bite of the chicken. *It* was *better than Mum's! I couldn't let this treat go to waste.* In one more minute, I was talking, laughing, and eating just like everyone else at our table. I even managed to find room for a slice of chocolate cake and a glass of milk.

At quarter to seven, Margaret and I slipped out of our room. Lucky for us, it was wash day and the babies' nappies were hanging out on the deck to dry. The rows of wet cloths hid us as we made our way to the stairs leading up to the first-class lounge doors. The thought of Miss Julia, or one of the other escorts, seeing us sent a cold shiver through me.

When we turned the corner, I saw Colin and two of his mates waiting for us.

"There you are," Colin said. "I was afraid you changed your mind. The gong just sounded, so we'll wait until the musicians leave. Then we can go."

I swallowed hard and nodded my head. I didn't feel good about this adventure at all.

"There, they're leaving," Colin whispered. "Let's go, mates."

He scooted under a rope with a sign that read FIRST CLASS PASSENGERS ONLY and started up the stairs. Margaret and I followed. The other boys were behind us watching for anyone who might come along. The metal railing was cold as ice and my shoes clanked and clanged on each step.

Colin's head reached the deck. He looked around before sliding under the rope at the top of the stairs and running across to the lounge doors. He held one door open and we all rushed in.

The lounge looked just like the fancy ones in the cinemas. There were groups of leather-covered armchairs arranged in circles around small wooden tables. Some sofas and fabric-covered armchairs sat against walls, or back to back. Dark green velvet drapes hung on the windows, and thick carpet in the same color covered the floor. There was a small raised platform in one corner of the room where the musicians played. Their music stands and chairs were still there as if they had just left for a short break. There was also a small bar against one wall with bottles locked behind the metal cage.

Glasses with half-finished cocktails, beer, and ale covered the tables. Smoke curled up from unfinished cigarettes left in ashtrays. It amazed me that anyone could be so rich they wouldn't finish their drink or cigarette. Uncle Bob smoked his right down to his fingertips. Mum always teased him that he'd burn his fingers off trying to get the last pull.

"Here Lizzie," Colin said, shoving a half-filled glass

at me, "try this one. It smells like one I had the other day. It's not too terrible. Some of them are horrid!"

"Colin, what are you doing? I can't drink this! It's whiskey! Only grown-ups can drink it. That's what Mum told us."

"Oh, come on, just try. Look, Margaret's having one."

I looked across the room. Margaret was sitting in an armchair with a drink in one hand and the remains of a cigarette in the other.

"Margaret! What are you doing?" I asked.

"We'll probably never get the chance to live like this, Lizzie, so I'm enjoying it now. It's like playing a role in a film. Please relax, Lizzie. It's jolly good fun and we're not hurting anyone."

I looked at Colin who was still holding the drink, waiting for me to try it. *Oh, why not. Margaret's right. It's our one chance to live like real first-class passengers.* I grabbed the glass before I could change my mind and swallowed the whole drink in one gulp.

"Eww! That was awful! How do people drink this and enjoy it?" I asked.

"Well, maybe that one wasn't your taste," Colin said. "Here, try this one. It looks pretty."

I took the glass from Colin. It was a pretty pale green and smelled like mint.

"I wouldn't mix that one with the one you just had," a voice boomed out.

I jumped and dropped the glass from my hand. Pale green liquid spilled all over the beautiful carpet before it soaked in, leaving a dark stain.

"Wh…Wh… Who's there?" Colin stammered out.

From a dark corner of the room, a chair spun around

and a very large man in a tan suit said, "Colonel Stafford, young man. And you are?"

"Colin Gunn, sir."

The Colonel stood and walked over to us. The first thing I noticed was his mustache. It looked just like the ones I had seen on photos of walruses in my geography book. In fact, he was shaped a little like a walrus – very round in the middle.

"Well, Colin Gunn," he said, "are you the leader of this foray?"

"Of what, sir?"

"Foray, boy, foray – this group of raiders, marauders, invaders, pirates," the Colonel said, giving me a quick wink.

"I, I, I guess so," Colin said.

"Speak up, young man. You're the leader or you're not." The Colonel's voice bounced off the walls of the empty room.

Colin rubbed his right thigh so furiously I thought he would wear his pants right through to the skin. That nervous habit always told me how he felt no matter what he said.

"I, I am," Colin said, standing a little taller. His right arm slowed down and stopped. "I'm this expeditionary force's leader. And this is my sister, Lizzie. I forced her and her friend, Margaret, to come with us tonight. I would appreciate it if you would let them leave. My men and I will take the blame and any punishment for this raid."

I was so proud of Colin. He was trying to protect Margaret and me. I began to think that maybe he didn't need me to watch over him every minute. Maybe he was growing up.

"Glad to see you accepting your role and the consequences. Of course, I'm sure you considered you would be caught by the stewards before long."

"Oh no, sir, we've been watching, and the stewards don't come to clean up until long after the gong. We usually have about an hour here before we have to leave."

"You've done your reconnaissance. Splendid, splendid!"

"My what, sir?"

"Reconnaissance, man! You've observed the area to see how and when the enemy moves through it."

"Yes, sir. That's how we knew we could come here after the gong. Everyone leaves to get ready for dinner and we had the whole lounge to ourselves," Colin said with a grin.

"Think you're pretty clever, don't you?"

"Well, yes sir, I do. We've done this dozens of times and never got caught, right mates?" Colin said turning to them.

They all nodded, but their trembling hands told me they weren't as brave as Colin right now.

"Until today," the Colonel said.

Colin turned around. His face was a mix of red and gray. I didn't know if he was going to be sick or try to run for his life.

"It seems that I now have a decision to make. Do I ring for the steward and have you thrown in the brig — that's the ship's jail, you know — for the rest of the voyage, or let you go with your promise never to return?"

Colin's mates all started talking at once, begging the Colonel to let them go and promising they would never leave their deck again. They surrounded the Colonel with tear-stained faces and hung onto his sleeves and pants' legs. I could feel my stomach bouncing around inside me. I imagined all of us being sent back home as criminals. *What would Mum say?* I looked over at Margaret who was sitting still as a statue, except for the tears flowing down her cheeks. *Will she still be my friend after this? Will she even talk to me in our jail cell? Would they let us stay together? Oh, why did I let Colin talk me into this and why didn't I stop him? Mum will be so disappointed in me.*

The Colonel stood stroking his massive mustache, eyes fixed on the ceiling, deciding our fate. Before, we had been a quiet band of brave burglars, now we were a sobbing pack of penitent pirates. I was sure someone would hear all the cries for mercy and burst through the doors ready to grab us and lock us up for the rest of the voyage. I wondered if we would have to stay in jail on the return voyage too. This was turning into the worst day of my life.

Chapter 16

"I've made my decision."

The Colonel had become our magistrate and I knew his decision would be final. I looked up and expected to see him put the black cap on his head. Whenever someone was found guilty of a serious crime in the films, that's what the magistrate did just before he made his decision. Instead, I saw the beginning of a smile. His mustache was twitching at the corners of his mouth, and his eyes seemed to twinkle just like Colin's did before he got into mischief.

"Ladies, gentlemen, it occurs to me that if you are going to continue with these raids the least I can do is prevent you from getting sick by drinking some of these abominations people call cocktails."

We all stared at him, and at one another. *I can't believe it. We aren't going to jail!*

"Colonel, sir," Colin said. "Do you mean we're free to go?"

"In a way, yes."

Our pack of pirates became merry once again. We hugged the Colonel's legs, wrapped our arms around his waist, and thanked him over and over again.

"All right, children, all right. Now, down to business. We don't have a lot of time left before the stewards come to clean up, and I must dress for dinner. Thank heavens it doesn't take me an hour to do so like those people who have never been in His Majesty's service."

The Colonel had become our hero and we looked at him with adoring eyes. By this time, Margaret had come back to life and stood next to me holding my hand while she used her other one to wipe her teary face clean.

"I suggest we meet again here tomorrow at the same time for your first lesson," the Colonel said. "Do you think you can do that?"

Colin looked around at all the nodding heads and said, "Yes sir. We'll be here a few minutes after the gong."

"Splendid, I'll stand outside the door to let you know when the coast is clear. Now, off you go. Be quick before someone comes."

We scrambled for the door and flew down the steps. When we reached the deck, I looked up; the Colonel was leaning over the railing, waving goodbye.

After that, we met the Colonel every day. He became a true friend to us. He taught us a little about everything, even cocktails. One day after we all sat down around the biggest table in the lounge, he brought over a cocktail called a G&T, or a gin and tonic. He said that was what most sensible people who drank alcohol would drink in the summer. He let each of us dip a finger in the drink and taste it.

"This is terrible," I said. "Do people really like to drink this? I'd much rather have a lemonade or hot cocoa."

Most of our little party agreed. Shudders rippled around the table as each of us tasted the awful concoction.

"I rather like it," Colin said.

"Oh really?" I said. "Well, you'll have to wait about ten years before you have another, so I wouldn't get used to it."

Colin's face turned red, and he mumbled something about just liking it a little, not wanting to have it all the time.

"Colin, it's perfectly all right to like it a little," the Colonel said. "Now when you're older and join His Majesty's service, you'll know what to order at your first formal reception."

Colin smiled, nodded, and stuck his tongue out at me. I rolled my eyes and said to Margaret, "Children!"

"Time for our lessons, boys and girls. Gather round."

The Colonel sat down in one of the large armchairs and picked up a book from the side table. We sat on the floor in front of him in a circle. This had become our daily routine. Each day, the Colonel would allow us to sample one item from first class. One day it was escargot, which I didn't like at all. They were slimy rubbery things, and when he told us they were snails, I was sure I would be sick. I thought about all the trouble they caused in Mum's and Grannie's gardens. I couldn't believe people really ate them and thought they were a delicacy. I would have to write Mum and tell her that all those creatures she was determined to kill were a luxury.

Another time, the Colonel gave us caviar. I didn't like that either. It smelled fishy and was so salty I thought I could never drink enough water to stop being thirsty. He told us caviar was eggs from a fish called a sturgeon. That made me feel really bad. All those little eggs would never become fish because someone thought it was a treat to eat them. Mister Larson used to tell us that he never collected all the eggs from his hens because some of them had to be left to grow up into chickens. I wondered if they left enough eggs to become fish, or if we would run out of sturgeon someday. I didn't know if anyone ate sturgeon, but since Colin and I were heading for a fishing family, I figured I could ask them.

The best part of every day was the Colonel's geography lessons.

"Children, today we're going to look at Canada, where all of us are headed. Let's start with our first port of call, Halifax, Nova Scotia."

I loved listening to the Colonel's voice. It was deep and rumbling and reminded me of Mr. Rawlings' motorboat.

"He's still there, Lizzie," Colin shouted, running ahead of me. "Hurry up before someone beats us."

I ran as fast as I could and soon caught up with Colin. Mr. Rawlings waited for us before casting off from the dock. If he had a good morning fishing, he came back to the dock early and sold his catch to Mrs. Stone, the fishmonger. Then he washed down the boat and whittled or read until school let out. He took the first two or three children who reached his boat out for the rest of the afternoon. Mr. Rawlings loved children but didn't have any of his own. Instead, he adopted everyone from the neighborhood.

"Mr. Rawlings, may we come aboard, sir?" I asked.

"Certainly, Lizzie, and who's that with you hiding behind your skirt?"

"My little brother, Colin. He's only six. This is his first year at school and he's a little shy. He's been watching you take us out to sea, and I've told him stories about our adventures. Do you think he can come today?"

"Well, let's have a look at you, son. Let me see if I can make a sailor out of you."

"Colin, come out from behind me and say hello to Mr. Rawlings. If you don't, you'll never get to go to sea. He'll take one of the bigger boys."

"Yup, might have to do that. Or maybe I'll take him

out and throw him back into the sea. Like I do to the fish that are too small to keep," Mr. Rawlings said, smiling and winking at me.

"Would you really throw me into the sea?" Colin squeaked, his eyes as wide as could be.

"Maybe, maybe. Let's get you on board and see what kind of sailor you are."

Colin and I jumped into the boat, Mr. Rawlings started the motor, and we took off. Once we cleared the dock, Mr. Rawlings pushed the boat faster and faster until we were all the way downriver at the opening to the sea.

"Now we can start fishing. Colin, ever fish before?"

"No, sir."

"Want to try?"

"Yes, sir."

"All right, here's what to do. Lizzie, you know what to do, so go to the other side of the boat while I get Colin all set up here. How do you like sailing so far, Colin?"

"I like it very much, sir. I don't think I ever want to go home. I could stay out here forever."

Mr. Rawlings and I laughed. Colin had never been in a boat before and didn't know what it was like when a storm came up. The rain pelted down, soaked your clothes, and made the deck so slippery you could hardly stand up. I was glad today was sunny for his first fishing trip.

"What are you thinking about, Lizzie?" The Colonel asked.

"Sorry, sir, I was remembering Colin's first time in a boat and first day fishing. That was three years ago, and now we're on the biggest ship ever and soon we'll be in Canada. We're going to a fishing family since Colin loves fishing so much.'"

"Well, I'd bet you're going to stay right in Nova Scotia. Don't you want to know all about your new home?"

"Yes, sir, sorry, sir. I'll pay more attention."

The Colonel showed us where Nova Scotia was on a map in the atlas. I loved that book. It was too big to hold, so he put it on the floor for us to look at.

"I calculate we're about here," the Colonel said. He pointed to a spot in the Atlantic Ocean.

"How do you know?" Margaret asked.

"Of course, I'm not positive, but since the Captain said we didn't have to wear our life belts anymore, I assume we're past the point where the Jerry U-boats patrol. We're out of the danger zone. By my calculations, that puts us around here."

We poured over the map like we could see our ship pushing through the water toward Canada.

"We beat Jerry!" one of Colin's mates shouted.

"Not so loud, my boy," Colonel Stafford said, "remember we're on a secret mission here. If anyone found us, we'd all be in the brig in no time."

We all looked over our shoulders, afraid a steward would pop up from behind one of the armchairs and march us to the Captain for our punishment.

"It seems we're safe this time," Colonel Stafford said. "Let's keep in mind that we can't be too careful, though."

Colin's mate was still shaking so the Colonel said, "Seems you're a bit chilly today. You just climb up here next to me and you'll be warm in no time."

He wrapped one arm around the boy and continued his lesson. He told us all about Nova Scotia, the great forests, and the animals who lived there. "See, here's

Sable Island. There are caribou, moose, bears, beavers, and muskrats there. And here on Cape Breton Island are black bears, bobcats, beavers, chipmunks, and snowshoe hare. Of course, there are porcupines, raccoons, pigeons, doves, ducks, and deer everywhere."

"What are caribou, sir?" Margaret asked.

"They're magnificent creatures. They're taller than I am with huge antlers and weigh 14 to 50 stone apiece. They look just like Father Christmas's reindeer, only bigger."

Everyone stared at him, mouths open, eyes wide. *Could there really be animals bigger than the Colonel?*

"Tomorrow, I'll try to bring some photos to show you, but the ship's library isn't the best. Stocked with lots of silly stories for the ladies to read and pass the time. Rubbish!"

"Have you seen caribou, Colonel?" one of the boys asked.

"Oh yes, on my first trip to Canada I went on a hunt with some other officers. Managed to shoot one and had his head mounted. Maybe I'll have it shipped back to England when this bloody war ends."

"We can bring it back with us," Colin said. "We'll be going back soon, won't we Lizzie? You could have it sent to us and we'll carry it back."

"Fine idea, my boy, fine idea. I just might do that," the Colonel said chuckling a little. "Now back to our lesson."

Chapter 17

That night, before lights out, Margaret and I sat on our beds talking about Nova Scotia.

"It sounds like a wonderful place, Lizzie. I'm sure you'll be happy there. I wish I knew where I was going. Maybe I'll wind up in Nova Scotia too. Then we could see each other. Wouldn't that be wonderful?"

"Oh Margaret, I can't stand to think we're going to be separated. You're my best friend. Who will I talk to every day?"

Miss Julia poked her head in the door. "Lights out, girls. Don't forget to say your prayers, don't forget to pray for the end of this war."

A chorus of "Good night, Miss Julia," rang out all along the hall as she went from room to room.

"We'll talk more tomorrow, Lizzie. Right now, we'd better get to sleep."

"All right. See you in the morning."

I turned off the lamp, pulled the blanket up and settled in; sure I would dream about my future home away from home.

BOOM!

The ship rocked and threw me out of bed. A lamp crashed to the floor.

WEEEEE-YOOOOO, WEEEEE-YOOOOO, WEEEEE-YOOOOO

I bolted up. My heart was pounding.

"Lizzie, it's the siren, the alarm siren, the emergency siren," Margaret babbled.

Mary and Jean started wailing. We didn't know what to do first. The room was pitch black since we closed the blackout curtains every night.

"Mary! Jean! Stop that awful racket!" I yelled. I couldn't think with the two of them howling like banshees. "Margaret, my lamp has been smashed. Can you reach yours?"

"I'll try."

After a minute, she said, "I've got it, Lizzie, but it's not working."

The whole time, the siren kept screaming. It was so hard to hear anything else. The door burst open.

"What are you girls waiting for?" a seaman yelled. "Didn't you hear the alarm? Grab your life belts and coats and get to your muster station. Now! The ship's been hit."

Of course, what's wrong with me? After all our practice drills, when the real emergency comes, I just stand here like a dummy.

With the door open, the emergency lights from the hallway lit our room. A wardrobe had been knocked over onto my nightstand. Pieces of broken lamp lay scattered on the floor. I couldn't believe this was really happening.

"Everyone, put something on your feet before you step on the broken glass," I said. "Come on, you heard the sailor. Grab your coat and life belt and let's go!"

Luckily, we still kept our coats and belts at the foot of our beds. Margaret held Jean's hand, and I helped Mary get ready.

"Wait," Jean cried, "my lamb, Fluffy, I can't leave without him. We have to find him."

She pulled away from Margaret and scrambled up her bunk ladder before we could stop her.

"Jean! Get down from there right now! We have no time for your nonsense. We've been hit by a torpedo. We have to go. Now!"

I had never heard Margaret yell or make demands on anyone, but I was glad she did. She was right. We had no time to look for a plaything. *We could be sinking right now! We might all drown if we don't get to the lifeboats in time!*

"Found him!" Jean said. "Naughty Fluffy. Why are you hiding from me? I've no time for your silly games right now."

Margaret glared at Jean and yanked her down from the top bunk.

"And I have no time for your silliness right now either. Let's go!"

Jean stared at Margaret with eyes twice as big as normal. But Margaret's commands worked. Jean stopped crying and fussing, put on her shoes, coat, and life belt, and grabbed Margaret's hand. We stepped out into a nightmare. Doors lay across the hallway. People screamed. Water dripped from the ceiling. Some of our mates stood like statues, dazed and confused. We hurried to the stairway, pulling and pushing anyone not moving. Some were barefoot, only wearing pajamas and life belts. We didn't have time to go back and look for their coats and shoes, so we shoved them forward.

When we reached our muster station, Miss Julia wasn't there. *Now what do we do? Should we go on to our assigned lifeboat? Should we wait for her?* The cries and screams of both grown-ups and children made thinking difficult. I looked around for Colin. His muster station was on the other side of the ship, but I kept hoping I'd see him.

"Lizzie, what should we do?" Margaret asked. "Do you think we should go to the lifeboat or wait for Miss Julia?"

"Oh, I don't know, Margaret. I'm as confused and scared as you are. Let's wait a few more minutes and see if Miss Julia gets here."

"There you are, children," a voice boomed out above all the noise. "I've been looking all over for you. Well, at least you're safe."

Colonel Stafford stood staring down at us, a huge grin on his face.

"Colonel!" I said. "I don't think I've ever been happier to see someone than right now."

"Come along, girls," he said. "I see we have two more little ones in our group. The boys are waiting for us."

"Colin?" I asked, grabbing his sleeve. "Is Colin all right? Did you find him? Is he injured?"

"He's just fine," the Colonel said. "You stop worrying about him like a little mother hen. He and all his mates are waiting for us in the lounge."

"The lounge!" Margaret and I shouted together.

"What are they doing there?" I asked. "We've been torpedoed! We have to get to our lifeboats!"

I started to think the Colonel must have hit his head or something, or gone completely barmy. Maybe he was injured in The Great War and hadn't told us. Maybe that's why he's been sent to Canada – to recuperate.

"Calm down, children," he said as he herded us along to the lounge. "I've already spoken to the Captain, and while we did get hit, the damage was not extensive and can be repaired. We'll be heading to Canada at top speed now. We won't have to stay with the convoy, and by tomorrow night we'll be out of range of the Jerry U-boats. Ah! Here we are, all safe and sound."

He pushed open the lounge doors and sure enough, Colin and his mates were sitting there pouring over the atlas trying to find our exact spot in the Atlantic like they did every day.

"Lizzie!" Colin yelled as I walked into the room. "I knew the Colonel would find you."

He ran over and hugged me. Now that I knew he was safe, I started crying and couldn't stop. Great sobs shook me from head to toe. I couldn't catch my breath. I felt just like I had on our walk to the bomb shelter the first night away from Mum.

"Lizzie, calm down. Stop crying," Colin said. "The Colonel says everything's all right. The sailors can fix the ship. We can still go to Canada. And I can be a cowboy. I can't wait to write to my mates back home and tell them all about it. Boy, they'll be jealous. Won't they, Colonel?"

"Quite, I'm sure they'll be quite jealous, Colin."

I didn't care about Colin's mates or whether or not they'd be jealous. I just wanted to get off this ship, get away from Jerry, and bombs, and U-boats, and this terrible war.

"Now girls," the Colonel said, looking over at Mary and Jean. "I think there are some introductions that need to be made here."

Margaret took care of that while I tried to stop crying and imagining the worst fate ever – drowning in the middle of this huge ocean.

"Colonel!" I said. "We have to let Miss Julia know where we are and that we're safe."

EEEE-EEEE-EEEE-EEEE

The all-clear siren sounded.

"There you are," the Colonel said. "I told you all was well. I should think your Miss Julia won't be worried about you now. But to be on the safe side, I'll send a message to her, and to Father Brown, to let them know you're with me. Now I think I still need to be introduced to the charming lamb little Jean is squeezing so tightly, and we all need a good cup of tea with plenty of sugar."

The Colonel rang for a porter. We stared, then everyone yelled, "No, no."

"Colonel, not the porter."

"We'll be found out."

"We'll be thrown in jail."

"We'll be sent back before we ever get to see Canada."

"Children, children, calm yourselves," the Colonel said. "The lounge porter and I have a special agreement. After all, where do you think I've been getting all your treats every day? You didn't think I was sneaking into Cook's pantry and stealing them, did you?"

He looked around from one frightened face to another, and let out a big roaring laugh.

"Oh children, you do bring me a great deal of pleasure. Now Jean, let's see about that little lamb before you strangle him to death."

The Colonel sat down and scooped Jean up onto his lap. When the porter appeared, he didn't act like there was anything unusual in a first-class lounge filled with seavacuee children. The Colonel asked him to take messages to Miss Julia and Father Brown, ordered tea, and joined us in our search to locate the ship's position in the Atlantic.

That day and the next, repairs were made to the rooms and the ship, and life returned to normal. Except for the fact that now we had to bring Mary, Jean, and Fluffy with us every afternoon when we went to see the Colonel.

Chapter 18

After our torpedo scare, it seemed we were given a lot more freedom on the ship. One day, tucked into my hidey-hole in the playroom, I overheard Miss Julia and Father Brown talking.

"The poor little things," Miss Julia said. "Imagine being taken away from their homes, put on a ship to sail across the Atlantic to a place they've never been, to a family they don't know. I can't imagine what they're going through. And after that frightful night with the U-boat encounter, well I just can't force them to buckle down and attend to their studies."

"I know what you mean," Father Brown said. "I feel the same way. Let them have a little fun while they can. Who knows what they'll face in Canada."

What are they talking about? "What they'll face?" I thought we were all going to wonderful homes and families. That's what the CORB man promised when he came to tell us about our evacuation. Even the matrons at the Fazakerley Cottage Home told us there were families waiting for us. Miss Julia must be wrong. She just must be.

After they left, I stayed in my hidey-hole where I had been reading. I didn't want to see anyone right now. *What if our family is mean? What if they don't like us? Can they send us home?*

I remembered how excited we all were when the letter arrived from CORB. It looked so important. It was in a brown envelope stamped "On His Majesty's Service." The letter said our application for emigration to Canada had been accepted. As war guests, we were expected to respect and trust our new "host family." Mum was so excited.

"Children, it says right here that your host family will be just like your family here. That makes me feel so much better sending you off. Now I'm sure you'll be safe and well-loved. I have to admit, I've had second thoughts about all this."

"Then why do we have to go?" Colin asked.

"Oh, Colin, we've gone over this a hundred times," Mum said, "I've tried everything to keep you here. But you know how difficult things have been since your Dad died. When I heard there was a maid-of-all-work position at Hornby Castle, I had to apply. I thought maybe, just maybe, you could come with me. That way you'd be away from these raids every night and we'd all be safe. But that's quite impossible. This is the best solution for all of us. Please try to understand."

Mum cried the whole time she told us her reasons. It didn't make me feel any better about leaving, but I knew she was right. We had ticks at the butchers, the grocers, the bakery, everywhere it seemed. Last month, our land-lord had even mumbled about our back due rent.

"Why can't we go live with Grannie or Auntie Mae?" Colin asked.

"I wish you could," Mum said. "But they're strug-gling too. Just last week, Auntie Mae had to take in a boarder to help with her rent. Now that Uncle Francis has been called up to serve in the Army, she needs some help herself."

"Could Grannie take us?" I asked. "We could be a big help to her. I could clean, and Colin could run er-rands. I wouldn't mind standing in those queues all day. I know it hurts Grannie's legs to do that."

"Oh Lizzie, that is so sweet, but Grannie's talking

about moving up North to her sister's house, Great Aunt Flo hasn't been well, and Grannie's been thinking about this move for a while. Now with Jerry bombing us every night, I think she's made her decision. But I promise I'll send for you as soon as it's safe to come home."

I knew then we would definitely be going to Canada.

For the next few weeks, we talked about what an adventure it would be. Mum said she was jealous since she had never left Liverpool and here we were traveling across the ocean to a different country! We spent days at the Bootle Library reading everything we could about our new temporary home. Colin and I even started to get excited about this trip.

Now after hearing Miss Julia, I wondered if it would be such a great adventure.

Chapter 19

"There you are!" Margaret said. "I've been looking all over for you. You have to come quick. The waves are crashing over the front of the ship. It's brilliant!"

"Margaret, it's called the bow. I've told you that a hundred times."

"All rights, the bow. Now, come on! The sailors have even roped off the deck so no one can go there and be hit by a wave."

That sounded interesting. The deck had never been closed off before. This must really be something to see!

I scurried out of my little hidey-hole, and we ran up the stairs to the deck.

When we got there, Colin and his mates were already there. Of course, he would be. If there was any danger, Colin wanted to be there. Now that he had friends and was used to the ship, he didn't need me all the time.

"Lizzie, isn't this wonderful?" Colin yelled over the roar and pounding of the waves. "The whole bow disappears under the waves, and pops right back up. We're taking turns running under the rope to the railing and back before the next wave can catch us. It's like a game of tag with the waves."

It feels like I'm on that giant rocking horse in the playroom. Maybe I should move over to the railing in case I need to throw up.

"Your turn, John," one of the older boys said.

I watched as the wave rose up above the bow. It crashed onto the deck and pulled back into the sea. It was fascinating, powerful, and frightening all at the same time. Another wave rose up and towered over the bow. Right after it pounded the deck, John ducked under the rope and ran to the railing. The deck was slick and he slid a couple of times, but never fell.

"Made it!" he yelled as he touched the rail. He slipped and slid his way back before the next wave pushed over the bow.

I watched in horror as each boy played with the ocean. *This is madness!*

"Colin, it's your turn. Let's go mate."

He turned away from me to take his place at the rope barrier.

"Oh, no you don't," I said grabbing his arm. "Are you barmy? Those waves could catch you and sweep you out to sea forever."

"That's the fun. Don't you see, Lizzie? You have to time it just right so the wave doesn't catch you."

"But the deck is so slippery. What if you fall? There's a reason the Captain put that rope up."

"You never want me to have any fun. I'm sorry I sent Margaret to look for you. I've already done it twice. We've been doing this forever and no one's been hurt yet."

Colin stood in front of me with his arms folded across his chest. I'd seen that stubborn look on his face before and knew I'd never win this argument.

"Peter, you go while Colin argues with his sister," one of the boys shouted.

"Yes, go, Peter," another one of the mates yelled. "Hurry! Don't want to let the wave catch you."

I looked over in time to see Peter duck under the rope and run towards the rail. But he had waited a few seconds too long to start. The wave rose above him. He looked up at the towering wall of water. It soared above his head then crashed down like a giant claw and scooped him up.

We all stood there, mouths hanging open, not be-lieving what had just happened. No one moved. I don't think I even breathed.

"Wh…Wh…Where's Peter?" one of the little ones asked.

"Quick, someone find a sailor," one of the old-er boys said. "Peter must be hanging onto the railing. They'll know how to rescue him."

We went from standing like statues to a panicked group of shouting children.

"Help!"

"Man overboard!"

"Peter's drowning!"

Everyone was yelling something. A few of the older boys ran off to find help. The rest of us kept staring at the spot where Peter had disappeared, hoping somehow he'd pop up and say, "Surprise! Had you worried, didn't I?"

But he didn't pop up, not then, not ever. The sail-ors came and tied ropes from their waists to bars on the side of the ship. They reached the railing at the bow and looked over hoping to see something. Others ran to the back of the ship or the side railing, but there was nothing there. Peter was gone.

Someone screamed, "Peter! Peter!" and ran toward the bow. A sailor grabbed him before he could duck un-der the rope. Everyone started screaming and crying.

Peter's gone? He can't be. We left home so we'd be safe. Now Peter's dead? How could this happen? What if that was Colin? I'm going to throw up.

The Colonel suddenly appeared on deck.

"Children, children, what foolishness have you gotten into," he circled all of us into his arms. "Come along."

He herded us up the stairs into the now-familiar lounge. Only today, it was full of people.

"May I have your attention, please," the Colonel said. "These children have just had a terrible fright. They need a good cup of tea with lots of sugar and some biscuits, I'm sure. I expect none of you will object. They are my very special friends."

People put down their books, or drinks, got up, and surrounded us. They took each one of us over to their table and wrapped a blanket around our shoulders.

One of the ladies went to Colin and said, "Here sweetness, you can come with me."

"No! I want to stay with you, Colonel. Please!"

"Of course, my boy, of course. You and Lizzie will come sit at my table."

"Can Margaret come too?" I held onto her hand afraid to let go. *If I do, a giant wave will crash through the window and grab her.*

"Certainly, Margaret is included," the Colonel said. "Don't think I've ever seen the two of you apart."

Things started to settle down a little after that. The porters ran from group to group with pots of tea and trays of biscuits. I could hear some of the women at the next table whispering to one another. "Poor little things. Seems they've had a dreadful shock."

"What in heaven's name happened? Does anyone know?"

"I certainly don't, but I'm sure the Colonel will tell us in his own time."

"I want to know now. After all, this is a huge imposition having these urchins in our lounge."

"Mildred! These children have obviously gone

through something just horrible. Have some Christian charity for their experience."

"It's just that I'm not accustomed to sharing my afternoons with any children, much less children of the lower class."

"Mildred! I for one am ashamed of you."

"Have a biscuit, Lizzie," the Colonel said, trying to distract me from the ladies' conversation. "It will do you good. Put a little color back in those cheeks."

I looked over and saw the Colonel had snuggled Colin next to him in his big club chair. I gave him a little smile and took one of the biscuits. I didn't think I could swallow it, but it tasted so sweet and buttery that before I knew it, I'd eaten three of them.

The Colonel started to tell us one of his stories from The Great War. They were always favorites of ours and before long, all of us were standing around his chair or sitting on the floor in front of him. I almost forgot why we were in the lounge at this time of day. But I soon remembered when the Captain came through the doors.

"Children," he said. "I need to have a word with all of you. Please come with me."

"Captain," the Colonel said, "if you don't mind, I'd like to accompany the children."

"Certainly, Colonel. Maybe you and I can have a little chat after I speak to them."

I looked up at the Colonel. He looked like one of my classmates who had just been told they had to see the headmaster. *Now he's probably in trouble for being our friend. We can't desert him. We'll have to insist we stay while the Captain speaks to him.*

"Of course, Captain. You're in charge here."

"I'm glad you realize that, Colonel."

We followed the Captain to his private dining room.

"Sit down children. I don't have tea and biscuits for you, but I think you've probably had enough already. Now, what happened today was terrible, and I'm very sorry it did. That doesn't change the fact that what you were doing was against the rules."

"Captain, if I may…"

"No, Colonel, you may not! We are lucky only one child was lost today. All of you could have been swept out to sea. We put those ropes up for a reason. We assumed all our passengers, children included, would realize the danger and stay far away, not go right up to the ropes. I still don't understand how Peter was the only one swept away. Can anyone explain that to me?"

We looked from one to the other. I realized the Captain thought we were just standing there watching the bow go under the waves, and come back up. I could see he was very angry with us. *What would happen if he knew what we were really doing?*

"Well, Sir," one of the older boys said, "we were playing a bit of tag, Sir. With the waves, Sir."

"I don't understand."

"Well, Sir, you see, we would wait until the wave left, duck under the rope, run to the rail, touch it, and run back before the wave came back up."

"YOU WHAT! In the name of all the stars whatever made you think you could play with the ocean like that?"

The Captain's face had turned as red as the apples at the grocer's. He was panting and puffing like an old train locomotive.

"Captain, if I may…," the Colonel said.

"YOU MAY NOT!"

"Captain, the children didn't realize…"

"And because they chose not to pay attention to a barricade put up for their safety, one boy is dead. Should I simply ignore that fact?"

The Captain's words shot out like bullets, hitting each one of us. I'd never felt so miserable, or guilty, or stupid in my life. Colin could have been swept away. Mum made me promise to look after him. How could I ever explain to Mum that I was too busy reading or playing with Margaret. *From now on, I'll be with him all the time, even if I have to tie him to me.*

The Colonel was talking to the Captain, but it didn't look like he was listening.

"No, Colonel, no. The children must be punished for this total disregard of my rules, which, I remind you, were done for their safety and the safety of all the other passengers. That is final! Children, you are confined to the playroom for the next day, or until we come out of this turbulence. You will only be allowed to leave the room for your meals, and to go to bed. Am I understood?"

"Yes, Sir," we all said.

"Good! Seaman Smith!" the Captain yelled.

A sailor came into the room and saluted the Captain. "Bring these children to the playroom and stay with them until one of their escorts arrives. Meanwhile, I will send a message to your escorts informing them of my decision. I will also speak with the ship's chaplain to determine a time for a memorial service for Peter, which you will all attend. Lastly, and this is my most dreaded task, I will have to write to Peter's parents to tell them what has happened. I don't know how I will be able to explain this."

"Yes, Sir," we mumbled.

"And there will be no more afternoon visits to the

first-class lounge. Understood children? Colonel?"

"Yes, Sir," we mumbled again

"Now, Captain," the Colonel said.

"NO MORE VISITS! Do I make myself clear, Colonel?"

"Yes, Captain, loud and clear."

I almost giggled when the Colonel said that, but one look at the Captain told me that would be a big mistake.

We filed out. Seaman Smith watched every move we made. No one was going to slip away under his watch.

Chapter 20

When we got to the playroom, Miss Julia was already there. I didn't think I could feel any worse, but once I looked at her, I did.

Her eyes were red and her face was blotchy. She had a handkerchief balled up in her hand and she kept dabbing her eyes with it. She took another handkerchief out of her pocket and blew her nose. She looked about as bad as I felt.

"Thank you, Seaman," she said. "I'll take charge now. You can go back to your duties."

"Yes, ma'am," he said giving a little salute.

Miss Julia turned and looked at us.

"Oh, children, what were you thinking? Never mind, I don't want to hear anything right now, no excuses or explanations. This is *my* punishment, too, for allowing you some extra freedom before you reach Canada. Now I want each of you to spend some time thinking about what happened today. I also want each of you to write a letter to Peter's parents telling them something about Peter and his time here on the ship.

"But please, don't mention anything that happened today or any other rules he may have disobeyed. This should be a letter with some loving memories of Peter that his parents can treasure."

I grabbed my book and went to my hidey-hole. I wasn't ready to write about Peter yet. I couldn't really believe he was gone. It all happened so fast. One minute he was laughing, running towards the railing, and pumping his fist in the air to show he had made it. The next minute, he was gone. Not one sign of him. Nothing. It was too fast. It couldn't have really happened. In a minute, he'd probably walk through the door laughing, and tell us what a fine joke he had played on us.

But when I looked around the room, I knew that wasn't true. Everyone was crying quietly.

"Can I squeeze in there with you?"

I looked up to see Colin standing in front of me, tears sliding down his cheeks.

"Of course, silly, there's always room for you."

I scooted over a little and Colin sat down next to me. His body shook with silent sobs. He tried to sniff back his tears, but that wasn't working.

As soon as I put my arms around him, he started to cry out loud. And so did I. We cried until I was sure there wasn't a tear left in either of us. My throat was raw from my cries. All around us, the only sounds you heard were sobs and sniffles. I knew no one would ever forget today. No letters were written that day. No one stopped crying long enough to write without soaking the paper with their tears. As I looked around the room, I thought we were the sorriest, most miserable group I had ever seen. Figures blurred in and out through my tears, but then I spotted Margaret. She was curled up in a ball on the couch. She looked like she was trying to disappear into the cushions. I had forgotten all about her.

"Colin, I think Margaret needs a hug too. What do you think?"

I pointed to the couch. Colin wiped his eyes and looked over. He jumped up, ran across the room, and hugged Margaret. I was right behind him and somehow the three of us pulled together into a little circle.

"I thought you'd deserted me," Margaret said. "I was afraid you didn't want to be with me anymore."

"Margaret! How could you think that? You're my

best friend. And you're like a second sister to Colin. Isn't that right Colin?"

"Oh yes, if anything ever happens to Lizzie, I know I can count on you."

We all started to cry again. I felt like I would never stop crying. I missed Mum, and Grannie, and Auntie Mae, and Uncle Bob, and home, and Peter, and everything.

Chapter 21

"Children, please try to eat something," Miss Julia said.

We were all in the dining hall for dinner. But no one was eating. Most of us just pushed the food around on our plates. I knew I wouldn't be able to swallow anything even if the food did make it into my mouth. My stomach felt worse now than it had during the first few days at sea.

"Well, there you all are!" a familiar voice boomed out from across the room. "I've been looking all over the ship."

The Colonel stood in the doorway, hands on his hips, looking very stern. He squeezed his way between the tables until he came to our sorry group.

Miss Julia went over to him and whispered something in his ear.

"What's this? Miss Julia tells me you're not eating. And after Cook spent all afternoon making this wonderful dinner for you? This won't do at all. Not at all, I say. Now everyone, sit up, no more sad faces. You've had a terrible loss and seen something you never should have had to see, but you did and it's done. You can't bring Peter back, and you'll only make yourself sick by not eating.

"I want everyone to take one bite of something on their plate right now."

We all stared at him like he had just asked us to row the ship to Canada. How could he think we could eat? I knew I would be sick the minute food touched my mouth.

"Come along, no more dawdling. We can't wait all night, you know."

One by one, we picked up our forks and put a tiny morsel of food on them. I looked at my plate and thought the mashed potatoes look like the easiest thing to swallow.

I'll try, but I won't apologize if I throw up all over the table. Why is the Colonel acting this way? He's always been so kind to us. Now he's just being mean.

I was amazed! The potatoes slid right down my throat with no problem at all. In fact, they tasted really good. My stomach started to rumble. I guess I was a little hungry after all. I realized I hadn't eaten anything since breakfast. We didn't even have tea.

The Colonel started telling us stories of his time in India. They were amazing, with tales of tigers, and rajahs, and princesses, and elephants. Before I knew it, my plate was empty. I looked around the table and saw that everyone had finished their dinner. I guess we were all hungrier than we thought.

"Now," the Colonel said, "I think you might still have room left for a little cake and tea. I checked with Cook before I came in and he said he would bake something special for you today. Something sweet to end your day. Think you can manage to find room for that?"

We all nodded, and the Colonel called our server over to remove our plates and bring dessert and tea. "And some for me as well, please," he said, winking at him.

After dinner, the Colonel went back to the playroom with us.

"As you heard earlier," the Colonel said, "the Captain is not pleased with our afternoon get-togethers. In fact, after you children left, he gave me quite a tongue-lashing. So, I'm afraid there will be no more secret visits to the lounge."

We all moaned when we heard this. Visits with the Colonel had become a highlight of my day. He always had some interesting treats for us, and after, we would either travel the world through the giant atlas, or he would read to us from one of his books. It looked like the rest of the voyage was going to be very dull.

"In light of these circumstances, I find I cannot disobey the Captain's orders. After all, he is in command on this ship."

"Yes, Sir."

"Yes, Colonel."

"We understand."

"We wouldn't want you to get in trouble."

We all tried talking at once.

"Hush, hush. I've thought it all over, and decided that while you can't come to my lounge, there is nothing the Captain said that prevents me from coming to yours."

We looked at each other wondering what he meant. *What lounge? We don't have a lounge.*

"Right here! This playroom is your lounge. From now on, I will come here every afternoon, right after the gong. We can still have our treats, and stories, and I'll even arrange to have the atlas brought down here so you can look through it any time you choose."

"Hurrah, three cheers for the Colonel!" one of the boys shouted. "Hip hip hurrah, hip hip hurrah, hip hip hurrah!"

Everyone crowded around the Colonel to thank him. The rest of the voyage wouldn't be dull and terrible after all. *The Colonel is one of the best people I've ever known. I wish Mum could meet him. I'll have to write and tell her all about him.*

The next day, the Captain announced there would be

a memorial service for Peter after tea. I had never been to a memorial service before. When Dad died, Mum held a wake at the house. We had a funeral service at the church. After that, our family and friends came back to the house to remember Dad and talk about him. But this was different. We couldn't say a proper goodbye to Peter since the sea had already taken him away. We didn't even have a lot of memories of him. We'd only known him for a little while. And there wasn't anyone from Peter's family here.

"Margaret, I don't think I'll go to Peter's memorial service," I said after we had finished breakfast.

"But you have to, Lizzie. We all have to go. The Captain said so and so did Miss Julia."

"The only people who knew Peter were a few of us seavacuees. The other people who will be there didn't know him. They probably never even saw him. They simply think it's their duty to go to the service for the 'poor little thing' as they're always calling us. I hate being called that. I hate all those people too. Just because they're in first-class doesn't mean they're any better than you or me."

"I don't like them much either. But I still think we should go. You don't want them to be the only ones there, do you? I think we owe it to Peter. I think we should think of him as a casualty of this war. We have to honor him, not ignore him."

I had to think about what Margaret said for a while. *Was Peter really a war casualty? Was this like a service that would be held for any serviceman who died away from home?* For a while, I guess I had forgotten about the war. There was no rationing on the ship. We were out of danger from the Jerry U-boats. It seemed like ages ago that we were running to shelters or basements to stay safe from the bombs. Without thinking, I reached into my pocket and rubbed my lucky charm, my piece of shrapnel. I had become so used to feeling it every day that I almost forgot where it came from.

Margaret had made me remember. There was a real war going on back home. People were dying every day. People were losing friends and relatives to Hitler's army and navy. Peter's family had lost him because we were on a ship sailing to somewhere safe. Somewhere his mum and dad thought would be a better place than England. Margaret was right. Peter was a casualty of war. He deserved to be honored by the people who knew him best – all of us seavacuees. And I wouldn't cry. I would stand there and be proud that I had been Peter's friend.

Chapter 22

"That was a lovely memorial service," the Colonel said. "Don't you think so, children?"

We all nodded our heads. Sad faces and feelings circled the table and our playroom. The Colonel had ordered tea and biscuits to cheer us up but it wasn't really working.

"Margaret, Lizzie," Miss Julia called, "I could use some help here with the little ones."

From the very first day, Miss Julia had counted on us to help her. There were still a few toddlers in nappies and the three-, four-, and five-year-olds needed constant watching and entertainment. If we left them alone at the table with paints and paper, one of them would have purple or green hair in minutes. Blocks became weapons, and paste turned into a favorite snack. The giant rocking horse was a favorite toy, but since it was so tall, the little ones needed help getting on and if they fell they had all kinds of bruises. Now that we were close to the end of our voyage, Miss Julia didn't want the children to look like casualties of war when they left the ship.

"All right, everyone sit down on the rug and I'll read you a story," I said.

I thought that would be a safe activity.

"Lizzie, Robert pinched me," Jean said.

"Did not," Robert protested.

"Yes, you did. Look, my arm is all red," Jean said.

"Maybe your silly lamb bit you," Robert said.

"Fluffy would never do that. Would you, Fluffy?"

Jean held her little lamb to her ear and listened while all the other children stared at her, waiting for Fluffy's answer.

"He said he would never bite me, and that he saw you pinch me. Lizzie, you have to punish Robert. He's a very bad boy."

Punish Robert? What was I supposed to do? I didn't want to call for Miss Julia. She and Margaret were busy with the babies. I couldn't send him away. I was in charge of watching all of them.

"Robert, come here," I said. "As your punishment, you'll have to sit right here next to me, facing the wall. You're not allowed to talk at all while I read the story, and you must apologize to Jean. Do you understand?"

"But Lizzie, I won't get to see the pictures," he said.

"Well, maybe next time you won't pinch someone."

I felt terrible punishing the little lad. I looked over to the table where the Colonel sat telling another of his wonderful tales, and he gave me a little wink. I felt better after that. Then I thought about Peter. If only he had obeyed the rules, he'd still be here with us and I wouldn't feel so sad.

Robert mumbled an apology and crawled over to the side of my chair facing the wall. Tears ran down his cheeks. I wanted to grab him, hug him, and tell him everything was all right, he was forgiven. But I didn't. *I wonder if this is how our teachers feel when they punish us. I don't think I want to be a teacher. I don't even think I want to be a grown-up, but I have no choice about that.*

By the time the story was over, half the children were curled up asleep on the rug. Robert had managed to half turn and kneel beside my chair peeking over my arm at the pictures. Since none of the children said anything, I let him.

"All right children, naptime," Miss Julia said.

Little cubbies with cardboard walls had been set up

along one wall of the playroom. Margaret and I carried the sleeping ones to their spots while Miss Julia led the others. Soon everyone was tucked in.

"Girls, I'm counting on you to stay here and watch over the children," Miss Julia said. "The Captain wants to see me to discuss our departure plans. I'll be back as soon as I can."

"Yes, Miss Julia," we both said.

"I guess we should tidy up while Miss Julia's gone," Margaret said.

"I guess so. These little ones certainly do make a big mess."

"Where's the Colonel? And the boys? They could have helped."

"I don't know. We were so busy getting everyone in for their naps, I didn't pay any attention to them."

"Do you think this means we're allowed to leave the playroom and go out on deck again?"

"I don't know," I said. "We'd better wait until Miss Julia comes back and ask her. Besides, she'll probably be back before we finish picking up."

I looked around at the mess in front of us – paints and glue pots with no lids on them, paper on the tables and floors, crayons out of their boxes, blocks scattered throughout the room, and dollies and toys off their shelves.

"Let's get started," Margaret said.

When we finished tidying the room, the first little one to wake up stood staring at us over his cardboard wall.

"Now you lay right back down and close those eyes," Margaret said. "You know you're not allowed to be up until Miss Julia gets back."

His head quickly disappeared, and we heard him

shuffling around on his mat.

"You'll make a good mummy," I said

Margaret giggled and said, "I'd love to be a governess, but I don't know about being a mummy."

"Maybe that's what you'll be when you get to Canada."

"Oh, that would be lovely. Do you think I might? Do you think I'm too young?"

"I don't know, Margaret. So many of the older girls back home left to join the Land Army, or the Ambulance Corps, there aren't many left for governess's jobs. Maybe it's the same way in Canada."

"Maybe, but we're only going to be there a short while, so I don't really care where I go or what I do. Do you?"

"Not really. Like you said, it's only going to be for a few months. We'll probably be back home when school's second term starts."

"Well, girls, this is just lovely," Miss Julia said. "You've done a beautiful job putting all things right. Thank you. Any problems?"

"No, Miss Julia," I said. "One of the boys woke up, but Margaret told him he had to go right back to sleep. And he did. She sounded just like a grown-up."

Miss Julia laughed, thanked us again, and told us we could go on deck for a while before dinner. The Captain had decided we had been punished long enough.

That was great news. I felt like I had been locked up in the playroom for ages, even though it was really only a day and a half. The sea air smelled wonderful when I reached the deck. I closed my eyes and let the wind blow through my hair. It wouldn't be long now before we reached Canada.

Chapter 23

"Look, Lizzie, look, Margaret," Colin shouted pointing out to the ocean. "It's a whale. We saw one a while ago with the Colonel. He's the one who spotted it and told us all about them."

"Where, Colin?" I asked.

"Keep looking right over there. The whales have to come up from the ocean for air. They break through the surface, and blow air out of the blowhole on top of their heads. It looks like a big fountain shooting water into the air."

"There! I see him," I shouted.

"Me too," Margaret said.

We stood at the ship's railing and watched as one after another, whales broke through the water.

"That was amazing," I said. "I can't wait to write Mum and tell her."

"My mates will be so jealous when I tell them about all of my adventures," Colin said. "I bet they'll wish their mums had let them go to Canada."

I still wasn't sure I really liked this journey, but it was a great adventure. Soon this part of our trip will end and another part will begin. *What will our host family be like? Will they have children our age? Will they live in the city or the country? Please, let them like me.*

"What are you thinking about, Lizzie?" Margaret asked.

"Just wondering about our host family. I hope they're nice. Do you wonder about yours?"

"Of course, but I'm not worried. I'm sure they'll be wonderful hosts, but I do wonder about school. I hope I'm smart enough to stay in the same grade. It would be awful if I had to be in a class with girls younger than I."

"I never thought about school. You don't think they have school in the summer, do you? I hoped we could see a little bit of Canada before we had to start our studies."

"Oh, I'm sure they don't have summer classes. I asked the CORB man about that. What do you want to see in Canada?"

"I'd like to see the Rocky Mountains and visit some Indian villages. I'd love to go into the woods and see the moose and caribou the Colonel told us about. What do you want to see, Margaret?"

"Some of the same things as you, but I'd also like to go to one of the big cities and see a play, or ballet, or some kind of dance recital, or maybe hear a big orchestra. We don't have anything like that in Manchester. The only dance recitals we have are from Miss Sophia's Dance Studio, but the soldiers took her away when the war started. She came to England from Poland, and once Hitler's army took that country over, she became our enemy."

"That's not fair. She had nothing to do with Hitler. Poland didn't declare war on us. I bet the Polish people hate Hitler as much as we do."

"I'm sure you're right, Lizzie, but now they're our enemy too. I just wish this war would end. I know at home everyone says 'Endure the Duration' but I'm already tired of enduring. I want to go home and see my Mum and Dad, and I want my brothers to come home and be safe."

"I want to go home too, Margaret. But now, my Mum works at Hornby Castle. I don't know where I'll go when I do go home. She lives there now, and Colin and I can't live with her."

"Maybe by the time we go home, you'll be old enough to work there."

"Even if I was old enough, what would happen to Colin? He'd still be too young."

"I forgot about how young Colin is. Maybe he could live with me at my house. At least until he's old enough to work at the Castle. You did say I was a second sister to Colin, didn't you?"

"Oh Margaret, you're the best friend I could ever have," I said hugging her. "Let's not tell Colin any of our plans. I don't want him to worry."

"All right, but I'll write to Mum this afternoon and tell her. I'm sure she'll be as excited as I am. Colin can bunk in with my brothers. It will be wonderful."

"It sounds like Colin and I will have another great adventure."

Chapter 24

That night, Margaret and I sat on her bed, and she told me all about her mum and dad, and her brothers. She described her room and the whole house.

"When you visit, you can stay in my room. If you want, I'm sure Mum could make us new curtains, maybe even a new bedspread."

"Oh no, Margaret, it all sounds beautiful. I've never had pink curtains. Mum never had time to make pretty things for my room. And since I shared it with Colin, his toys were always all over the place. I can't believe you have a room all to yourself."

"I am lucky, but Dad said he didn't want me bunking in with the boys, so I shared the room with Grannie until she died. After that, Mum and Dad said that I could stay there all by myself. I love my room. Dad built a little bookcase for me and I keep my toys and books there. I get a new book every Christmas, and I've kept all of them since I was a little girl. Now I have a whole shelf. Maybe there are some you haven't read yet."

"I'm sure there are. Mum takes us to the library every week, so I've read a lot of books, but it must be lovely to have your very own books. You can read them anytime you want."

We talked until it was time for lights out.

I fell asleep dreaming about Margaret's home.

At breakfast the next morning, Miss Julia and the other escorts went to each table and told us to go to the playroom when we finished eating.

I wonder why? I hope there hasn't been another accident or a problem of some kind.

When we were all assembled, Miss Julia said, "Children, we want you to know we will be arriving in Halifax, Nova Scotia tomorrow. We want you to get dressed in your best clothes in the morning and pack all your belongings in your suitcases. Check your rooms carefully because you certainly can't come back for something you left behind. I expect the older boys and girls to help the little ones. The other escorts and I will, of course, take care of the toddlers.

"When we arrive at the port, the first-class passengers will debark. After that, we will be taken to a special area where the Canadian customs officers will review our paperwork before we leave the dock. This may take a while, so I expect everyone to be on their best behavior. Are there any questions?"

"Miss Julia," one of the girls said, "will our host families be at the dock?"

"I don't believe so. As I said, the customs officers have to review your papers, so that may take some time. But don't worry, CORB made arrangements for all of you in Halifax. Some of you will be matched up with a local family, while others will travel by train to different parts of Canada."

Matched up? I thought we already had a family waiting for us. Why couldn't they come to meet us at the dock? Miss Julia talks like she doesn't know which family we will be living with. She must be wrong. The CORB man promised our host family would be just like our real family. Maybe Colin's stowaway idea isn't so dumb after all.

"Lizzie, isn't it exciting?" Margaret asked. "In just one day, we'll be in Canada. I can hardly wait to meet my host family. What's the matter, Lizzie? You don't seem very happy."

"I don't know, Margaret. I thought there would be a family waiting to take us home with them, I didn't think we'd have to go somewhere else and wait for them."

"What's the difference whether we meet them on the dock, or somewhere else? I'm sure they'll come to get us as soon as they hear the ship has arrived. Sometimes you worry too much, Lizzie."

I guess Margaret's right. It really doesn't make any difference if we meet our host family tomorrow or the next day. I have to stop worrying about everything – except making sure Colin is packed and ready.

Chapter 25

"Well, children," the Colonel said, "tomorrow starts a whole new life for you. I envy you – getting to start up in a new country, no one knowing anything mischievous you did before, finding new mates, maybe even making Canada your new home, for you older ones that is. Ah, yes, what a great opportunity."

Making Canada my new home! What does he mean? We're only going to be here a few months.

"Colonel," Colin said, "are you going to be in Halifax? Can we still see you all the time?"

"No, my boy, I'm afraid not. I've been assigned to Toronto to help train the new recruits. Some of our Canadian soldiers are already fighting in France, and it's important that we train more of our men to join them."

"Won't we ever see you again?" Colin asked.

I could see his eyes starting to water and hear the sniffles of some of the others.

"Oh, it's not such a disaster, Colin. You can write to me and tell me all about your adventures. I'm sure you'll all have many great stories to tell me. I've given my address to your escorts, and they can give it to you after we disembark. And I expect to hear from each and every one of you," the Colonel said pointing his finger at each of us.

"Ah, here's our tea. I thought for a minute Cook forgot all about us."

The Colonel got up to inspect the tea tray, and I saw him brush his hand across his eyes.

I'm going to miss you, Colonel. You've been a real friend, even if you are a grown-up.

We sat quietly and had our tea, tears slipping down

our faces.

"Now, now, children," the Colonel said, "why all the sad faces? You are about to embark on the greatest adventure of your young lives. You should be excited, not gloomy. Come on now, tell me what each of you is most excited about seeing or doing in Canada."

One by one, we told the Colonel our dreams and hopes. Thanks to the Colonel, we had learned a lot about Canada. Some wanted to go out west and be lumberjacks or trappers. Some wanted to become mountain climbers. Soon there was a whole list of possibilities – farmers, teachers, soldiers, governesses, big-city successes.

"And Lizzie and I are going to be fishermen," Colin said.

"Well, that's quite an ambition," the Colonel said. "Why do you think that will happen?"

"When we left Liverpool, the matron asked us if we wanted farming or fishing and I told her I liked fishing, so that's what she marked on our papers."

"I guess you're all set, Colin. Not afraid of going out in this big ocean again?"

"No sir, I love the sea. When I finish being a fisherman, I'm going to enlist as a sailor."

"Colin, when did you get that idea?" I asked.

"I've been thinking about it for a while, Lizzie. I'm sure the Navy could use some men who are used to being on the sea. And the sailors have taught me how to tie knots and lots of other things."

"When you're old enough to join the Navy, the war will be over."

"I know, but I can still become a sailor, can't I, Colonel?"

"Certainly, my boy, certainly. The Navy is always

looking for good seaworthy men," the Colonel said.

What will Mum think about that? I don't like it one bit. I don't want to think about not seeing Colin every day.

"And what about you, Lizzie? Do you want to be a sailor too?"

"Oh no, Colonel, but I do want to meet some cowboys and Indians and I want to see the mountains. The CORB man showed us pictures of them in the summer and they still had snow on the tops. They must be wonderful. I just know this will be an amazing holiday adventure."

"I hope it will be, Lizzie. I hope it will be a wonderful holiday for all of you. And as soon as our boys squash Jerry, you can all go home and tell everyone what a marvelous visit you had in Canada.

"Look at the time," the Colonel said, pulling his watch out of his pocket. "I'm having dinner with the Captain tonight. Mustn't be late and keep him waiting. I won't see you children tomorrow, so I'll say goodbye now. Make sure you write and tell me all about your life in Canada."

Like one massive wave, we crashed upon the Colonel. We blubbered our goodbyes mixed with tears and sniffles. The Colonel was sniffling too as he walked out of the playroom.

How many more people will I have to say goodbye to?

Chapter 26

I woke to a calm, sunny day. Last night after dinner, we stood on deck and watched as the Canadian shoreline got closer and closer. This morning after breakfast, we ran outside and there was Halifax. We could see the docks and the city. It was crowded with buildings. Some taller than I had ever seen. My stomach started jumping around like it had the first day on the ship. But I knew I wasn't going to be sick this time. I was just nervous and excited.

"It looks so big and busy," Margaret said.

"Look, here come the tugboats to take us into port," Colin said.

"How do you know that?" I asked.

"I told you. The sailors have taught me a lot about being on the sea."

Colin has certainly changed. He isn't the same scared boy he was when we left Liverpool. He's really ready for this new life.

We watched the tugs line up next to our ship. The sailors waved up to us and yelled, "Welcome to Canada."

This is going to be a great adventure.

"Children," the Captain's voice boomed over the loudspeaker. "Today is August 19th. We will be pulling into the port of Halifax, Nova Scotia shortly. Collect your bags and report to the dining hall."

We waved goodbye to the tugboat crew and ran downstairs to our cabins. We had packed last night and only had a few last-minute items to put in our suitcases.

"Mary, Jean, make sure you pack your toothbrushes, and your hairbrushes," Margaret said. "And Jean, don't forget Fluffy. You won't be allowed to come back to look for him."

"Oh no, Margaret, I've got him right here. I tied him onto my wrist so he doesn't get lost."

I looked over and laughed. Jean had used one of her hair ribbons to tie Fluffy to her.

"I guess we don't have to worry about losing him," I said.

Margaret and I picked up our bags, and Mary's and Jean's, and headed for the dining hall. Colin was waiting for us at the door.

"I didn't want to go in without you, Lizzie. It's so crowded in there I figured I'd never find you."

"Colin, you're getting smarter every day," I said.

He flashed a big grin at me and we went into the hall.

I stopped as soon as we went through the doors. I forgot how many of us were on the ship. The hall was packed with 350 CORB children, their suitcases, and the escorts.

I'm so glad Colin waited for me. I never would have found him in this crowd.

"Children, quickly find a seat," one of the escorts said. "We'll be docking soon."

We put Mary and Jean at a table saved for the little ones, and we made our way towards the far end of the hall.

"There, Lizzie, I see three seats at that table," Colin said, pushing through to save them for us.

"Let's try to stay together," Margaret said. "Maybe we can even go to the same host family."

I gave her a small smile, but I knew that would never happen. *Who would want three seavacuees? Would a family even want two? What if they tried to separate Col-*

*in and me? I couldn't let that happen. I promised Mum
I'd stay with him, protect him, keep him safe. Oh, why
did we ever leave Liverpool?*

"Oh, I forgot," I said, "I stopped at the sweets shop
yesterday and got each of us a Mars bar. I don't know
if they have them in Canada, and I thought we could all
use a treat."

"Thank you, Lizzie," Margaret said. "How ever
could you manage to buy three?"

"I asked Miss Julia if I had enough money left and
she said I did, so this is what I decided to spend it on."

"You're the best sister in the whole world," Colin
said through a mouthful of candy.

"Children, your attention please," Miss Julia said,
speaking into a microphone. "We are all going to go out
on deck in a minute and wave hello to everyone waiting
to greet us on the dock. Check your luggage and make
sure your name is on it. The porters will come around,
collect it, and bring it to the customs house where we're
all headed to have our passports stamped.

"I don't think I need to remind you that you are to be
on your best behavior. We don't want our host families
thinking we don't know how to conduct ourselves, do
we?"

There was a general murmur of agreement, but everyone wanted to get outside and get a close look at our
new home.

"Do you think there'll be cowboys and Indians on
the dock to meet us?" Margaret asked.

"Wouldn't that be wonderful," I said.

"Maybe one of the cowboys will be our host family," Colin said. "I might decide to become a cowboy
instead of a sailor. Or maybe an Indian family will be our

host family. Wouldn't that be brilliant?"

"I'll be happy just to meet them," I said.

"All right, children, the escorts will dismiss you one table at a time," Miss Julia said.

Of course, that didn't work out very well. As soon as she stopped speaking, everyone got up and headed for the doors. You would think the ship was sinking the way everyone was pushing to get outside.

"Come on, Lizzie, Margaret, this way," Colin said.

He pulled us away from the direction everyone else was going.

"Where you going, Colin?" I asked.

"I know another way to get to the deck. Follow me."

He wound his way around the tables and through a set of doors into the kitchen. He ran through the empty room to a door at the far end. It led to a narrow hallway I had never seen before.

"This way," Colin said.

He turned left and ran down the hall to a metal door at the end.

"Give me a hand," he said.

Margaret and I grabbed hold of the round wheel in the middle of the door and pulled. The door was very heavy, but once we got it open a little, it swung the rest of the way easily.

"Here we are," Colin said beaming.

We stood on the deck looking down at the dock.

"How did you know about that way out of the dining hall?" I asked.

"I told you, Lizzie, I made friends with some of the sailors. They've shown me all different parts of the ship. You should see the engine room, and their quarters, and…"

"Stop! I don't think I want to know anymore."

"Look, the people are throwing things up to us," Margaret said leaning over the railing.

Colin and I ran over. They were throwing sweets and coins to us. Some had signs that said, "Welcome to Canada." Others waved small British flags. Everyone was shouting a hello or welcome.

I can't believe it. They seem really happy to see us. They must be very rich. How can they throw away sweets? Isn't sugar rationed here?

"I caught it. I caught a coin," Colin said.

"And I got a sweet," Margaret said.

I stopped thinking about why they were throwing things and tried to catch something myself. We all grabbed at whatever came our way. Between what we caught, and what landed on the deck, our pockets were soon full.

"All right, children, pick up whatever you can and let's go," a sailor said as he herded us along to the gangplank.

We were all laughing, excited, and happy.

I think I'm going to like Canada. I don't know why I was so scared of the people here. They certainly seem happy to see us.

Chapter 27

The escorts led us off the ship to the customs house. It looked like a big old barn with wooden walls and doors. Inside wasn't very welcoming either. There were rows of wooden benches and men sat at long wooden tables at the end of the room. Three light bulbs hung from the high ceiling and made our shadows look long and scary. My thoughts of the warm welcome from the people on the dock quickly faded. *This place is as bad as the warehouse in Liverpool. I'm beginning to get bad feelings again about this adventure.*

We sat on the benches and waited for our names to be called. At least they didn't separate Colin and me, or Margaret. One by one, boys and girls went up to the table, spoke to the officers, and went through a door to another room.

Finally, it was our turn. Colin and I were called together. I squeezed Margaret's hand and said, "I'll see you in a few minutes."

She nodded, tears in her eyes. *She looks so scared. I would be too if I had to sit alone in this place. It's so gloomy. It reminds me of the air raid shelters back home.*

The officer asked us our names, where we came from, our mother's name, and our age. Then they stamped our passports. Another officer took us through the door where everyone else had disappeared.

Now we were in a smaller room painted bright white, with lots of ceiling lights. Rows of cots lined the room. Doctors and nurses moved from one cot to another. Boys and girls from the ship sat or lay on the cots with their sleeves rolled up.

"What's going on?" Colin whispered to me.

"I don't know."

"All right, let's get you two settled, shall we?" one of the nurses said. "Come with me, sweetie."

She took Colin's hand and started to lead him to an empty cot.

"No, I'm not leaving Lizzie," he shouted. "You can't make me." He pulled away from the nurse and grabbed my arm.

"She won't be far away. Now come along. Be a big boy and get your shots."

"Shots? What shots?" I asked. "No one told us about getting shots. I don't want any and neither does Colin."

"I'm afraid you don't have a choice about it," the nurse said. "Now stop your nonsense and come over here."

"No," Colin screamed, "I'm not leaving Lizzie."

"Nurse," one of the doctors said, "just have them sit together on the cot. I'll do both at the same time. We can't have screaming like that in here. Before you know it, they'll all be screaming for their mommies or something else."

"Yes, Doctor, the two of you sit over here and behave."

Colin wiped his eyes and looked at me.

"Come on, Colin, it'll be all right."

At least I hope it will be. Miss Julia would be upset at the fuss Colin was making, I'm sure. But no one told us about getting shots. What are they for anyway?

We sat for a minute and another nurse came over.

"We have to weigh and measure you. Come over here and step on the scale."

Colin went first, now it was my turn. The nurse wrote everything down on a chart. Then the doctor came over.

"It seems you're not malnourished. Guess the food on the ship was pretty good. Let's look down your throats and see how they look."

He sat in front of Colin on a little stool with wheels. "Open wide. Say aaah." He put a wooden stick in Colin's mouth. "Tonsils intact, no sign of disease," he said to the nurse. "You're next," he said to me. "Amazing. She still has her tonsils too. How old are you?"

"I'm thirteen."

"Seems they don't believe in removing tonsils in England," he said to the nurse. "I could count on one hand the children who have had a tonsillectomy."

"Yes sir," the nurse said, writing on our charts.

"All right, roll up your sleeves," he said. "You're each going to get some vaccination shots. We don't know whether or not you got these, so we'll just give you another to be sure."

"What are they for, Doctor?" I asked.

He smiled and said, "I doubt you know about any of these diseases, but you'll be vaccinated against small-pox, inoculated against diphtheria, and tested for tuberculosis. Ever hear of any of them?"

We both shook our heads. They all sounded terrible.

"The needle might hurt a little, but it's necessary. With the tuberculosis test, your arm may get a little itchy, but that's normal. If you see a hard, red bump at the test spot in two or three days, you'll need to see a doctor. Do you understand?"

"Yes Doctor," we both said.

"Good. I'll leave you in the good nurse's hands. Oh, and welcome to Canada. I hope you enjoy your stay here."

"Thank you, Doctor," we both said.

The nurse gave us our shots and the tuberculosis tests, and told us to go through a door to another room.

This one was a little smaller than the first one but just as scary. When there were about twenty of us sitting there, a matron told us we were going to the Fairview Home in Halifax. *The Fairview Home? Where is our host family? We aren't supposed to go to a home. This is not what the CORB man promised would happen.*

"We'll leave here and take a Birney Car to the Home," the matron said. "You can have lunch when you get there."

Lunch?

"What's lunch?" Colin whispered to me.

"I don't know. Maybe it's like our dinner."

"Then why didn't she say dinner? And what's a Birney Car?"

"I don't know Colin. I guess we'll have to wait and see what happens."

I don't think I like Canada. I don't understand why we had to get shots, or what lunch is, or a Birney Car. And the matron sounds funny. I don't understand some of the things she's saying. Why did I think this was going to be great fun? Maybe I'll tell them we want to go home. We've changed our minds about spending the duration in Canada.

Chapter 28

"Find your suitcases, and let's go. We have to walk down to the corner to catch the streetcar," the matron said. "As quickly as possible, please, boys and girls."

The porters had written our CORB numbers on the side of our luggage, so everyone found theirs quickly. We walked down the street to the corner. People stopped and stared at us. Some said, "Welcome to Canada." Others spoke to each other, not to us.

"Poor things."

"So far from home."

"Can't imagine my child going through what they've seen."

I was getting angrier and angrier.

I'm not a poor thing. I'm sure we made a mistake coming here. I'll talk to Colin tonight about a plan to run away and get back to Liverpool.

"Here we are, boys and girls. Here's our streetcar."

I realized I hadn't paid attention to anything on our walk to the corner. Now I looked around. The streets were filled with automobiles and people. I don't think I had ever seen streets so crowded.

The Birney Car screeched to a stop in front of us. It had two levels, ran on tracks in the ground, and had a rod on the roof that attached to wires running above the street. I had never seen anything so big.

"Lizzie, what is it?" Colin asked. "Are we going to get in that thing?"

"I guess so. This must be the streetcar the matron said would take us to the Fairview Home."

"This is an adventure. Come on Lizzie, let's get on."

As usual, Colin was ready for any daring scheme. I

wasn't as adventurous.

"Let's get a seat by the window so we can see the city," Colin said.

I let him drag me down the aisle. When we didn't find two seats together, Colin headed for the stairs.

"Let's go upstairs. I bet you can see forever from up there. Maybe we can even see some cowboys and Indians."

Before I could say anything, Colin was half way up to the second level. We sat down just as the streetcar pulled away from the stop.

Liverpool was a big city, but the docks and warehouses covered most of it. Halifax was different. Some buildings were so tall I couldn't count all the floors before we passed them. There were shops with big windows filled with ladies' and men's clothes. Newsagents and bookstores were on every corner. We passed huge parks with statues. I could see large flower gardens and people walking on the paths or riding bikes.

"Look, Lizzie, there are boys and girls swimming in the middle of the park."

And there were. The pool looked much bigger than the pools in Stanley Park back home.

"Maybe if we stay here in Halifax, we can go there someday," Colin said.

He was so enthused and excited about everything that it was hard for me to think about a plan to get back to Liverpool.

"We're here, boys and girls," the matron called up the stairs. "Hurry up. We can't keep the streetcar waiting for you forever."

We hurried down the stairs with the others who were on the upper deck.

"Just a short walk up the hill to Fairview Home. Stay together. I don't want anyone to get lost on your first day in Canada," the matron said.

We walked behind her like goslings following their mother goose. She turned into a long drive. At its end stood a massive white house with green shutters. There was a large porch that stretched across the entire front of the house, brick chimneys popped up from all four corners as well as two more in the middle. It was the biggest house I had ever seen. The front door opened, and two ladies came out to meet us.

"Helen, we wondered when you would get here," one of them said to our matron. "The children must be starving by now."

"Better a little late lunch than none at all," said the other lady. "Let's get them inside and fed. We can worry about dorm assignments later."

The ladies told us to leave our luggage in the hall and go right into the dining room. It was a long room that went from the front of the house all the way to the back. There were two rows of wooden tables and benches.

As soon as we sat down, someone put a plate in front of us. I didn't know what kind of sandwich it was, but I was hungry. I pulled a corner open. There was a brown paste spread across the bread. I took a bite. It was delicious. Someone put a tall glass of milk in front of me.

"Is that whole glass for me?" I asked.

"Yes, of course dear, and you can have more, and another sandwich if you want."

Colin looked at me with wide-open eyes.

"We can have as much milk as we want?" he asked, "and more to eat?"

"Of course, dear, just raise your hand if you want

more."

After my second sandwich, I heard one of the ladies say, "I think we're going to need more peanut butter if they keep eating at this pace."

Peanut butter! That's what I'm eating. I've never had it before, but it's my favorite food now. Maybe I can learn to like Canada.

After lunch, one of the ladies took us upstairs to the dormitories. The boys and girls were separated again. I didn't like being away from Colin, but I knew there was nothing I could do to change that.

A few girls were already living here, and they showed us where we could put our things.

I don't know why they're bothering. We're only going to be here for a day – just until our host family comes to get us. I'd better not say anything though. Maybe their host family never came to get them. That's a scary thought. What if our host family never comes? Will we have to go back to Liverpool? Now I'm not sure if I want to stay or leave. I know Colin wants to stay. I wish Margaret was here so I could talk to her.

"Lizzie!"

I turned around and there was Margaret. We ran to each other and hugged like we had been separated for ages.

"Margaret, I was just wishing you were here. I'm so happy to see you. When did you arrive? Did you eat yet? They have the most delicious paste called peanut butter that you spread on bread to make a sandwich. It's heavenly, it's…"

"Lizzie, slow down. I just got here. I hoped I would get here before your host family did. Do you know when they're coming to pick you up?"

"No, the matrons haven't said anything to us about that. Do you know anything about your family?"

"Not yet. I guess we'll find out more tomorrow. Meanwhile, I hope they have tea soon. I'm starving."

"Come over here, I'll show you where to put your things. And you can have the bed right next to mine."

"It's so lovely here. I wish we could stay here for the duration."

"Girls and boys, wash up and come down for supper," a voice yelled up the stairs.

"Supper?" Margaret asked.

"I don't know, but I think that's what they call tea here. They called dinner lunch."

"How odd. Why would they do that?"

We hurried downstairs. I saw Colin sitting with a couple of boys his age. *Colin seems to make friends wherever he goes. He probably doesn't want anything to do with me now that he's found new mates.*

"Lizzie, come meet my new friends. Wait a minute – is that Margaret?"

Colin jumped up from the table and ran over to give Margaret a hug.

"I'm so happy to see you," he said. "I was afraid your family picked you up at the dock, and we'd never see you again. Lizzie, isn't it wonderful that Margaret's here with us?"

"Yes, Colin it is. But right now, I think we'd better all sit down before the matrons get mad."

One of the matrons was staring at us already. Colin went back to his place and Margaret and I found seats next to two girls from our dormitory. Once everyone was settled, the matron at the head of the table said, "I'm Mrs. Cabot. Mr. Cabot and I are in charge of you while you're here. He's out visiting a sick parishioner, but he hopes to get back before your bedtime. Meanwhile, we will say grace now, and thank the Lord for your safe arrival and the food on our table."

We bowed our heads while she said grace. The kitchen door opened, and a line of ladies carrying platters of food started going around the table.

It was a feast! We had roast beef, potatoes, rolls, gravy, two kinds of vegetables, and glass after glass of milk. The food was even better than what we had on the ship.

"I think I'll burst. I'm so full," one of the boys said.

"Too full for some pudding?" a matron asked.

"Pudding? Well, I guess I still have a little room left."

What the matron served us didn't look like any pudding I had ever seen. It was in a big bowl and wiggled a little when she scooped out a spoonful. And it was chocolate. It didn't have any fruits or nuts in it either, but it was so good.

"Is this what Canadians call pudding?" someone asked.

"I don't care what they call it, it's delicious," one of the boys said.

We all laughed and quickly finished our dessert. *Peanut butter, chocolate pudding, all new foods, but I like them. Maybe I should give Canada a chance.*

After supper, we were allowed to go to the front parlor and listen to the radio for a while. *Radio, not wireless, another new word.* We all wanted to hear news about the war, but instead, there was a variety show on the station. By the time that was over and the news was about to start, half of us were asleep and the other half were barely able to keep our eyes open.

The matrons managed to get us up to our rooms and helped us get into our nighties. I was asleep before my head touched the pillow.

Chapter 29

The next morning was warm and sunny. Everyone washed and dressed quickly. Maybe our families would come for us today.

Boxes of cereal, pitchers of milk, and bowls were placed down on the table. At home, I had hot porridge, not cold cereal for breakfast. But I remembered how delicious yesterday's meals were and I was ready to try it.

Mrs. Cabot sat down and we said grace. She told us to choose whichever cereal we wanted. I didn't know one from the other, so I took the box closest to me. I liked it, but I think I liked my porridge more.

After breakfast, Mrs. Cabot took us into the front parlor to meet Mr. Cabot.

"Welcome to our new arrivals," he said.

He was very tall and skinny. His black suit and vicar's collar made him look stern, but his smile was kind and his eyes sparkled.

"I'm sorry I wasn't here to meet you last night, but as I'm sure Mrs. Cabot told you I had to visit one of my parishioners. Anyway, we're all here together today, so what shall we do on this glorious day?"

Do? I thought we would meet our families today. I want to stay right here so I don't miss them.

"Why don't we go to the park?" one of the boys said.

"Maybe we could play that game, baseball, you taught us," someone else shouted.

In a minute, a dozen suggestions were made.

"Mr. Cabot," I said, "aren't our host families coming to pick us up today? I don't want to miss them."

He looked at Mrs. Cabot, and she shook her head.

"Silly," one of the girls from our dormitory said,

"there's not one family that comes for you. A whole bunch of them come. They look us over, and if we suit, they take us home with them."

"Oh no," I said, "you must be wrong. The CORB man said there was a family waiting for us. A family just like our family back home."

"Well, he lied."

"No, he couldn't have. He promised."

I felt tears filling my eyes. Colin squeezed closer to me. Margaret sat staring straight ahead.

"Mrs. Cabot? Mr. Cabot? Is she right? There's no special host family coming to get us? What will happen to us? What if no one wants us? Will you send us back to Liverpool?"

My tears started to fall. *Now I'm scared. What will we do? Where will we go? We never should have left. Maybe we can find the Colonel. Maybe he'll let us live with him.* I wrapped my arms around Colin. *He looks more scared than me. I have to be brave for him. I have to keep him safe.*

"Children," Mr. Cabot said, "I'd like to speak to our new arrivals privately. The rest of you may go outside to play."

After they left, Mr. and Mrs. Cabot tried to explain how we would meet our host families.

"You see, children," Mr. Cabot said, "when the idea of all of you coming here for the duration began, there were dozens of families who wanted you to come live with them. The government officials and the Bishop met and decided that those people should apply to become a host family. After all, we couldn't send you off to someone's home without making sure they were good people who would take care of you, just like your own mom and dad would. Each family had to get a letter from their pastor saying they were a good Christian family. They had to prove they could provide for you and see that you went to school and church. All their applications were reviewed, and the selected families are notified as soon as a ship arrives with evacuee children on board."

"But don't they know who we are?" Margaret asked.

"No dear," Mrs. Cabot said, "not specifically who you are. They just know they will be offering a home to a needy child during this terrible war."

Needy? We're not needy. Mum would never have sent us if she thought we would be treated like a poor charity case. I don't care what she said about not having any money and needing to find work. We would have been fine. I know we would. I hate being a "poor little thing."

Colin grabbed my hand. I could feel him shaking next to me.

"Lizzie, can we go back home, please?" he asked.

"Oh, don't feel that way," Mr. Cabot said. "These are all wonderful families who can't wait to meet you and take you home. You'll see. Why I bet you'll be gone and living in a lovely home by this time tomorrow."

"I don't like this at all," Colin whispered to me.

"Me neither. Colin, Margaret, why don't we all go outside?" *The three of us will have to come up with a plan. I want to ask the others about what actually happens.* "May we go join the others outside, Mr. Cabot?"

"Yes, of course. You'll see. Everything will work out. I'm sure you'll be very happy you made this trip."

Margaret, Colin, and I ran outside to try to get some real answers to our questions.

"There she is," Margaret said pointing to a bench in

the far corner of the yard. "She's the one who said the CORB man lied."

We ran over to ask her the thousand questions we had.

"Hi," I said. "I'm Lizzie. This is my brother, Colin, and my best friend, Margaret. What's your name?"

"I'm Patricia. I'm sorry no one told you what happens when you get here. I thought you already knew. Our escort told us all about it."

"What exactly does happen?" Margaret asked.

"Since your group arrived late last night, there was no selection meeting this morning. But there probably will be one this afternoon."

"A selection meeting? What's that?" Colin asked.

He still held onto my hand like he was terrified I would run away. *All his independence from our time on the ship has disappeared. He's back to being a scared little boy.*

"The pastor, Mr. Cabot, calls us into the dining room and we all line up against the wall. The families come in and 'inspect' us. They walk along the line and look carefully at each one of us. Sometimes they ask you a question, like how old you are, or what you like to do, or if you know how to milk a cow, or herd cattle, or some other silly thing. Then they tell him if one of us suits them. If no one does, they leave and come back when the next ship arrives."

"Milk a cow?" Colin barely whispered the question. "How would we know how to milk a cow? There are no cows in Liverpool."

"Silly," Patricia said, "not everyone comes from a big city."

"I think you're wrong, Patricia," I said. "No one

from the country would leave to come here. They weren't getting bombed every night."

"Maybe you're right. I don't know. I just know what happens every morning and afternoon."

"How long have you been here?" Margaret asked.

"A whole week. No one seems to want me because of my leg."

We all looked at Patricia's leg. It was turned in and she wore a big special shoe on her foot.

"I was born like this," she said. "People call me a cripple, but I can walk. It just takes me a little longer to get places, that's all."

"And that's why no one's picked you?" I asked.

"I guess so. No one tells you why you weren't chosen. Mrs. Cabot just says, 'That's all for today. You can go back outside.'"

I don't know what to say to her. Could she be telling the truth? This is not what the CORB man told us. Colin and Margaret looked shocked. They remind me of the way Mrs. Brown looked when we came out of the air raid shelter, and she saw her house bombed to a pile of rubble.

"Lizzie," Colin said, his voice trembling and barely louder than a whisper, "what if no one picks us? What if they pick you and not me?"

He started sobbing and grabbed me around the waist. His whole body shook and his cries grew louder and louder.

"Colin, calm down," I said rubbing his back. "You know I'll never leave you. We're a team, remember? Mum made me promise to keep you safe. How can I do that if you and I are apart? Now, dry your eyes. No more nonsense about us separating, all right?"

Colin looked up at me and nodded.

Oh please, don't let anything like that happen. And what if the family wants Colin and not me? I can't think that way. I have to be strong.

I looked up at Margaret. Tears ran down her face. Her shoulders bobbed up and down with silent sobs.

"What am I going to do without you to talk to every day?" she said. "I don't want to be all alone. I hate it here. I want to go home."

She plopped down on the grass and started crying again. Colin and I sat on either side of her, hugged her, and cried.

I don't know how long we stayed like that. The next thing I knew one of the ladies from breakfast came over to take us to lunch.

"Come along now. You'll feel better once you wash up and have something to eat. Patricia, can you show them where to go?"

"Yes, ma'am. Come on mates. I'm sorry I had to tell you how it works here. At least you won't be surprised. I'm sure some of your group will be. Those are the ones I feel really sorry for. It's like the first air raid you went through. You don't know what's happening. You're just terrified."

Chapter 30

We struggled through lunch. I don't know what we ate. I'm amazed I ate anything at all. *The CORB man lied to us and to Mum. She never would have sent us over here if she knew what was really going to happen. Would she? Of course not. She's our Mum. She loves us. What can we do? I have to think of some way we can go home.*

"Everyone done?" Mrs. Cabot asked. She looked around the table and nodded. "Well children, I want to tell you what we are going to do this afternoon."

Mrs. Cabot tried hard to make the "selection meeting" sound like fun, but I knew it would be just like Patricia described. We were sent upstairs to clean our faces and brush our hair. If anyone looked particularly dirty after their morning in the yard, he was told to change clothes. A little while later, Mr. Cabot called us downstairs and told us to go into the dining room.

Just like Patricia said.

He lined us up against the wall.

"All right, children, the host families will come in to meet you. If they ask you a question, please answer politely. Stand up tall. No fidgeting."

He gave us one last look and told Mrs. Cabot to bring the families in.

Husbands and wives came in and walked down the line. Sometimes, there was a lady by herself. Each "host family" looked us over, and spoke quietly to Mr. Cabot. One by one, children were led away. Most looked confused and scared. They sat at a table with their future family for a few minutes. Some left with them. Other children came back to the wall, either crying or angry.

"Colin," Mr. Cabot said, "the couple sitting over

there would like to speak with you."

"Come on, Lizzie, let's see what they say."

"Oh no, Colin," Mr. Cabot said "they only want to speak to you, not both of you."

"No," Colin said.

"No?"

"No. Lizzie and I are a team. I won't go anywhere without her."

"Now Colin, let's not make a fuss. They just want to talk with you, ask you a few questions."

"Like if I can milk a cow? No, I can't," Colin yelled over to the couple. "I've never even seen a real cow."

"Colin! Go to your dormitory right now," Mrs. Cabot said. "That was extremely rude. My apologies, Mr. and Mrs. Fiske. I don't know what got into him. He must still be tired from his voyage."

"I'm not tired. I don't want to be inspected, and I won't go anywhere without Lizzie. And you can't make me."

I'm so proud of you Colin, and terrified. Will we be punished? Will the Cabots decide we have to be separated? This is definitely not a great adventure. It's a nightmare.

Chapter 31

Neither Mr. or Mrs. Cabot said anything to us about Colin's behavior. Supper was quiet. Over half our group had been chosen that afternoon. Margaret wasn't one of them.

After supper, we went to the front parlor to listen to the radio. There was news about the war. None of it was good. Bombing continued in England. More soldiers died in France. No one seemed to be winning. No one knew when it would all end.

After the news, we went upstairs.

"I think I have a plan," I said to Margaret and Colin. "I thought about this the other day, but after today, I decided it's something I have to do."

"What? What's your plan?" Margaret asked.

She leaned over and whispered in my ear, "Can we include Patricia?"

I looked over to see Patricia sitting on her bed. She had a book in her lap, but I could see she wasn't reading.

"Patricia," I said, "would you like to join us?"

"Oh yes, thank you. No one ever wants me to join them."

"Well, we do. Now listen to my plan."

I told them I decided to find the Colonel and ask if we could live with him.

"I'll tell him the CORB man lied to us, and our mums, and remind him that he said we should let him know how we were getting on. Well, we're not getting on very well, are we?"

They all shook their heads.

"Who's the Colonel?" Patricia asked.

"He's the most wonderful man I've ever met," Margaret said. "We met him on the ship on our way over. He arranged for treats for us every day, told us all about Canada, and stood up for us when Peter drowned, and –"

"What! Someone drowned on your voyage? We never heard about that," Patricia said.

"That's not important right now," I said. "The thing is we'll have to sneak out of here, get on the train, get to Toronto, and find where he lives. It's dangerous, and it won't be easy, but it's better than staying here and having people inspect us twice a day. What do you think?"

"I think it's a wonderful plan," Colin said jumping up and down on the bed. "I can't wait to see the Colonel again."

"Colin, get down before Mrs. Cabot hears all the commotion and comes up," I said.

"It sounds like a fine plan to me, but how can we pay for the train?" Margaret asked.

"We each got a dollar when we landed, remember? We'll use that and the coins people threw to us. It should be plenty for our fare and maybe something to eat. To-morrow, we'll all sneak a little something extra from each meal. That way, we won't have to spend a lot on food. We'll plan on leaving after lights out. What about you, Patricia? Will you join us?"

"I want to, but I'm afraid I'll slow you down. I told you I can't walk as fast as you can. I wish I could go. The Colonel sounds wonderful."

She started to walk back to her bed. Her head drooped onto her chest and she dragged her leg more slowly than before.

"Wait a minute," Colin said. "There's a wagon in the yard. I saw it today. You could sit in it, hold onto our luggage, and we'll take turns pulling you."

"Do you think that will work?" Patricia asked, turning back towards us.

"Of course."

"Yes."

"What a splendid idea."

Patricia grinned at us and hurried back to my bed to listen to the rest of the scheme.

Chapter 32

The next morning I was up with the sun. I wanted to get packed and make sure Colin was too. I didn't want us to make any noise during our escape that night.

"Margaret, Patricia," I whispered, shaking them awake. "Get up and pack before anyone else wakes up. I'm going to sneak into the boys' dormitory and wake Colin. We all have to be ready to leave tonight."

I crept down the hall to Colin's room. The only sound in the house was my breathing. It sounded as loud as the bellows Grannie used to stoke the fire in her hearth. The door's loud creak as I pushed it open turned me into a statue. *What should I do now? I'm sure that noise woke Mrs. Cabot. Should I go in, or run back to my room?*

"Lizzie? Is that you?"

Colin's loud whisper sounded like a bomb exploding in the quiet room.

"Shhh, yes it's me."

I hurried over to Colin's bed.

"I came to wake you and help you pack. We have to be ready to leave tonight, and this may be the only time we can do it without anyone knowing."

"You're too late. I packed last night after everyone went to sleep. I was afraid I wouldn't wake up early enough to do it in the morning."

"That was good thinking, Colin. I'm proud of you. Now remember, try to steal a little something from breakfast for our trip tonight."

"Like what?"

"I don't know, maybe a piece of toast, or muffin. I guess it depends on what Cook makes this morning."

"You know, yesterday I snuck into the kitchen and

Cook gave me a biscuit. She called it a cookie, but it was a biscuit. I bet I could do it again today."

When did he manage that? Not that it surprises me. Colin always finds a way to get an extra treat.

"Colin, you amaze me. Try to get her to give you a few of them. Tell her you want one for your sister and her two friends. That way, she'll think you're being generous. You know, sharing, that kind of thing."

"All right. I'm sure she'll give me a few biscuits. She's very nice."

"Good, we're all set for this morning. I'll see you at breakfast."

I tiptoed back to my room. Margaret and Patricia were finishing putting the last few things in their luggage. None of us had very much to pack so it didn't take long. Soon we were all back in bed waiting for Mrs. Cabot's call to wake up.

Everyone seemed a little nervous at breakfast. Maybe they were thinking about the next "selection meeting." I wasn't sure, but I didn't care. It just meant our little group's jitters and fidgets wouldn't be noticed. *How are we ever going to pinch some food? Between Mrs. Cabot and the other ladies, someone is always watching or standing right next to us. We need to distract them, but how? I've got it!*

"Oh, I'm so sorry," I said as my glass of milk crashed to the floor. "It just slipped out of my hand."

"It's all right, dear," Mrs. Cabot said. "Are you hurt? Did you spill any on your dress?"

"No, I'm fine, just clumsy. I'm terribly sorry."

Mrs. Cabot and one of the ladies were on the floor sopping up the mess with napkins while another lady ran into the kitchen for a mop. Someone brought out a broom to sweep up the glass. All of them chattered away at the same time.

"Be careful, Mildred. Don't cut yourself."

"Helen, just move over a bit so I can mop there."

"Mrs. Cabot, can the children stand so I can sweep under their chairs?"

"This milk seems to spread faster than I can mop."

Margaret, Patricia, and Colin were scooping up pieces of toast and wrapping them in napkins while the ladies cleaned up my mess.

"I can't tell you how sorry I am," I said.

"Now, now, dear," Mrs. Cabot said, "nothing to be sorry about. Accidents happen. It's not like you did it on purpose."

I could feel my face burning when she said that.

"All right everyone, let's settle down," Mrs. Cabot said. "Is everyone finished? Well then, you can go outside and play for a while but don't get dirty. We'll have our morning meeting with your host families in a little while."

When everyone got up and started to go outside, the four of us ran upstairs to hide our stolen treasures. We quickly joined the others before anyone missed us.

"I'll pull the wagon over close to the house," Colin said. "Patricia, come with me and we'll see how you fit in it."

They went off to see to that part of our scheme while Margaret and I planned our escape.

"I thought I would ask Miss Burns about the street-cars," Margaret said. "She's the lady who brought my group here and she talked to the ticket taker a lot, so maybe she knows how late they run."

"That's a great idea," I said. "I'm not sure I know

the way to the train station. It can't be far from the harbor, but it's probably a pretty long walk from here."

"You know, Lizzie, maybe we should walk. I don't know if they would let us take the wagon on the streetcar."

"You might be right, but we can try. If they say no, we'll ask for directions and walk."

"Lizzie, Margaret, give me a hand," Colin yelled. "I'm having some trouble pulling the wagon."

We looked over to the other end of the yard. The wagon was stuck in a rut.

"Colin, you can't pull Patricia across the yard," I said. "The ground is too soft. We'll be fine on the sidewalk though. Patricia, are you comfortable in there? Do you think we can fit our bags in there with you?"

"Oh yes, Lizzie. I'm fine, and there's room for everything in here. It might be a little tight, but I don't mind."

"It's settled. We'll pinch what we can from lunch and supper today, but I don't think we can have another 'accident.' Colin, we're counting on you to get something extra from the kitchen."

"I'll go there right now. Don't worry, Lizzie, I'll come away with something for our trip."

A little while later, Mr. Cabot came out onto the back porch and rang a big bell.

"Time for our morning meeting," he announced.

We looked at each other and slowly walked toward the house. *I hate this. I can't wait to leave here. I'm not some "thing" to be put on display and chosen like a treat in the sweets shop.*

"Come along children, don't dawdle," Mr. Cabot said as we climbed the steps to the porch. "Run upstairs, wash your hands and face, and brush your hair. Come down as quickly as you can. We don't want to keep everyone waiting, do we?"

They can wait forever. I don't care.

"No, Mr. Cabot," we mumbled.

When we were all gathered in the dining room, Mr. Cabot said, "Sit down children. Today, we have a special guest. The Chief Housekeeper of Government House, Mrs. Collingsworth, has come to select some of you to join her staff, and work for the Lieutenant Governor. Since the war started, many young girls have enlisted to go overseas and work as ambulance drivers, or nurses, or even join the ranks of the Land Army. Many young men have enlisted in the Royal Army. As a result, Government House has some openings for household help. We feel privileged to be considered for the honor of filling those positions, and I expect everyone to act accordingly. Now, let's stand in a nice straight line by the wall and I'll bring in our special guest."

I wasn't expecting this. What if she calls one of us? Can we say no? What is the Lieutenant Governor anyway?

"Sir," I said, "what is the Lieutenant Governor?"

Mr. Cabot looked at Mrs. Cabot. They both looked shocked.

"Why, why, he's the Lieutenant Governor," Mr. Cabot stammered. "His Honor, Frederick Francis Mathers."

"No sir, I mean, not who is he, but what is he?"

"What? What? I told you he's the Lieutenant Governor."

"My dear," Mrs. Cabot said, "I don't think she understands what that means. Lizzie, dear, he is the most important government official in all of Nova Scotia, which is where you are right now. He's appointed by the Governor General who receives permission to name him from King George VI himself. Does that answer your question?"

"I guess so."

"I think he's like our Lord Mayor," Margaret whispered to me.

Mr. and Mrs. Cabot just shook their heads.

"Let's get on with this," he said throwing his hands into the air. "We can't keep Mrs. Collingsworth waiting."

He left the dining room and when he came back, there was an older lady with him.

"Children, this is Mrs. Collingsworth, Chief Housekeeper at Government House. Say good morning to her."

"Good morning, Mrs. Collingsworth," we said.

"Good morning, children. I want you to know that His Honor, Lieutenant Governor Mathers, has been watching your journey here closely and admires the courage you have shown in leaving your families and traveling to our great country. He has decided he would like to help provide a secure, safe home for you while you are here. In light of that, he sent me here to Fairview Home to select a few of you to come live and work at Government House. This is a great honor. Normally, any employees of Government House must go through several interviews and have references from their pastors and local government officials. However, in your case, we are abandoning all that. We are relying on your inherent goodness, and gratitude to be chosen, to stand in good stead. We know you will welcome this opportunity to serve the government and, indirectly, King George himself."

Serve King George? How can any of us refuse to serve the King? We would be traitors.

The whole time she talked, Mrs. Collingsworth walked up and down inspecting us. Now she sat at the table and called Mr. Cabot over. They sat whispering to each other, she got up, thanked us for our attention, and left.

What's happening? Doesn't she like any of us? Doesn't she think we're good enough to serve the King? If I get picked, do I want to go? Will she pick Colin if she picks me? Why doesn't Mr. Cabot say anything?

Mrs. Cabot sat next to Mr. Cabot and they whispered back and forth. Finally, he stood, walked over to us, and said, "Mrs. Collingsworth has graciously decided to accept three girls and three boys to join her household. When I call your name, please go upstairs, pack your bag, and return to the front hall. Miss Burns will escort you to Government House. Matthew, James, and Philip, please go pack your things. Jean, Barbara, and Margaret, please do the same."

"No," I cried. "Margaret, you can't leave. Please don't make her go, Mr. Cabot."

"Lizzie, really," Mrs. Cabot said, "this outburst is outrageous. Yesterday, Colin was rude to the Fiskes and today, you. I should think your mother would have taught you better manners."

"My Mum did teach us manners," Colin said. "But we don't want Margaret to go anywhere without us. Please let her stay."

"I'm afraid that's quite impossible, Colin. Mrs. Collingsworth has made her selections and that's final."

Chapter 33

I sat on my bed and watched Margaret put the last few things in her luggage – the items she would have packed tonight for our escape.

"Margaret, what am I going to do without you? You're my best friend," I said, wiping silent tears from my face.

Colin sat next to me sniffling.

"You can write to me, Lizzie. You have to let me know if you find the Colonel. If you do, maybe I can join you. If he asked, maybe the Lieutenant Governor would let me leave. And now you have Patricia to talk to. I think she'll be a very good friend."

"I'm sure she will be. It's just not the same."

"Promise me you'll still go ahead with our plan and leave tonight."

"I promise. Now I want to get away from here more than ever."

"I spoke to Mrs. Cabot, and she said she would write down the Government House address for you. Don't forget to ask her for it."

"Come on, Margaret," Barbara said, "they're waiting for us downstairs."

Colin and I gave her a last hug and she ran out of the room, down the stairs, and out the door. I held on to Colin. *At least Mrs. Collingsworth didn't take Colin away from me. I know I would just die if she had.*

"Lizzie, let's go find Patricia," Colin said. "She probably feels as sad as we do right now."

"You're right, Colin. I guess I was just feeling sorry for myself."

We went outside and found Patricia sitting on the

bench in the far corner of the yard. I sat next to her. Colin sat on the ground in front of us and pulled on the grass.

"I'm sorry Margaret's gone," Patricia said. "I mean, I'm sorry she won't be coming with us tonight. I guess it's good that she's going to live in Government House. Do you think it's like Buckingham Palace? Do you think it's grand?"

"Maybe, I don't know. I know I'm going to miss her terribly."

"I already miss her," Colin mumbled, pulling a whole fistful of grass out of the ground.

"Colin, you'll make a big bare patch in the ground if you don't stop," I said.

"Who cares? They shouldn't have the right to send us wherever they want. What if Margaret's not happy there? Will he let her leave? Where will she go? It's not fair."

Colin's right. It isn't fair. We should be the ones inspecting the host families, not the other way around. If they're so happy to have us, we should get to pick which family we want to live with.

"Maybe we can ask Mrs. Cabot if we can choose the family we want to live with," I said.

Patricia and Colin stared at me.

"Aren't we leaving tonight?" she whispered.

"Yes, Lizzie, aren't we?" Colin asked.

"Of course we are. I forgot for a minute. I didn't expect Margaret to leave us. Guess my thoughts are a little fuzzy."

"You're always a little fuzzy," Colin said.

I leaned over to push him down, but he jumped away and ran across the yard.

"Can't catch me, can't catch me," he yelled.

"Can too," I shouted, and ran after him.

I stopped and looked back. Patricia was sitting all alone picking at a loose thread on her skirt. I walked back, ashamed that I had left her. She didn't know Margaret as well as I did, but I could tell she missed her. *She's probably thinking no one will ever choose her. All because of her leg. If they can't find a place for her in Government House, who will find a place for her? We have to find the Colonel. He won't care about Patricia's leg. I know he won't.*

"Children, time for lunch. Come in and wash up," one of the ladies called from the porch.

On our way upstairs, I reminded Colin and Patricia to try to sneak something off the table for our trip tonight. Neither looked very excited. I told them when we found the Colonel, I was going to ask him to send for Margaret. The Lieutenant Governor couldn't refuse a Colonel in the Royal Army, could he?

"That's a wonderful idea, Lizzie," Patricia said.

"Good old Lizzie, always coming up with a scheme. I feel better already," Colin said. "I'll make sure I pinch something at lunch, then I'll go to the kitchen and see what I can get from Cook."

We all felt a lot better when we headed down to lunch.

Peanut butter sandwiches – perfect. I could eat half, hide the other half under my napkin, and ask for another. I got Colin's attention and showed him my plan. He understood right away and did the same thing. I poked Patricia and showed her a half sandwich sitting on my lap. At first, she looked puzzled, but she smiled and soon she had half a sandwich on her lap too. It was a little tricky walking away from the table with them wrapped in our skirts, but the usual rush of everyone trying to get outside helped.

"That was clever," Colin said when we got outside.

"I'm just happy we had sandwiches today and not soup," I said.

We all laughed.

"Imagine trying to carry soup in our skirts," Patricia said. She walked around making believe she had a ladleful of soup in her skirt. She looked so funny Colin and I laughed until I couldn't catch my breath.

"Patricia, you should go on the stage when you grow up," Colin said. "You're a great actress."

"Well, maybe I will," she said. "Who knows what will happen when the war ends."

The war. Always the war. It changes everything. Where we live, who we live with, what we eat. I'm sick of this bloody war.

The bell rang out from the back porch.

"Come inside children. We have some families who would like to meet you," Mr. Cabot said. "Quickly run upstairs, wash your hands and faces, brush your hair, and come down to the dining room."

We lined up as usual and waited for the people to inspect us. I hoped no one would choose us today. The only place I wanted to be, aside from home, was with the Colonel. And tonight, we would leave here and find him.

As each couple passed, I silently said the words "Don't pick me, don't pick me."

The last couple walked past and I sighed with relief. We were all still standing together.

"Sorry I'm late. Got stuck at the market behind some fool who insisted on arguing about the price for his catch. Damn fool."

"Mr. Harris, your language," Mrs. Cabot said, "the children shouldn't hear such things."

"Yes, yes, I know. Just annoyed, I guess. Now which ones are mine?"

"Well, that's up to you, isn't it? Isn't Mrs. Harris with you?"

"No, no need for her to come into town. We're sixty miles away, you know."

Everyone stared at this man who stood talking to Mrs. Cabot. The people who came to Fairview Home were always dressed in their best clothes. The men wore suits with sharp creases down the front of their trousers. The women wore pretty dresses, and hats, and gloves. They all looked like they were on their way to Sunday church services.

This man wore overalls, a plaid shirt, and a stained fedora. His boots were muddy and he smelled of fish. I don't think he even shaved today.

"Well, let's get this over with. I told Mr. Cabot I need a boy to work on my lobster boat with me. He said he had one. Where is he?"

Colin grabbed my hand. *No, he can't mean Colin. He can't. Colin's too little to go out on a lobster boat. Oh, why didn't we leave last night.*

"Mr. Harris, I presume," Mr. Cabot said. "So sorry. I was saying goodbye to one of our boys."

"Don't have much time if I want to get home before midnight. You said you had a boy for me."

"Yes, yes, he's right over here. But I'm afraid there's a little teeny problem. It seems he insists his sister go with him."

"His sister?" he boomed. "What in blazes am I supposed to do with her?"

"Maybe she could help Mrs. Harris around the house," Mrs. Cabot said, twisting one hand against the other. "Sort of a mother's helper."

The man stared at Mrs. Cabot until she backed away and hurried out of the room. He turned back to Mr. Cabot.

"I wasn't counting on having to provide food for two."

"Um, yes," Mr. Cabot said.

"Do I get paid for both, or just one?"

Paid? What does he mean 'paid'? Are we being sold? I thought we were going to a family who would treat us like their own children. That's what the CORB man told us. He didn't say we would be bought or paid for. If we are, can we ever leave and go home? Why did we come to Canada? Why didn't we leave last night?

"Oh, both, of course," Mr. Cabot said. "And the Lord will bless you twice for your Christian generosity."

"Don't give a hoot about that. I'm looking at what it means to my pocketbook."

"Yes, well, they're right over here."

Mr. Cabot stopped in front of us. "This is Colin and his sister, Lizzie. Say hello to Mr. Harris, children."

Neither of us could speak. I looked up. The man stared at me and looked over at Colin.

"Not much to him, is there? If I caught one this small, I'd have to throw him back."

"Oh, how funny, Mr. Harris," Mr. Cabot said. Now his hands twisted around one another faster and faster. "Colin here is quite the little seaman. Isn't that right, Colin? Why he's shown me all kinds of knots he can tie, and told me he wants to be a sailor in the Royal Navy. Don't you, Colin?"

Colin never said a word.

"Cat got your tongue, boy?" the man asked. "Can you speak? Answer me, boy."

"Yes, sir," Colin stammered.

"Don't yell at my brother," I heard myself say. I didn't even realize I was going to speak.

"I wouldn't have to if he'd answer when spoken to. And you, little missy, need to keep a civil tongue in your head."

He looked us up and down one more time.

"Know anything about lobstering?" he asked Colin.

"No sir, but I used to go fishing with Mr. Rawlings when we lived in Liverpool."

"You did, huh? Got any other boys?" he asked Mr. Cabot.

"No, Mr. Harris, I'm afraid all the other boys have already gone to host families. We did expect you yesterday, you know."

Mr. Harris glared at Mr. Cabot but never answered him.

"Can't afford to take another day off to come up here and see what you've got, so I guess these two will have to do."

"Splendid, splendid, Mr. Harris. They are lovely children. I'm sure they'll bring you great joy."

"Humph," Mr. Harris grunted. "You got some papers for me to sign or what?"

"Yes, yes, of course. Children go get your things while Mr. Harris and I finish our business."

They walked to the table and sat down. Mrs. Cabot came back in with some papers and a pen.

"Go along children," Mrs. Cabot said, "get your luggage."

Patricia stood next to me, crying quietly. "I guess

I'll never get to meet the Colonel," she said.

"Mr. Harris," I called across the room.

He turned and stared at me with those dark mean eyes.

"Mr. Harris, can Patricia come too?"

Patricia looked at me in shock. I was a little shocked myself. I certainly hadn't planned on asking him to take Patricia. But now that I had, I was glad.

He stood up and looked at Patricia.

"It's bad enough I'll have to explain you to Mrs. Harris. How do you think I could explain bringing a cripple home to her?"

I felt like he had punched me in the stomach. *I can't believe you said that. You are the meanest man I've ever met. I hate you.*

Patricia whimpered and slumped down to the floor.

"Patricia, get up, come upstairs with me, please," I said.

She looked up with tear filled eyes. "No, Lizzie, you go ahead. I'll just hold you up. You know it takes me a while to climb the stairs."

"Patricia, listen," I said kneeling down next to her. "I'll write to Margaret and give her my address. She can give it to you, all right? Mrs. Cabot has the address for Government House. Somehow, we'll get back together. We will find the Colonel and you will meet him. I promise."

Patricia nodded, but she never looked up.

Chapter 34

When we came downstairs, Mr. Harris was already outside waiting for us.

"Behave yourselves, children," Mr. Cabot said. "Remember, the Harrises are taking you in out of good Christian charity. You should thank the Lord every day for their generosity."

"Here's a little something to eat on your trip," Miss Burns said, handing each of us a paper sack.

"Thank you, Miss Burns," we both said.

We stepped outside. A beat-up, rusty old truck sat in front of the house.

"Get in, get in, I don't have all day. Already spent too much time up here. Mrs. Harris will be angry enough I'm late for dinner. Wait till she sees I've brought two mouths home with me."

He threw our luggage into the back of the truck and Colin and I got in the front seat.

Mr. Harris drove through the traffic in Halifax and mumbled about "stupid drivers" and "damn fools." Once we left the city, he calmed down. We drove through forest so thick they formed a solid wall on either side of the road. We passed water that could be lakes, or rivers, or even the ocean. Mr. Harris never told us what they were. He never said a word to us.

We finally pulled into a little village. There was a church and houses were painted blue, yellow, white, and red. They must have looked pretty and cheery once, but now the paint was chipped away, and they were run-down. The most unusual building was a round tower with glass windows at the top. It was on the edge of a group of huge rocks surrounded on three sides by the ocean. Giant waves crashed over the rocks into the side of the tower. *They remind me of the waves that took Peter away. I can't let Colin go there.*

"Mr. Harris," I said, "what's that tower?"

"It's the lighthouse. Haven't you ever seen a lighthouse?"

"No, sir," Colin said. "What is it?"

"What is it?" Mr. Harris bellowed.

His voice bounced off the metal roof of the truck.

"It's a lighthouse. It shines a light out at night and on foggy days to make sure ships don't run aground on the rocks. Aren't there any lighthouses in England?"

"I'm sure there are, sir," I said, "but not in Liverpool where we're from."

"Humph, useless know-nothing children, just as I suspected," he mumbled.

We are not useless know-nothing children. You're just a mean man.

Colin stared at me with tear-filled eyes. I grabbed his hand and squeezed. *We'll be all right as long as we're together.* I gave him a smile and he relaxed a little.

The truck pulled up in front of a run-down blue house that sat right at the edge of the land. Another blue building next to it was built half on land. The other half had stilt legs that went from the floor into the harbor.

"All right, get out," Mr. Harris said. "Don't know how I'm going to explain you two to Millie."

We got out and picked up our bags that Mr. Harris had thrown down from the back of the truck. He grabbed a box and headed for the house. I ran ahead of him to open the door. *Maybe if I'm polite he won't think I'm useless.*

"'Bout time you got home," a woman's voice said.

We walked into the kitchen just as she turned from stirring a pot on the stove.

"Wh…Wh… What is this? Who are these children, Tom? You were supposed to pick up one boy to help on the boat, not a child and a girl. What am I supposed to do with them? It's bad enough you're late for supper, now I have two more mouths to feed? How do you think I can manage that? The stew's already boiled down to almost nothing with you taking your sweet time in the city. And now you bring home two orphans?"

"Not now, Millie, I'm tired and hungry. We can talk about them later."

I got madder and madder. "We're not orphans," I shouted. "Our mum sent us over here to keep us safe. Don't you ever call us orphans again."

"Well, she's got a mouth on her, doesn't she?" Mrs. Harris said.

"Little missy, I talked to you once about keeping your mouth shut. I won't tell you again. Next time, I'll reach for the belt instead."

Colin stared at Mr. Harris. "You'd better not," he said. "You'd better not even try to hit my sister."

"Oh, so you have a sassy mouth too, do you? Maybe I should take the belt to both of you right now. Maybe that will teach you to mind your manners."

"Tom, stop," Mrs. Harris said. "Is this what this house is going to be like now? You fighting with these children every day? Take them back."

Maybe he will. Then we could get Patricia and leave right away to find the Colonel.

"Millie, I'm too tired to do anything but have some supper and go to bed. We'll talk about it later."

"Still don't know how I'm supposed to feed two extra mouths. Some of this is for your lunch tomorrow. If I give it to them, there won't be any left."

Mr. Harris rubbed his hands over his face, stopped, and looked at us. "Wait a minute, one of the ladies at the Home gave each of you a paper sack, right?"

We nodded our heads, afraid to open our mouths.

"Well, that's your supper. Problem solved, Millie."

"Fine for tonight, I guess. Don't know what I'll do tomorrow. Sit down, Tom. I'll bring your plate over."

Mr. Harris sat down and Mrs. Harris filled a bowl with some stew. *I don't know what it is but it smells good.* She filled a second bowl and brought it to the table. Before she sat down, she looked over at us.

"Well, sit down and have whatever it is in your sack. Lucky for you someone at that Home took pity on you and sent you with food. Otherwise, you'd be going to bed hungry."

I looked around. There weren't any more chairs in the tiny kitchen. *I guess we'll sit on the floor. Tomorrow I'll figure out how we can run away.*

While we ate our peanut butter sandwiches, I looked over at Mrs. Harris. She was skinny, like Mr. Harris and her hair was brown and gray. She had on a faded cotton dress that I could see had been mended in a few places. *She's not like Mum. The CORB man lied about our host family. He lied about everything. We're not going to see the mountains, or ride horses, or even see the cowboys or Indians. I have to think of a plan to find the Colonel.*

Mr. and Mrs. Harris ate their stew without saying a word. *When Dad was alive, we always talked over tea. Why don't they talk to each other?*

"Thanks, Millie, that was good," Mr. Harris said as he sopped up the last of the stew with a piece of bread.

"Have little missy there wash the dishes. I want to talk to you."

I sat on the floor and stared at both of them.

"You heard him," Mrs. Harris said. "Clean up after yourselves and wash these dishes and the pot. Put the rest of the stew in that jar over there, and put it in the icebox."

"Yes, ma'am," I mumbled.

They left the kitchen and went into the front parlor. Colin and I were alone.

"Lizzie, I don't like it here," he said, crying softly. "Do we have to stay?"

"Shhh, quiet, Colin. We don't want them to hear us. Come on, let's get these dishes done before they come back in. I don't want to stay here either, but we can't leave tonight. Tomorrow we'll look around and see how we can run away, all right?"

"All right, but let's get up early. Maybe we can run away before they wake up."

"What are you two whispering about?" Mrs. Harris said. She stood in the doorway with her fists on her hips.

"Nothing, Mrs. Harris, really," I said.

"No, you're probably too stupid to talk about anything that's worth listening to."

She walked over to the sink and inspected the pot and the dishes. "They'll do," she said. "You two can sleep here."

She walked over to a curtain at the end of the room and pulled it aside, pointing.

"Like I said, I wasn't expecting two of you so you have to share the bed."

We picked up our bags and walked over.

"But this is the pantry," I said.

"What did you expect? A fancy bedroom like the Princesses have at the Palace? This is fine for the likes of you. You can try to clear a space on one of the shelves for your clothes, and put those bags where I won't trip on them when I come in here."

This is awful. What would Mum say if she saw this?

Colin started crying and I felt tears run down my face.

"Lizzie, do we have to stay here? Can't we run away now?"

"No, Colin, we have to wait until morning. We don't even know which road leads back to Halifax. It'll be all right. We can both fit in that bed. Just think of it as part of our adventure."

Not the great adventure I dreamed of. Now it's a great nightmare.

Chapter 35

"Get up, boy. Plan on sleeping all day?" Mr. Harris boomed from the doorway. "And you, little missy, should be getting firewood and helping Mrs. Harris with breakfast."

What time is it? How late did I sleep? I can't believe I even went to sleep.

"It's still dark out, sir," Colin said.

"What of it? By the time we load the boat and get out on the water, the sun will be up. You don't catch anything lying in bed. Now let's go."

Colin and I felt around in the dark for our clothes.

"Lizzie, I have to go to the toilet. Where is it?"

"I don't know. I'll ask Mrs. Harris."

I stepped into the kitchen. Mrs. Harris never turned around. "You can wash your face here in the sink. If you need the toilet, there's a privy outside."

A privy? Don't they have an indoor toilet?

"A privy?" Colin asked.

"Yes, you know what that is, don't you? Or are you so highfalutin you've never heard of one?"

"No, Mrs. Harris, we know what it is. Thank you. Come on, Colin."

I grabbed his arm and pulled him out the back door. Colin stopped as soon as we got outside.

"How are we going to get away? It's too dark to see anything and in a little while, I'll have to go with Mr. Harris to his boat."

"While you're gone, I can walk around and figure out a plan. You'll just have to go along with Mr. Harris for today. You can do it. I know you can."

"All right, but I don't want to stay here another day."

We both used the privy and went back inside. Mr. Harris was already yelling at Mrs. Harris.

"Why isn't she making breakfast? Did she get wood for the stove? Did she get the eggs? Where is she? Oh, here's the little Princess. I suppose you think we should wait on you. Well, think again. Now, get back out there and bring in some wood. That's the least you can do since Mrs. Harris already made the oatmeal and tea. Millie, tomorrow I want to see this girl in this kitchen before you. Make sure you tell her what her morning chores are. If she's to live here, she'll earn her keep."

Mrs. Harris never answered him. She put a bowl in front of him and scooped some oatmeal into it. A plate of toast and a pot of tea were already on the table.

"Sit down," she said to Colin. "You can't go out on the boat without some breakfast."

Colin sat and she gave him some oatmeal.

"Got boots, boy?" Mr. Harris asked.

"No, sir," Colin said trying to swallow the lump of oatmeal in his mouth.

"Well, that's just fine. Isn't it, Millie?"

"Now Tom, I think there's an old pair of mine in the shed. Maybe they'll do for today. I'll go to the Pastor and see if he knows any family with boy's boots."

She looked over and saw me standing in the doorway. "Wood, missy?" She shook her head.

I ran outside and tried to find the woodpile in the dark. *While she's visiting the Pastor, I'll look around and find a way to escape.*

When I came back in with an armload of wood, Colin was putting on a pair of boots.

"They're too big, sir," he said.

"Millie, where are your rags? He can stuff them in

the boots. They'll be fine."

Mrs. Harris dug around the cabinet and found some old dirty rags. "Here, shove these in the toes."

Colin did, and put the boots back on. "There's still too big, sir."

"Can you walk in them without falling down?"

Colin walked across the kitchen, and didn't fall.

"They'll do. No need to bother the Pastor, Millie. He'll be fine."

Oh no, if Mrs. Harris doesn't go out today, how am I going to plan our escape?

"If you say so, Tom. But he needs long pants. Those shorts won't do."

"We can talk to the Pastor after Sunday's services. The waders will cover his legs. Of course, they'll be too big, but I'll roll up the cuffs and put a belt on him. Let's see how he takes to fishing."

Mr. Harris finished his breakfast and he and Colin left for the day.

"All right, missy, sit down and have some tea and toast."

"Can I have some oatmeal?"

"No. That's for Mr. Harris and his worker. You can make do with toast, or nothing at all."

I sat down and took a piece of toast. Mrs. Harris sat opposite me and stared. "What's your name?"

"Lizzie."

"And your brother?"

"Colin."

"Hmm, well we have a lot to do today, so don't take forever with your toast. Do you know how to bake bread?"

"No, Mrs. Harris."

"Useless, just like Tom said," she mumbled.

I am not useless! She's just as mean and ugly as Mr. Harris. We have to get away from them.

Chapter 36

I spent the day learning what my daily chores would be and how to bake bread. Before Mr. and Mrs. Harris wake, I have to bring in wood and get the fire going in the stove, put the kettle on for tea, and start the oatmeal.

"While the oatmeal cooks, you can make toast," Mrs. Harris said. "After Mr. Harris leaves, do the breakfast dishes and clean up the kitchen, just like you did today. Only tomorrow, I expect you to do a better job. I want everything to shine in here."

"Yes, Mrs. Harris."

She took me outside to the chicken coop. "Get in there and collect the eggs," she said, handing me a basket.

As soon as I stepped into the pen, the chickens started squawking and running around. *Do chickens always make this much noise? They look like they want to attack me. Where are the eggs? I don't see any.*

"Well, what are you waiting for?" Mrs. Harris asked. "The eggs won't pop out of the coop and fly into your basket. Go get them."

Get them? From where?

"I'm sorry, Mrs. Harris. I don't know how."

"My word. You've never done this before?"

"No, ma'am. We didn't have chickens at home."

"I see I'll have to teach you everything. Don't know why Mr. Harris thought you'd be a help to me. Seems I still have to do it all myself."

She walked into the pen, grabbed my basket, and went over to a wooden box. It was high enough off the ground so she could reach inside without bending down. There was a ramp at one end, like the ship's gangplank, for the chickens to walk up and down.

"Well, come over here. You won't learn anything standing over there."

Mrs. Harris lifted a hatch on the side of the box and reached in. She pulled an egg out and put it in the basket.

"Your turn," she said handing me the basket. I took it and reached in.

"Ow!"

I pulled my hand out. "Something poked my hand."

"You probably poked the chicken first. She's just defending her territory. Look around before you stick your hand in there. Sometimes if there are no eggs in the straw, you have to reach under the hen and see if she's sitting on one. But be gentle, if you know how. They don't like to be disturbed."

I tried again and this time I saw an egg. I grabbed it and pulled my hand out before another chicken pecked at it.

"Hooray, one egg," Mrs. Harris said. "Now get the rest of them. There's a hatch on the other side too. And hurry up about it. Can't spend all day collecting eggs, there's lots to do."

Mrs. Harris walked back to the house and left me alone with the chickens. They still looked like they would love to attack me and were waiting until we were alone. Somehow, I managed to collect ten eggs. I felt around for more. I didn't want to go inside unless I had all the eggs Mrs. Harris thought I should.

"I got all of them, I think."

"Let's see," Mrs. Harris said. She counted them and clucked just like the chickens. "Not bad, could be worse. Now, go over to the sink and scrub them clean and make sure you don't break any."

Scrub them? How do you scrub eggs?

"Mrs. Harris, what do I scrub them with?"

"Oh, for goodness sake, you must be the stupidest child I've ever met. Just use the dishrag and scrub off all the dirt and feathers. And don't use cold water. Fill up that basin and put some water from the kettle in it to warm it up. Never seen such a useless child," she mumbled tossing flour onto the table. "Don't take all day, either. We have bread to bake and you are going to learn how."

"Yes, Mrs. Harris."

Why is she so mean? Doesn't she know that we don't have chickens roaming around Liverpool? Maybe she's the one who's stupid.

I finished scrubbing the eggs clean and Mrs. Harris came over to inspect them.

"Humph, they'll do. Put them on the counter and come over here so you can knead the dough."

Need the dough? What does that mean?

"Now watch me. Take the dough and push it with the heel of your hand, like this."

She pushed the dough, folded it, flipped it, and pushed it again.

"You try."

I tried, but it was harder than it looked. The dough looked soft but it was thick and heavy. By the time the dough was smooth, my arms felt like loose rubber bands.

"That'll do. Now get the big blue bowl out of the cupboard, spread butter around the inside, and make a ball out of the dough. Put the dough into the bowl, rub it all around so the butter covers it, put a damp dishtowel over the top and leave it on the counter next to the stove. It has to rise before we can bake it."

I did everything she said. The whole time she never took her eyes off me. *I don't know why she has to watch me like that. Does she think I'm going to steal something? There's nothing here to steal. I think the Harrises are poorer than we were.*

"Done? Good. I have to go to the market. Clean up this kitchen. It's a mess. There's flour everywhere. And make sure you sweep and scrub the floor. I want everything to sparkle when I get back."

"Yes, Mrs. Harris."

Scrub the floor? I don't think this floor has ever been scrubbed. The stains look as old as me. How can I find a way to escape if I'm stuck in this kitchen all day? Maybe if I work really fast, I can finish before she gets back and still have time to look around outside.

I flew around the kitchen picking up all the measuring cups, spoons, and bowls. I put the flour canister, yeast, and salt back in the cupboard. I washed everything and left it to dry on the drain board. I swept and scrubbed the floor. I finished the scrubbing right at the back door, and stood up on the back porch. *Done! Now for our escape route.*

I ran down the steps to the yard.

"Where do you think you're going, missy?"

Mrs. Harris stood by the side of the road, arms crossed against her chest. She was with another lady who looked at me like I was a criminal.

"That the Home girl?" she asked. "Doesn't look like much."

"She's not. Doesn't know how to do anything, or what her place is, do you missy?"

I wanted to run across the yard and punch both of them. What does she mean "my place"? They're sup-

posed to be my family while I'm here. Mrs. Harris treats me like a servant.

"I'm all finished cleaning up. I thought I'd take a walk around the village to see what it's like."

"Oh, you did, did you? You'll go for a walk when I say you can. Right now, get inside and make tea for Mrs. Robinson and me. You have time for a cup of tea, don't you, Lucy?"

"That would be lovely, Millie."

The two women marched through the kitchen leaving dirty footprints on my scrubbed floor.

"We'll have our tea in the front parlor, missy. And clean up this floor. I told you I want it to sparkle."

"Did she think the floor was clean with those dirty footprints all over it?" Mrs. Robinson asked.

"I don't know, Lucy. Who knows what kind of filth she lived it. They're nothing but poor trash, you know."

"Yes, real guttersnipes. I admire you for taking her in. You're a real Christian, Millie. Don't know if I'd sleep a wink with one of them under my roof. I mean, not knowing where they come from and all that."

"As Tom says, it's just our way of doing a little something to help out during these terrible times.

"Missy! Are you getting our tea or not?"

Poor trash? Guttersnipes? I hate you both.

"Yes, Mrs. Harris."

I fixed a tray with the tea things and searched through the cupboards for some biscuits, but I couldn't find any. As soon as the water boiled, I filled the teapot and carried the tray into the parlor.

"Mind if I wash up, Millie?" Mrs. Robinson asked.

"Of course not, Lucy. You know where it is," Mrs. Harris said.

I put the tea tray down on the table and watched Mrs. Robinson go into a room I'd never seen. *Of course, I've never seen it. I've never been out of the kitchen. It's a toilet. I guess Colin and I are the only ones who have to use the privy. I have to find a way to get us out of here.*

"Don't stand there gaping. You'd think you'd never seen a washroom before. You have seen one, haven't you?"

"Yes, of course. But why can't Colin and I use it? Why do we have to use the privy? That's not right."

"You watch your tongue, missy, or I'll have Mr. Harris take the belt to you when he comes home. And where are the cookies for our tea?"

"I couldn't find any biscuits. Do you want bread and butter?"

"Don't be ridiculous, girl. Bread and butter? Is that what you serve with tea where you come from?"

"No, Mrs. Harris, we don't have butter. Everyone in England uses margarine since the war started, even the King and Queen."

"My, my, sassy little thing, isn't she?" Mrs. Robinson said as she walked into the room.

"I'm sorry you had to hear that, Lucy. Now you see what I have to put up with."

"Millie, is it really worth it? Couldn't you and Tom find another way to contribute to the war effort?"

"I don't know. I'll have to see what he says when he comes home. He took her brother out on the boat with him today. If he's as useless as she is, Tom might agree to take them back."

"I hope so, for your sake. I can't imagine having to put up with her every day."

"Why are you still standing there?" Mrs. Harris said

when she realized I hadn't moved an inch. "I told you to bring us some cookies. They're in the jar on top of the ice box."

I walked into the kitchen and realized tears were running down my face. *Why did I let Mum send us here? These people hate us. They think we're trash. I have to get us out of here. We have to find the Colonel. He didn't think we were trash.*

"Missy, what are you doing? We're waiting for our cookies," Mrs. Harris yelled from the parlor.

"Yes, Mrs. Harris." *Tomorrow you'll have to get your own cookies.*

Chapter 37

"It's about time," Mrs. Harris said as I walked into the parlor with a plate of cookies. "While Mrs. Robinson and I have our tea, you can go into the yard and dig up some carrots, onions, and potatoes for dinner."

"How will I know where they are?" I asked.

"Really, Millie, she's quite impossible," Mrs. Robinson said. "You have to tell Tom to take her back. She's more trouble than she's worth."

"You're right, of course, but I'll have to see what Tom thinks of the boy tonight. Now, as far as you go missy, do you mean to tell me you never grew vegetables in your yard?"

"No, ma'am. Mum was going to start a garden, but we got the letter about being accepted with the next ship, and she got –"

"Enough! I don't need your whole history. I think I may have put labels on them when I planted them months ago. If not, you'll just have to root around until you find what I need for dinner. Get four or five carrots, two onions, and three potatoes. That should be enough."

"I should hope so," Mrs. Robinson said, "unless you plan on feeding the whole village."

"Tom's always so hungry when he comes home, and I want enough left for his lunch tomorrow as well. Well missy, what are you waiting for? Those vegetables won't pick themselves."

She turned back to Mrs. Robinson and the two of them started trading stories about someone else they knew. I went into the kitchen, found a big bowl, and went outside to search for vegetables.

Doesn't she know I grew up in the city? I'm not a

farm girl who knows about any of this,

I wiped the tears from my face and looked around. There were other people out in their yards and down by the water, so I watched to see if any of them looked like they were headed for Halifax. Everyone seemed to be gardening, or at the waterfront working on nets or some kind of wooden crates with curved tops. The road that ran past the house didn't seem to go anywhere. One end stopped just past the house, and I couldn't see where the other end went. *I'll have to wait until I can go down this road. That's the only way I'll be able to find a way out to Halifax.*

I found the vegetable garden and looked for the markers. There were some old faded strips of rags with letters on them, but I couldn't make out any words. *Guess I'll just start digging and see what I come up with.* I had found a small scoop under the sink, so I used that to scrape away some dirt. As soon as I felt something hard, I dug in with my hands. It was a potato, and there were a bunch of them all in the same place. Now I had to find the onions and carrots. I moved to another part of the patch and started digging.

"Hello, Frank," I heard someone yell. "Any mail for me today?"

Mail? The mail must come from Halifax. Where is he? Where's the post carrier?

I stood up and looked around. I spotted a horse and cart down at the end of the road. *I'll watch him and see where he goes. If I can just see which road he takes, that will be the one we can use to run away.*

"Nothing for you today," I heard him shout back. "Got something for the Harrises though."

Something for this house? He's coming here? If I

can get to him before Mrs. Harris does, I can ask him which road to take. Maybe we can leave tonight.

I snuck over to the corner of the house so I could run out and talk to him as soon as he stopped.

"Morning, Frank," Mrs. Harris said. "I heard you yelling about my mail all over town."

Oh no, why did he have to yell out her name. I can't run out there now. She'll never let me talk to him. Maybe I'll have a chance tomorrow.

"Now Millie, I think you're exaggerating a little. Just mentioned it to Flo, that's all."

"Well, maybe. Let's see what it is. Probably no good news."

He handed her a letter and turned the cart around to head back. Mrs. Robinson came out and joined her. They talked for a few more minutes, and she left. The post carrier was two houses down the road by then. *I'll have to look for him tomorrow. I know, I'll tell Mrs. Harris that I'll get the post for her so she doesn't have to come outside. Then I can talk to him all I like.*

I went back to the vegetable patch, found the carrots and onions, put them in the bowl and went inside. Mrs. Harris sat at the table frowning and read her letter. I put the vegetables in the sink and started washing them.

"Humph, inspection! Wait until Tom hears this. It seems, missy, that they'll be an inspector coming to visit in the next month to make sure we are treating you two well. I'll expect you to say we are, or I'll have Mr. Harris take the belt to you. Do you understand?"

"Yes, ma'am." *In a month, we won't be here. Wonder what you'll tell the inspector then.*

I spent the rest of the morning doing chores. I dusted furniture, washed clothes, and brought in more firewood.

Lunch was a piece of bread with butter and a glass of water. I didn't complain. I thought if I did, she would probably take that away from me too. I don't know the last time I felt so tired.

"Mrs. Harris," I said between bites of my bread. "I'd be happy to wait for the post carrier for you tomorrow so you don't have to walk outside."

"You would, would you? You're a sneaky little one, aren't you?"

How could she know we're planning to run away?

"Think you can get out of your chores and just stand outside waiting for the mail, do you? Well, forget that, missy. The only reason Frank came to the house today was because the letter was a Special Delivery."

"If he doesn't come to the house, how do you get the post?" I asked.

"It's called the mail, and I go to the post office down the road and pick it up, that's how. Not that it's any of your business."

"I could do that for you, Mrs. Harris. Then you wouldn't have to walk all that way."

"I don't think so. You have plenty to do here. I don't mind going. It gets me out of the house for a while."

Now what? The post doesn't come here and I can't go there. I'll have to figure out something else. Maybe we should take our chances and just leave. How lost can we get? Anything is better than staying here.

"Plan on taking all day to eat your lunch? Maybe I shouldn't even give you any."

"No, I'm finished," I said shoving the last bit of bread into my mouth. I took my plate and glass to the sink to wash them.

"Soon as you finish that, go outside and feed the

chickens. There's a sack of feed next to the coop. While they're eating, check for more eggs. Sometimes there are some late layers. After that, you can scrub down the washroom, then I have some mending for you to do. You know how to sew, don't you?"

"Yes, ma'am."

"Good. Well, don't just stand there. Go feed the chickens," she said, shaking her head and rolling her eyes.

I fed the chickens, found a couple more eggs, and came inside to scrub them and clean the washroom. When I finished, I looked for Mrs. Harris. She was sitting in the front parlor flipping through a magazine.

"Mrs. Harris, I finished cleaning your washroom." *The one Colin and I can't use.* "Do you want me to start the mending?"

"No, I want you to stand there like the simple-minded fool you are. Of course, I want you to start the mending. I left a pile of Mr. Harris's clothes on the kitchen table. Seems he's always catching them on something and ripping them. I left my sewing basket there too. I'm going to my room to take a nap. I'm exhausted from having to teach you how to do everything. Make sure you wake me at four o'clock so I can show you how to make supper."

"Yes, ma'am." *She's exhausted? She hasn't done a thing all day except have tea with Mrs. Robinson. Wait a minute. Maybe I can sneak out while she's asleep and walk up the road. Maybe I can find the road that leads to Halifax.*

I went into the kitchen. The table was piled with overalls, and shirts, and socks. Some of them looked like pieces of rags held together with a couple of threads.

What does she think I can do with these? No one could sew these rags back together. I'll never finish all this mending before four o'clock. Maybe I should just leave them here on the table and go find our escape route. Yes, that's what I'll do. I'll hurry back and try to work on some of these clothes that aren't too badly torn apart. And she'll never know the difference.

I tiptoed to the screen door and pushed it open.

"Where do you think you're going?"

Mrs. Harris's voice filled the room. I froze. *What can I say? What excuse can I make up?*

"I thought you might try something funny to get out of doing your work, so I figured I'd check up on you. It seems I was right. As soon as my back is turned, you're ready to go off and wander around town. Think you're on a holiday, do you? Well, missy, think again. I didn't want to take in any of you street urchins, but Mr. Harris needed help on the boat so I agreed. I didn't count on an extra child, but since you're here, you'll earn your keep. Now, where were you going? And don't lie. I won't abide lying."

I stood at the door like a block of stone. *I knew it! She never wanted either of us. Street urchin? Earn my keep? The bit of bread and butter she gives me every day?*

"ANSWER ME!"

"I was going to the privy. I guess I'm allowed to do that, aren't I? And I'm not a street urchin. We have a lovely home in Liverpool, and a mum who loves us. Stop saying ugly things about us."

She flew around the table and slapped me across the face so hard I fell against the stove. It was still warm, but not hot enough to burn through my clothes.

"I warned you about talking back to me. If you ever speak to me like that again, or use that tone of voice, you'll get more than a slap. Now sit down at that table and get to work. I'm going out. I can't stand to look at you."

She pushed the screen door open so hard I thought it broke. It slammed back against the house and stayed there. I got up to close it and watched her stomp down the street. *Probably going to Mrs. Robinson's to complain about what a terrible girl I am. Well, I don't care. We're leaving here tonight. I'll find a road to get us out of here and if we have to sleep rough, we will. It'll be better than another night here.*

I sat at the table and looked over the pile of rags. I finally settled on one shirt that I might be able to mend, and got out a needle and thread. *Tomorrow we'll be in Halifax. We'll get Patricia and head off to find the Colonel.*

Chapter 38

When Mrs. Harris came back, I had just finished stitching one shirt back into one piece.

"Is that all you've done while I've been gone? You are the laziest girl I've ever seen. No more time for that now. Put Mr. Harris's clothes in your room. You can work on them in your free time."

Free time? What's she talking about? I haven't had a free minute since I woke up.

"Right now, you have to get supper started. You'd better bring in some more firewood. I'm not sure there's enough. Then start to peel the potatoes and cut them up. I'm making stew tonight. Mr. Harris doesn't like the potatoes too small, so cut them into chunks, and slice the onions and carrots. Put everything into the stew pot and cover it with water. Let me know when you're done."

Mrs. Harris left me alone in the kitchen. All I wanted to do was put my head down and cry. *Oh Mum, why did you send us here? I'd rather be in Liverpool in our Anderson shelter than here. I want to go home. I want to be with Mum and Colin. Poor Colin. What has he been doing all day? Mr. Harris better not have hit him. Maybe he won't work out on the boat and Mr. Harris will take us back. That would be wonderful. I'll keep my fingers crossed.*

Eww – why are my arms and legs so itchy? And when did I get these red bumps all over me? Oh no. Could I have the disease the doctor told us about when we got our shots? Am I going to die? Oh, what was that called? Maybe Mrs. Harris knows. I hate to ask her but I guess I'll have to.

"Mrs. Harris?" I stood in the parlor doorway. She

lay on the couch with her eyes closed. Slowly she turned her head and opened one eye.

"What? Can't you even peel potatoes without help?"

"It's not that, Mrs. Harris. I have these itchy red bumps all over my arms and legs and when we landed the doctor gave us some shots and told us to watch and see if we got a hard, red bump. That would mean we have that disease. I think I have it, but I can't remember what he called it."

"Oh, my word, one more catastrophe you brought to this house. Come here, let me see what you're talking about."

I walked over to the couch and showed her my arms and legs.

"You stupid girl," she said. "Those are mosquito bites, not some dreadful disease. Don't you even know a mosquito bite when you see it?"

"A mos…mos…what?"

"A mosquito. Don't tell me you've never heard of mosquitoes before."

"I never have, Mrs. Harris. What are they? Is it contagious, like measles?"

"I cannot believe how stupid you are. Of course, it's not like measles. It's a bug bite, that's all. You probably got them when you were outside picking the vegetables. They'll be itchy for a day or two then they'll go away. Don't you have mosquitoes in England?"

"No, ma'am. I've never heard of them before."

"Well, now you have. Disease. Really. Get back in the kitchen and finish getting the stew ready. I need to close my eyes. Wait till Lucy hears about this one."

She turned on her side with her back to me. My face was hot and, I was sure, red. *What did she call them?*

Mosquitoes? Bugs? One more thing the CORB man never told us about. She shouldn't have called me stupid, though. It's not my fault we don't have pesky bug things like that in England. And who cares anyway? It doesn't matter. Colin and I are leaving here tonight.

I went back to cutting up the vegetables and putting the stew on the stove. I made sure the fire wasn't too hot, just enough to keep everything simmering.

"Mrs. Harris, I put the stew on, but I don't know what else to add to it," I yelled to her.

She came into the kitchen, rubbing her eyes. "Never mind, I'll take care of it. You'd probably just make a mess of it. Mr. Harris is very particular about his stew."

She came into the kitchen, reached into the cupboard, and took down some spice jars. She added a little from some and a lot from others, and gave the broth a taste.

"Perfect. I won't add the fish until Mr. Harris gets home. If it cooks too long, it gets rubbery. There. That's your first lesson in making stew. Keep your eye on it and make sure it doesn't boil. That will ruin it."

"Yes, ma'am."

"I'm going to sit outside and wait for Mr. Harris. It's too hot to stay in this kitchen."

"Yes, ma'am." *Too hot for you, but fine for me. You are the meanest person I've ever met.*

Chapter 39

"Mr. Harris and your brother are just docking the boat. While they're cleaning the nets and bringing their catch to the fish factory, we can cut up the fish and add it to the stew." Mrs. Harris stood inside the door holding a big fish by the gills. She slapped it down on the counter and started to cut it up.

"Watch carefully, missy. I'll expect you to be able to do this from now on. Certainly no reason for me to slave over making supper for you and your brother. If you want to eat, you'll have to learn how to make your own meals."

She talks like she and Mr. Harris aren't going to eat any of the stew. I bet we're only going to get the vegetables anyway. She'll save all the fish for the two of them.

"I hope you had a better day than I did," Mr. Harris said, bursting into the kitchen like an explosion. "It's a wonder I didn't get killed out there trying to do everything myself and watching that this mongrel didn't go overboard or worse."

"Tom, calm down. The day's over and I've made some delicious mackeral stew for supper. After we eat, we can sit in the parlor and figure out what to do about the two of them. Believe me, my day was no better than yours. Now go get cleaned up for supper."

Mr. Harris mumbled and grumbled his way out of the kitchen. When he left, I could finally peek around Mrs. Harris to look for Colin.

"Colin," I yelled, "are you all right?"

He stood just inside the door and looked like he was about to fall over. His face was a sickly gray color and his shirt was ripped open down its right side. I pushed past Mrs. Harris and grabbed him

"Colin, it's me, Lizzie. Say something. Look at me."

His eyes rolled up to my face, and he started to cry. His whole body shook with his sobs. He started to fall down and I grabbed him under his arms and led him to a chair.

"Colin, Colin, talk to me. Are you hurt? Did Mr. Harris hit you? What happened?" But he didn't answer. He just kept sobbing and gulping down mouthfuls of air. I ran over to the sink and got a glass of water.

"Here Colin, drink this. Calm down, please, Colin. You're scaring me."

I knelt in front of him and rubbed his back. I had never seen him look like this. Colin was always the daredevil, the adventurer, the brave one. Now he looked like a lost, frightened, little nine-year-old boy. He took little sips of the water and his sobs got quieter. I felt tears running down my face.

I've failed him. I promised Mum I'd keep him safe. I don't know what happened today, but I'll find out and Mr. Harris will pay for it.

"I think that's enough hysterics for today," Mrs. Harris said. "Stop acting like such a baby. You'd think a little hard work would kill you. It won't. You've both obviously been spoiled rotten all your lives. Well, that ends now. Get washed up for supper, boy. And you, missy, get the table set. The two of you can eat in your room. I'm sick of the sight of you."

Good, I'm sick of the sight of you too.

"Come on, Colin, wash your face and hands and go to our room. I'll bring your supper into you."

"Real little prince, isn't he? Can't even carry his own bowl? Needs you to wait on him, does he? Maybe he's too delicate to eat stew. Maybe he should just have some bread and butter."

"No, Mrs. Harris, he's fine. I'm sure he's just tired after a whole day of fishing. I don't mind taking care of him a little. Please don't punish him."

"Fine, but it's only because I'm such a softhearted person. Don't think you can take advantage of me like this all the time."

"No, Mrs. Harris, thank you."

Softhearted? I don't think she even has a heart.

"Millie, is supper ready?" Mr. Harris yelled from the hall.

"Yes, Tom, come right in and sit down."

She ladled the stew into a big bowl and set it down on the table just as Mr. Harris came into the kitchen.

"I have some nice fresh bread for you too, Tom. I made it this morning."

"Thank you, Millie. You work too hard, you know. Don't know how you manage to do it all in one day."

She put another big bowl of stew on the table, and got two small bowls from the cupboard. She scooped some vegetables and a lot of broth into the bowls and fished around for the tiniest pieces of mackerel she could find. She put one piece in each bowl.

"Here, missy, for you and the boy. Don't spill any. And make sure you clean up everything when you're finished. Mr. Harris and I will be in the front parlor after supper. You can bring us some tea and cookies. That all right with you, Tom? I didn't have time to bake today."

"Sounds fine, Millie. Besides, we need to talk about these two tonight."

"I agree. Why are you still standing there, missy? If you don't want your supper, I can always pour it back

Into the pot."

"No, ma'am. I'm sorry, ma'am. I'll bring you your tea after supper."

They act like I'm not right here in the room with them, like I can't hear them. They're rude and mean. I can't wait to leave here tonight.

I put our bowls on the tray and carried them into our room. Colin lay across the bed fast asleep. *He looks so little. I hate to wake him, but he has to eat something. We have a long walk ahead of us tonight.*

I put the tray on the floor and shook his shoulder. "Colin, wake up. I brought you some stew," I whispered. *I don't want Mrs. Harris to know he's fallen asleep. She'll probably come in and take away his supper.*

"Come on, Colin, wake up. You have to eat. You have to keep your strength up."

He opened his eyes a little. "I'm too tired," he mumbled.

"I know you're tired, but you have to wake up. Please, Colin."

He pushed himself up on his elbow. "Do I have to? Why?"

"Because I have a plan and you have to eat so you have something in your stomach so we can run away tonight."

That got him sitting up. "Run away? Really? To the Colonel? Will we get Patricia? Will we finally see some cowboys and Indians and the mountains?"

"Shhh, not too loud. We don't want them to hear us. Now eat your stew and I'll tell you my plan."

Chapter 40

"That girl is useless, Tom, just useless."

Mrs. Harris's words hit me as hard as her slap across my face did. *Useless? After all I did today? She's the one who's useless.*

"… doubt she's ever seen a chicken before."

I placed the dishes in the sink and tiptoed to the hallway so I could hear what they were saying.

"What do you want me to do, Millie? I can't go back to the city tomorrow. That one trip already cost me a day's fishing. And if I don't catch my quota, we won't be seeing our portion of the government's bounty this year."

"Was the boy any help at all?"

"What do you think? The only fishing he's ever done is a little bit of sport fishing. If he caught something it was great fun. If he didn't, at least, 'I had a nice afternoon out on the water' he told me. Nice afternoon. I'm not breaking my back every day so he can have a 'nice afternoon.'"

I could hear Mr. Harris stomping back and forth in the parlor. *I'd better move closer to the sink in case one of them decides to come in here.*

"I tried to show him a few things, Millie, I really did. He's too young and too small. It's a wonder he didn't wind up going down with the line.

"I never should have agreed to take them. But that Mr. Cabot told me there'd be no more boys until the next ship docks in a week or so. I thought maybe this boy would be able to do a few things, but I guess I was wrong. When that hook grabbed hold of his shirt, I was sure he was a goner. Lucky for him he just lost his shirt. Might not be so lucky next time."

"Could you just have him bait the hooks, or throw the nets over, or something simple? Just until we can trade them in for some others who at least know what a day's work is."

"I don't know, Millie. I don't want to be responsible for that boy's death."

Trade us in? Colin could die? We have *to leave.*

They stopped talking. I turned on the water, piled all the dishes in the sink, and put the kettle on.

"Aren't you done yet?" Mrs. Harris asked.

I looked over my shoulder. She stood in the doorway, fists bunched at her hips.

"No, ma'am, but I will be in a few minutes. I'll bring your tea in as soon as the water boils."

"That girl wastes more time than anyone I've ever met," she said heading back to the parlor. "Do you see what I'm talking about, Tom? I don't think I can put up with her for another week or so. Why don't you plan on bringing them back on Sunday? You never take the boat out on Sundays. Even if there aren't any other boys, you can't do much worse alone than with him. What do you say, Tom? Sunday?"

"Maybe you're right, Millie. Let me think about it."

The kettle whistled and I ran back to the stove from my listening spot at the doorway. I poured the water into the teapot, got some cookies down from the jar, and brought the tray into the parlor.

"Finally," Mrs. Harris said. "Tom, turn on the radio. Let's see if there's any news about our boys over in France."

"Mrs. Harris, could we listen to the news too, please? I'm awfully worried about Mum and Grannie, and everyone back home. Please."

Mr. and Mrs. Harris looked at each other.

"Let them listen, Millie. We've had our say about what's to be done."

"Get the boy. You can sit on the floor."

I ran to our room and dragged Colin, who was half asleep, out to the parlor just as the news started.

"In the latest news," the announcer said, "we've received word that a ship, the SS *Volendam*, carrying 600 passengers including 321 children and a crew of 250, traveling from Liverpool to Canada, was torpedoed in the Atlantic by a German U-boat. The passengers all escaped in lifeboats and were rescued by nearby vessels. According to sources on one of the rescue vessels, the children's behavior was amazing. Although they were awakened in the middle of the night and rushed up on deck to get into their lifeboats, they showed true British spirit singing *Roll Out the Barrel* until the rescue boats picked them up. The children were all evacuees sponsored by the Children's Overseas Reception Board, known as CORB. They are now on their way back to Scotland. In other war news –"

"Well, that could have been you, children," Mrs. Harris said. "You could have been floundering around in the Atlantic hoping another ship would rescue you. Instead, you're here warm, comfortable, and well fed. You should be extra grateful that we took you in."

"I wish it *was* us on that ship," Colin said. He stared at Mr. and Mrs. Harris with a look I had never seen before. He scared me. He looked like he could kill them right then. "We'd be headed back to England, and we wouldn't have to live here with you. Lizzie, I want to go home, now."

Before I could do or say anything, Mr. Harris reached

over and grabbed Colin. He lifted him up so they were eye to eye and shook him. "So, you don't like it here? You don't like us? You don't like having to work with me every day? That's too bad, boy. Your mother sent you here and you'll stay here until the war ends. You'll work as hard as any mate I've ever had on my boat, or you'll suffer the consequences. DO YOU UNDERSTAND?"

I sat there staring up at him. I didn't think I could move. No one had ever spoken to either of us like that before. Before I realized it, I was on my feet kicking Mr. Harris's leg.

"Let him go. Let him go."

"Millie, grab her."

Mrs. Harris's arms clamped around me and dragged me away. I tried to get loose, but she was too strong.

"Who do you think you are?" she screamed in my ear. "You think you have the right to kick Mr. Harris? I'll show you."

She whacked my face and sent me across the room. I hit my head on the table and blood ran down my cheek. I tasted blood in my mouth and realized my lip was bleeding too.

Mrs. Harris stood over me, snorting. Her chest and shoulders moved up and down every time she breathed. Her fists were clenched and ready to hit me again.

Colin was still held up in the air staring at me and looking more frightened than I've ever seen. *I have to calm down before Mr. Harris starts hitting Colin. I have to let him know I'm all right.*

"Please, Mrs. Harris, please stop. I'm sorry. It's just that the news was a shock. A shock for both of us. I'm sure Colin didn't mean it. It's just that our ship was hit too and I'm sure that's what he was thinking of, isn't it

Colin? You didn't mean anything you said, did you? We just miss our mum."

I looked at Colin. *Please, Colin, please play along with me. I promise I'll get us out of here.*

Mr. Harris dropped Colin to the floor. He crawled over to me and I wrapped my arms around him.

"Go to your room. Get out of my sight," Mrs. Harris said.

Mr. Harris clicked the radio off. "Well, Millie, they were certainly a mistake. And now it seems they'll be no new children arriving here anytime soon. Still want me to bring them back on Sunday?" I heard him say as we left the room.

He is going to take us back on Sunday? I looked at Colin and squeezed his hand. Maybe we don't have to walk all the way to Halifax after all.

We stopped in the kitchen and I wet a rag to wipe the blood off my face.

"Lizzie, are you all right? I can't believe she hit you. I hate her. Are we leaving tonight? Can you walk very far?"

"I'm all right, Colin. Are you? Mr. Harris shook you pretty hard."

"I'm fine. The sea banged me around worse today than he did."

Back in our room, I tucked Colin into bed. "I think we should wait until Sunday, Colin. It'd be a lot easier than walking. Do you think you can wait? It's only two more days."

But Colin was already asleep. *I guess today was too much for a nine-year-old boy. Well, he wouldn't be able to walk very far tonight anyway, so we may as well wait until Sunday.*

Chapter 41

The next day, we woke before Mr. and Mrs. Harris. I brought in firewood, put the kettle on, and started the oatmeal. While that cooked, I set the table. Colin dressed in his torn shirt, which I had somewhat sewn together last night, and his too-big boots. He sat at the table waiting for Mr. Harris.

"Lizzie, I thought we were going to leave last night."

"I thought so too, Colin. But you were so tired you fell asleep while I was talking to you, and I didn't want to wake you. Besides, I heard Mr. Harris say he's going to take us back on Sunday. I think it might be better for us to wait. That way, we won't have to walk, and since I don't really know how to get to Halifax, we won't have to worry about getting lost. Do you think you can manage two more days on the boat?"

"I guess so. How about you? Can you manage two more days with Mrs. Harris? She hit you, Lizzie. What if she hits you again? What if she really hurts you next time?"

I reached up and felt my swollen lip. The side of my head that had hit the table throbbed.

"I'll be all right. I'll be real polite, make sure I stay out of her way, and keep my mouth shut. That's why I made sure we were up early today, so they couldn't yell at us about sleeping in."

"If you can do it, so can I."

I gave Colin a hug. We'd be all right. I knew we would.

"How sweet," Mrs. Harris said from the doorway, her arms folded across her chest. "Do you think you could break away from him long enough to get breakfast started?"

"Good morning, Mrs. Harris. The oatmeal's cooking, the kettle should boil any minute, and I have the bread ready to make toast as soon as Mr. Harris comes down."

"Humph, maybe you've learned your lesson. I'll see how the rest of the day goes. And what about you?" she said turning to face Colin. "Have you learned how to behave? Or docs Mr. Harris have to take the belt to you this time?"

"Good morning, Mrs. Harris."

Good, Colin's being real polite too. Thank you, Colin.

"I'm ready to go to work. I already have my boots on. I'm just waiting for Mr. Harris to have breakfast and leave for the day."

"Humph, well, try not to get in the way today. Mr. Harris has too much to do to play nanny to you."

"Yes, Mrs. Harris."

Mr. Harris charged into the kitchen and threw himself into his chair. "Oatmeal ready yet, missy? Or have you been standing around doing nothing, waiting for Mrs. Harris to do it all?"

"Good morning, Mr. Harris. The oatmeal's ready. Would you like some tea first?"

"No, girl. I have my tea with my toast. Pay attention, would you? It's not so hard – oatmeal, then tea and toast. Think you can remember that?"

"Yes, sir."

"Don't count on it, Tom. She has a brain the size of a pea."

I clamped my teeth together and took a deep breath. *You can do this, Lizzie. Stay calm, don't let them make you angry.* I stirred the oatmeal.

"I think the oatmeal's ready, Mrs. Harris. Would you check it, please?"

"You see what I mean, Tom? I have to watch her every minute. She's more trouble than a newborn."

Mr. Harris shook his head. "Only a little while longer, Millie. Give her a list of chores, go spend the day with Lucy or Flo. Get yourself out of the house for a while, maybe pack a picnic lunch and go up by the lighthouse while the weather's still warm."

"That sounds wonderful, Tom, but I'm not sure I trust her alone. Heaven knows what might happen. For all I know, she could burn down the house. Then where would we be?"

I can't stand it when they talk about me like I'm not even here. I have to keep telling myself only two more days, only two more days.

"Oatmeal's ready."

Mrs. Harris dished it out and I made the toast. I piled the slices on a plate, poured water into the teapot, and sat on the floor to wait until they had finished. As soon as Mr. Harris reached for his toast, I jumped up and scooped his bowl off the table and into the sink. I looked at Colin's bowl. He still had a little left, so I signaled him to finish up before Mr. Harris got mad. He shoveled the last few spoonfuls into his mouth and reached for a slice of toast. I pulled his bowl off the table and brought it over to the sink.

"Mrs. Harris, would you like me to get the eggs now, or do you want me to wait until after I've had my breakfast?"

"Did you wash their bowls yet?"

"Yes, ma'am."

"Then you may as well go get the eggs. Don't take all day about it. You have to make my toast and tea when they leave."

"Yes, ma'am."

I gave Colin a little kiss on his forehead. "Be careful today," I whispered in his ear. "Don't let anything upset you. Remember, two more days."

"What are you whispering about, missy?" Mrs. Harris asked.

"Nothing, Mrs. Harris. I'm just wishing Colin a good day of fishing."

"Wishes don't catch fish, missy. Skill does," Mr. Harris said. "Skill, not stupid mistakes. You understand, boy?"

"Yes, sir."

I ran outside to the chicken coop, happy to be out of the house even if it was only for a few minutes. I fed the chickens, collected the eggs, and was just putting the latch on the gate when Mr. Harris and Colin came out the back door.

"Have a good day," I yelled waving to them.

Mr. Harris grunted something, but Colin smiled, waved, and blew me a kiss.

"Are you done, missy?" Mrs. Harris called from the doorway.

"Yes, ma'am. There are more eggs today than yesterday."

"Probably means you missed some yesterday, that's all. Well, come on, I'm waiting for my breakfast, you know."

"Yes, ma'am." *Maybe she'll go on a picnic today if I prove to her that I can be trusted.*

I ran to the house, put the eggs on the counter, and

started to make toast. The kettle was still hot, so I made a fresh pot of tea for her too. After breakfast, I asked Mrs. Harris what my chores were for the day.

"The usual – dust the furniture, clean the washroom, wash the floors, and try to finish that mending. Do you think you can remember all that?"

"Yes, Mrs. Harris. I'm not sure I'll finish all the mending though. There's a lot to be done."

"But I see you made time to mend the boy's shirt, didn't you?"

"Yes, ma'am. He doesn't have a lot of shirts so I thought it would be better if he wore a mended one than a good one. If he keeps ripping shirts, he'll have nothing to wear to Sunday services."

"Sounds like you might be using your head for more than a hat rack today."

"Yes, ma'am."

"As soon as I finish breakfast, I want you to start the bread. Let's see how much you remember from yesterday."

"But Mrs. Harris, you didn't teach me what the ingredients are, just how to knead the dough."

"And you didn't pay attention when I was putting everything together, did you?"

"No, ma'am. I was outside collecting the eggs."

"Oh, all right, I swear my work never ends. Get the flour, yeast, sugar, and salt and I'll go through it with you one more time."

You never went through it with me before.

"Yes, ma'am."

So, we made bread. She yelled at every little mistake I made. "Too much flour, not enough sugar, too much salt, too much butter in the bowl." On and on she went

until I thought I would scream. I had to keep saying over
and over, two more days, two more days.

Chapter 42

Colin came home looking as tired as he did yesterday, but at least his shirt was still in one piece. We ate supper in our room again and he told me about his day.

He told me how they set the nets and jigged for cod. *He doesn't seem as tired as I thought he was. He sounds like he enjoyed his day today. I hope he hasn't decided he likes it here.*

"What did you do today, Lizzie?"

"The usual, cook, clean, bake bread, bring in firewood, collect eggs, make supper, wash dishes, pots, pans, and clothes. And mend Mr. Harris's pile of rags. I don't think there's an end to the mending."

"It is pretty hard to get through the day without catching your clothes on something and ripping them."

"You managed it today, I see."

"Only because Mr. Harris didn't let me do a lot today. I tried to stay out of his way, like you told me to, Lizzie. And I was polite all day, even when I wanted to call him a bloody fool."

"Colin! Your language. Just because you're working on a boat doesn't mean you get to swear like a sailor. What would Mum say if she heard you?"

Colin's chin hit his chest and he started sniffling.

"Colin, it's all right. I'm sorry. I didn't mean to yell at you. I just don't want you to pick up Mr. Harris's bad habits, like swearing. You know Mum and Grannie wouldn't like it."

"I know. I'm sorry, Lizzie. I won't do it again."

I put my arm around him and gave him a little hug.

"I didn't get a chance to tell you yesterday, Mrs. Harris got a letter telling her that an inspector will be here in a month to check up on us. I wonder what he'll say when he sees we're not here."

"I bet he'll be mad. Do you think he'll yell at them?"

"Probably."

Colin jumped up and pretended he was the inspector. He paced back and forth, hands behind his back, and shook his head. Every once in a while, he stopped in front of me, shook his finger in my face, and acted like he was yelling at me. I started laughing and couldn't stop.

"What are you two doing in there?" Mrs. Harris yelled from the kitchen.

I covered my mouth with my hands and tried to stop laughing, but Colin started imitating Mrs. Harris and that made it worse.

"Mr. Harris and I can't even hear each other talk," Mrs. Harris said pulling the curtain aside. "What's going on in here?"

Colin stood frozen in the middle of the room. His face turned red and he looked down at the floor.

"Sorry, Mrs. Harris, Colin was telling me about something that happened on our trip here. Just something funny that he and his mates did."

"I'm sure it's nothing that would interest me. In the future, I don't want to hear so much noise while we're eating supper."

"Yes, ma'am.," we both said.

"Mr. Harris and I talked it over and decided if you can behave yourselves, you can listen to the news on the radio. But if you create another disturbance like last night, you won't get another chance. Do you understand?"

"Yes, Mrs. Harris," I said, "thank you. We'll behave. We just want to hear what's going on at home."

"We'll see. Meanwhile, missy, you have dishes to

do and the kitchen to clean before you can do anything else."

She spun around and left our room.

"Come on, Colin. You can sit and talk to me while I do the dishes."

That night, we listened to the news without any problems. We heard about the battles in France, and the bombings in Liverpool and London. Nothing had changed. The war was still going on, the same as when we left home. *Would it ever end? Would we ever get to go home? I'm not sure I even want to listen to the news anymore.*

Chapter 43

When I woke up, it was still dark. But I knew it would be a beautiful day. It was Sunday. We were going back to Halifax today. I couldn't wait to see Patricia again, if she was still at Fairview. If she wasn't, Mrs. Cabot could give me her address and I could write to her. All we had to do was pick a day, meet at the train station, and go find the Colonel. *I wonder if Margaret would like to join us. Maybe I can visit her and ask. She lives in Halifax. She can't be that far away from Fairview.*

"Colin, wake up," I said shaking him. "It's Sunday."

"Huh?"

"Sunday, silly, it's Sunday. We're leaving today, remember?"

"I forgot. I've been working so hard that one day seems the same as the one before or the next one. Sorry, Lizzie."

"It's okay. Come on, get dressed. Be sure to put on your best clothes for church while I get breakfast started."

I ran outside, got some firewood, and came back in to get the oatmeal and kettle on the stove. *I hope the pastor doesn't give a long sermon. I can't wait to get started for Halifax.*

"What do you think you're doing, missy?" Mrs. Harris said.

"Oh, good morning, Mrs. Harris. I'm getting the oatmeal ready for breakfast. I hope I didn't wake you."

"It's Sunday, missy. Mr. Harris has eggs and ham on Sunday. Oatmeal's for workdays."

I can't believe it. The first thing I do today is a mistake. Oh, please don't let the rest of the day go wrong.

"I'm sorry, Mrs. Harris. You never told me that, so I figured I'd make breakfast, same as every other day."

"Maybe you should ask before you 'figure' things. No sense in wasting it. Move it to the back of the stove. You and the boy can have that today. Now go get some eggs for Mr. Harris's and my breakfast."

"Yes, ma'am." *How was I supposed to know that Sunday was different? She should have told me that last night. Calm down, Lizzie, before you break the eggs. Remember, you're leaving today.*

"Here you are, Mrs. Harris. I'll just scrub them, and they'll be all ready," I said when I came back into the kitchen with the eggs. Colin sat on the floor dressed in his best clothes, and rubbed his palms up and down his thighs.

"Colin? What's the matter? What's wrong?" I asked.

"Nothing's wrong with him, missy. Just thinks he's too special to sit on the floor. Thinks he should sit at the table. And where does he think I should sit? He probably thinks I should sit on the floor. Maybe he thinks Mr. Harris should sit on the floor too. Is that what you think, boy?"

"No, Mrs. Harris."

"Mrs. Harris, I'm sure he didn't mean anything by it. It's just that he's used to sitting at the table for breakfast, that's all. Isn't that right, Colin?"

"That's what I do every morning. I didn't know today was different."

"Of course, Sundays are different. Does Mr. Harris have eggs and ham every day? No. Do we go to church services every day? No. Do you wear your best clothes every day? No. You need to think before you act, boy."

Colin looked at her, sniffed loudly, wiped his eyes, and said, "I'm sorry, Mrs. Harris. It won't happen again."

"It certainly won't. You'll be off right after church, and good riddance to both of you."

"What do you mean, Mrs. Harris?" I asked. *I can't let her know I listened to them the other night.*

"Mr. Harris and I have decided that you're not working out, so he's going to take you back to Fairview today. As soon as you finish your breakfast, go to your room and pack your things."

I wanted to jump up and down and scream hooray, hooray, but I was afraid that might make her mad. Instead I said, "Yes, Mrs. Harris," and sat on the floor next to Colin.

"Missy, if you and the boy want breakfast, you'd better get up and dish out your oatmeal. I'm certainly not waiting on you."

"Yes, ma'am."

I scooped oatmeal into bowls for the two of us. I could hardly eat I was so excited. *Tonight, we'll be back with Patricia, and away from these two horrid people.*

Mr. Harris thundered into the kitchen and sat at the table. Mrs. Harris dished out their breakfast and they ate in silence, as usual. *I don't understand why they never talk to each other while they're eating. It's not like they don't want us to hear them. They never seem to care if we're in the room or not when they talk about us.*

Colin and I ate quickly, washed our bowls, and went to our room to pack.

"I'm so excited, Lizzie. I didn't think I'd ever want to go back to Fairview, but I really do."

"Me too. Maybe the next family who chooses us will be like the ones the CORB man told us about. Maybe they'll take us to see the mountains, and maybe we'll meet some cowboys and Indians."

Colin stared at me, his mouth hanging open.

"Aren't we going to find the Colonel? I don't want to go to another family. They may be just as horrible as these people."

"Oh, of course, Colin. I meant that we might have to wait a day or two before we can leave for the Colonel's. And maybe some family will choose us before then."

"Don't worry, Lizzie. I'll make sure no one chooses us."

What is he thinking? I can't worry about that now. The only important thing is to get back to Halifax.

"Boy, missy, let's go," Mr. Harris bellowed.

"Yes, sir," we both said.

We walked up the road to the church. I looked around at the little village. There wasn't much to see. We passed a general store, the post office, and some houses. Other people going to church walked along with Mr. and Mrs. Harris. The way they looked back at us, I knew they were talking about us. I saw some children, but when they started to run over to us, their parents grabbed them and pulled them back.

We don't have a disease. Why won't they let their children talk to us?

The sign in front of the church said "St. John's Church. Rev. A Sheppard, Rector." It was very pretty with white walls and a red roof. The tall steeple had a cross on top. I thought about our church at home. *This church is so little. It could fit into one corner of our church.* We followed the Harrises inside.

"Sit here," Mrs. Harris said, pointing to the last pew in the church. "And wait for us when the service is over."

Why can't we sit with them? Are they ashamed of us? Who cares. We're leaving right after services. That's something to be thankful for today.

A couple of boys climbed over me to sit next to Colin. *Maybe all the boys and girls sit back here, or maybe these two are just curious about who we are.*

"My name's Pete, and this is Jim. Who are you? We've never seen you here before," one boy whispered loudly.

"I'm Colin and this is my sister, Lizzie. We're living with Mr. and Mrs. Harris."

"Where are you from? You talk funny."

"No, I don't. You talk funny."

"You take that back."

"Will not."

"Oh yeah," he said raising a fist.

"Stop it," I whispered. "Do you want us to get in trouble on our last day here? All of you be quiet. You're in church, not on the street. You boys sit there quietly and listen to the pastor."

"Is she always so bossy?" Pete asked.

"Not always," Colin said grinning.

He and Pete started poking each other and soon they were giggling, whispering, and pointing to different people in the church.

"Shhh," I said to the two of them. Pete made a face which made Colin laugh. A few people turned around to stare at them.

"Colin, stop it now. Do you want to get a beating on our last day here?"

Colin took a deep breath and shook himself.

"Sorry, Lizzie, I'll stop."

But I could see that wasn't going to happen. He was having too much fun with his new friend. *Please Rev. Sheppard, make this a short service.*

Finally, after lots of angry looks and a few shushes, the service was over. Pete and Jim climbed over us and pushed past everyone to get outside. Colin was all set to join them.

"Stay right here. You heard Mrs. Harris. We have to wait for them."

"Aw, Lizzie, can't I go play with Pete and Jim for a little while?"

"No, you can't. Besides we're leaving as soon as we get back to the house. Remember?"

"I remember."

Colin pouted and folded his arms across his chest. *I feel as mean as Mrs. Harris right now, but I don't want Colin to go running off with those two boys. Knowing him, he'll only get into trouble.*

"Let's go," Mrs. Harris said as she passed our pew.

"Lovely service, Rev. Sheppard," she said stopping to greet the pastor at the door.

"And who might these two children be?" he asked.

"They're Home Children, two of the evacuees from England. We wanted to do something to help the poor little things so they're staying with us for a while."

"What a wonderful act of Christian charity. Rev. Pilkington did leave a note saying there might be some children coming here to Peggy's Cove but he wasn't sure when."

"Dear Rev. Pilkington, we do miss him so. He was a lovely man."

I stood there staring up at Mrs. Harris. *Is this the same woman who yells at me all day long? As Grannie says, 'Butter wouldn't melt in her mouth.' I wonder if she acts like this with other people? Maybe she's only mean to us.*

"And what are your names?" Rev. Sheppard asked looking past Mrs. Harris to talk to us.

"I'm Colin and this is my sister, Lizzie," Colin said before I could open my mouth. "And we're going back to Halifax today 'cause they don't want us anymore."

"Colin!" I said.

"What?"

"Reverend," Mrs. Harris said, "I'm sure the child misunderstood me this morning. I was chatting with them and wondered if they were disappointed we didn't have any children for them to play with. They seem so sad all the time. So, Tom and I thought we might take a ride up to Halifax so they could visit with some of their friends at the Fairview Home. A simple misunderstanding as you can see."

"Yes, yes, I see how a young child could have misinterpreted that. Well, children, have a pleasant day. I'll look forward to seeing you next Sunday. Maybe you can tell me about your excursion today. Good day, Mrs. Harris."

"Good day, Rev. Sheppard. Come along, children."

She put her arm around my shoulders and led me away. I grabbed Colin's hand and glared at him.

"Tom," she yelled over to Mr. Harris. He was standing a little way off the road talking to some men. "I'll take the little ones back to the house. Come along when you're finished. Remember, we promised them an excursion to Halifax today."

Mr. Harris waved over and went back to his conversation.

An excursion. Is that what she's calling it? I wonder what she'll tell the Reverend next Sunday when we're not here. Probably another big fat lie.

Chapter 44

"Damn engine. Damn truck." Mr. Harris threw his door open, went to the front of the truck, and pushed up the hood.

"Is the truck broken, Lizzie?" Colin asked.

"I hope not. This is our chance to get back to Halifax. Maybe Mr. Harris can fix it."

But I didn't think so. All I heard were sounds of metal banging against metal, and Mr. Harris swearing "damn" this or "damn" that.

He came around to the side of the truck, stuck his hand in, and turned the key. Nothing happened. He stared at us, spit on the ground, and stomped back to the house muttering and swearing the whole way.

In a few minutes, Mrs. Harris came out to the truck. "Get your bags and come back inside. Seems you won't be going to Halifax today after all."

She turned around and marched back to the house looking just as angry as Mr. Harris.

"Come on, Colin. Let's go inside and see what they plan to do with us."

Colin climbed up into the back of the truck and tossed our bags down on the ground. When we walked inside, Mr. and Mrs. Harris were sitting at the kitchen table.

"Guess you'll both be here with us until I can get the truck fixed," Mr. Harris said.

"Tom, do you think Henry can fix it today?" Mrs. Harris asked.

"Well, I certainly don't know the answer to that until I ask him, do I, Millie?"

"No, of course not, I just thought if he could work

on it right away…"

She stopped talking when Mr. Harris stood, grabbed his hat, and slammed out the back door.

"Now see what you've done," she said glaring at us. "Now Mr. Harris is mad and it's all your fault. I'm going to Mrs. Robinson's for a while to calm down. You two can amuse yourselves. Since it's Sunday, I can't have the neighbors see you work, so find something to do that won't get you into trouble, or embarrass Mr. Harris or me."

She stormed out the door and down the road.

"Lizzie, did she mean it? We can do whatever we want today?"

"I guess so."

"I want to find Pete and spend the day with him and his mates. Oh boy, a whole day to do nothing but explore and have fun. See you later."

"Wait! We have more important things to do than play games and go exploring. We have to find the road that will take us back to Halifax."

"Aw, come on, Lizzie, as soon as Mr. Harris gets that old truck fixed, he'll drive us back. That's a lot better than walking."

"And what if he doesn't get it fixed? What if it's too broken to fix? What if we have to wait weeks or months before it can be fixed? Do you want to have to go out on that boat every day and work like a slave? How long do you think you can do that? Every night you come home so tired you can hardly eat your supper. And you fall asleep as soon as you finish.

"Why do you think I waited to leave until today? Because I know you're too tired to walk to the end of the road when you come home, that's why. I thought that if Mr. Harris drove us, you could sleep the whole way. That's why I put up with Mrs. Harris calling me stupid, and useless, and lazy, so you wouldn't have to walk all the way to Halifax."

I threw myself into a chair, covered my face with my hands, and started to cry. I thought about Mum, my promise to keep Colin safe, to protect him. I thought about all my dreams of having great adventures, seeing the Rocky Mountains, meeting cowboys and Indians, walking through the pine forests, visiting the museums in the city, everything the CORB man promised us would happen. I missed Mum, Margaret, Patricia, the Colonel, and home. Oh, how I wanted to go home and be with Mum again. My sobs shook the table.

"I'm sorry, Lizzie. Please stop crying. You're right. I'm being a stupid spoiled boy. Of course, we'll go look for the road to Halifax. And we'll leave here as soon as we can. And I'll try not to be so tired anymore. I won't work as hard on the boat, that's all. What can Mr. Harris do? Throw me overboard?"

"Oh, Colin, don't even say that." I grabbed him and held him tight. "What would I do without you? How could I ever go home without you?"

"Don't worry, Lizzie. I won't let him get that mad at me. I was just kidding."

We held onto each other for a few minutes, then Colin said, "We'll never find the road unless we get out there and look for it."

I wiped my eyes and smiled at him. "Let's go."

We walked down the road, past the general store and post office. Everything was closed. There was no one around. We walked further to the church.

"Maybe the pastor's home. We could ask him," Colin said.

"What if he tells Mrs. Harris? We'll really be in trouble."

"We could make him promise not to tell. He can't break a promise. He's a pastor."

"Maybe you're right. All right, let's see if he's in the church."

I pulled on the door, but it was locked.

"Now what?" I asked.

"He must live somewhere near here. Come on. We'll go to that house and ask. There's nothing wrong with asking if we can talk to the pastor, is there?"

"I guess not."

We walked over to the closest house and knocked, but there was no answer. We went to the next house, and the next. Finally, someone said, "Can I help you?"

"Yes, ma'am," I said. "We're looking for the pastor. Does he live here?"

"You must be the two little children from England. Poor things. We all feel so sorry for you. What you must have seen over there, and what you must be going through now, I just can't imagine."

She kept wiping their hands on the dishtowel she held and shaking her head.

"Yes, ma'am. Is the pastor here?" I asked again.

"Oh, I completely forgot that's what you wanted to know. No dear, I'm afraid not. He has a few congregations he preaches to on Sunday. I'm not sure where he lives, come to think of it."

"Thank you, ma'am," I said.

"Why don't you come in and have some cookies and milk?" she asked.

"No thank you, ma'am. We have to be going."

"Well, stop by anytime. You're always welcome here."

"Thank you, ma'am," we both said.

We walked back to the road. "Why can't we go live with her?" Colin asked.

"We can't just ask people if we can live with them."

"She's a lot nicer than mean old Mrs. Harris."

"Come on, let's go down this road and see if it will take us out of town."

We followed the road up and around until we got to a fork.

"Which way?" Colin asked.

"Let's go to the right. There's a lot of houses that way. Maybe that's the main road out of town."

"It's so quiet. It's like one of the ghost towns in a film at the cinema," Colin said. "Maybe it *is* a ghost town."

He closed his eyes, put his arms out straight in front of him, and walked ahead, wailing, "Whooo, whooo."

I started laughing and he kept walking around in circles until he almost fell into the water.

"Colin! Open your eyes, the water."

He jumped away from the dock. "One more step and I'd have gone right in. Maybe the ghosts don't like me to make fun of them."

"Maybe not, come on, let's keep going."

We walked a little further up the road.

"What's that red building up on the hill, Lizzie?"

"I don't know. Maybe it's a meeting place, like a union hall, or something. Come on, let's go see."

When we got there, we tried the door, but it was locked. Colin peeked in one of the windows. "It's a classroom, Lizzie. Look, there are desks and a slate at the front behind the teacher's desk. Do you think this is where we'll go to school when summer's over?"

"Colin, we'll be gone by then. Remember?"

"Right. Sometimes I think we'll never leave here."

"Don't say that. We will. I've been thinking that maybe your idea about becoming stowaways isn't so bad."

"You mean instead of going to find the Colonel?"

"Exactly. I've thought about it a lot. We can't live with him, I don't think, not on an army base. I thought he could find a way to get us home, but maybe we shouldn't bother him at all. Maybe we should just find our own way home. What do you think?"

"I think that's a grand idea," Colin said jumping up and down and clapping his hands. "Oh Lizzie, this might be the best adventure of all. Even better than seeing cowboys, or Indians, or the mountains. When can we leave? Tonight?"

"I think we'd better make some plans before we go, if you really want to do this."

"I do, I do."

"All right, tonight I'll write to Margaret, tell her our plans, and ask if she wants to go with us."

"What about Patricia?"

"I almost forgot about Patricia. We can't leave her here, all alone. We'll bring her too, if she wants to come. I'll write to her tonight too."

"This is so exciting. I can't wait."

"You'll have to wait a little while. We have to find out when the next ship sails to England. I don't think we can wait for another ship with CORB seavacuees on it. Remember the wireless broadcast? They might not send any more children for a while. At least not until our Navy gets rid of the Jerry U-boats."

"How will we find out when a ship is sailing home?"

"I bet Margaret could find out. She lives in Halifax. I bet the Governor gets the newspaper every day. Remember at home, the news always had a list of all the ships coming in and leaving? That's how Mum knew when Uncle Joe was coming home."

"You're right. Oh, Lizzie, this is the best idea ever. I can hardly wait. And don't worry about me on the boat. I'll be careful and I won't make Mr. Harris mad. I'll just keep thinking about going home and seeing Mum again. Won't she be surprised when we show up at Hornby Castle?"

"She certainly will be. Come on, let's not worry about the road to Halifax right now. I've got letters to write."

Chapter 45

On the way back to the house, we talked about how we could sneak aboard a ship, where we could hide, how we could get food from the kitchen, and a hundred other things. Since Colin had spent most of our voyage to Canada exploring the ship and talking to the sailors and crew, he knew quite a lot about places the passengers never see.

We reached the back door still talking about our plans.

"Finally decided to come home, did you?" Mrs. Harris asked. "Where have you been? Gallivanting all over town, I suppose. And why do you want to see the pastor?"

We looked at each other. *How does she know we looked for the pastor? What else does she know?*

"Never mind, I don't really care. What I do care about is Sunday dinner. Or did you think that I should do all the work today while you two roamed the streets like you did in England? Well, think again, missy. There are vegetables to pick, chickens to feed, eggs to collect. Don't stand there staring at me like a simpleton. Go! Get to work!"

"You told us we could do whatever we want today," Colin said.

"Do I hear back talk out there, Millie?" Mr. Harris yelled from the front parlor.

"No, sir," Colin said. "I'm sorry, sir, ma'am."

"That's better. Now go," Mrs. Harris said.

We both ran out the back door to the vegetable patch.

"Colin, why did you say anything?"

"Because she's so mean. She told us to amuse ourselves. Well, we did. She didn't say we had to do chores. And I don't even know what to do. I'm always on the boat."

"Come on, I'll show you."

I brought him over to the vegetable patch, pointed out the carrots, onions, and potatoes, and went back inside to get two big bowls, one for the vegetables and one for the eggs. I heard Mr. and Mrs. Harris talking.

"… he could get it fixed by next Sunday?"

"Like I've already said, Millie, it depends on whether or not he can get into town this week."

"Here's an idea, Tom. If Henry is going into town, why can't he take the two of them back?"

"Do you want our business spread all over the village? If he takes them, we'll have to tell him why, or make up a lie, and you know I don't lie well."

"We won't lie. We'll just tell him they're useless children who didn't work out."

"That would be fine, Millie, if you hadn't already told everyone we were doing this because we felt so bad for these 'poor little war refugees.' You always have to play the martyr, don't you, Millie? Well, this time it backfired on you."

"Maybe so, but what are we going to tell everyone when we come home without them?"

"I don't know. I'm sure you'll think of something, but if Henry takes them, they'll probably tell him why we're sending them back. That wouldn't make us look like such great Christians, would it?"

Mrs. Harris didn't answer. I was afraid she'd come into the kitchen and find me there, so I tiptoed back to the door, pushed it open, and walked over to get the bowls.

"What are you doing in here?" Mrs. Harris asked

standing in the doorway with fists clenched at her hips.

"I just came back to get bowls for the vegetables and eggs."

"Well hurry up about it. We don't want to eat at midnight."

"Yes, Mrs. Harris."

I ran outside. Colin had picked the onions, potatoes, and carrots already so we only had to feed the chickens and gather the eggs. While we did that, I told him what I heard while I was inside.

"If the truck gets fixed, we'll be on our way to Halifax next Sunday, right?" he asked.

"I guess so, but I've been thinking. What if there's no ship leaving for England for another month. What will we do? If we go back to Fairview, Mr. Cabot will try to put us with another family. Maybe even one who lives further away. How will we get back to Halifax then?"

"Maybe, so what do you want to do?"

"I'm not sure. I'll write to Margaret tonight, and this week, let's both try to be really helpful. That way, maybe they'll let us stay until Margaret writes back and tells us when another ship is leaving. Then we can figure out how to get to Halifax."

"But we have been trying to be good and do everything they say. It doesn't seem to matter. They hate us as much as we hate them."

"Colin, don't say that," I whispered, quickly looking around to make sure no one was listening. "We'll take everything inside and tell them we're sorry we haven't been very helpful. I'll tell them we just didn't know about some things because we grew up in a city. But now we do, and we'll try harder to do better. Maybe they'll let us stay at least until we hear from Margaret."

"All right, we can try, I guess."

We gathered our bowls, went inside, and I apologized to Mr. and Mrs. Harris. I told them we had spent the day thinking about it and that's why we wanted to talk to the pastor – to ask him how we could be better children. Colin sniffed loudly, and I knew he was trying to stop a giggle from exploding out of his mouth. I crossed my fingers and waited for Mrs. Harris to say something.

She stood there with her arms crossed in front of her chest and listened. She squinted her eyes and bit her lower lip. *Does she believe me?* I kept moving from one foot to the other, and Colin started rubbing his palms up and down his thighs. *I wish I had my lucky shrapnel piece to hold onto, but I'm glad I buried it in my clothes. If she ever found it, I'm sure she'd throw it away.*

"I'm not sure if this is a game you're playing or not, missy. But if you're telling the truth, I'm glad to see you realize what a burden you've been to Mr. Harris and me."

"Yes, ma'am."

"All right, enough talk. Get those vegetables peeled and cut up. I'm making a roast tonight and it needs to get in the oven. You can make tea for Mr. Harris and me and bring it into the front parlor. We need to have something to eat to tide us over until supper. I brought home some spice cake Mrs. Robinson made. You can put that out with our tea."

"Spice cake! I love spice cake," Colin said.

"It's not for you, boy. And see that I don't find you've taken any, or they'll be the belt for you."

"Yes, ma'am," Colin mumbled. He shuffled over to the sink and started to wash the vegetables.

"I only wanted a little taste," Colin said looking over

his shoulder to make sure she was gone.

"Never mind, soon we'll be gone and on our way back to Mum. She'll give you all the spice cake you want."

Colin grinned at me and went back to scrubbing the vegetables while I set up the tea tray. *I hope I can make my plan work. It's certainly not the great adventure I looked forward to, but it is an adventure, of sorts, I guess.*

Chapter 46

"Mrs. Harris, may I go to the post office to post this letter?" I asked.

"What letter?"

"This one," I said holding up the envelope. "It's to my friend, Margaret."

"I think I should read it before you send it."

"But it's private. It's just to tell her my address and ask her how she likes living in Government House."

"Government House! You have a friend living in Government House. I don't believe it. How could you know anyone in Government House?"

"I do, Mrs. Harris. Margaret was on the ship with us, and we became best friends. A lady from Government House came to Fairview and chose her and some others to go live there. It's true, I swear it is."

"What does she do there?" she asked folding her arms across her chest and leaning back in her chair.

"I'm not sure. I think she's a maid-of-all-work."

"Oh, a maid? So, she's not a friend of anyone at Government House?"

"No, no, she just got picked to work there, that's all."

"I still think I should see the letter before I let you send it."

"Please, Mrs. Harris, there's nothing bad in it. I only want Margaret to know where I am so she can write and tell me what it's like to live in Halifax."

I can't let her see the letter. All our escape plans are in it. We'll both get the belt if she reads about them.

Mrs. Harris took another sip of her tea and drummed her fingers on the table. I cleared the plates, brought them to the sink, and started to wash the breakfast dishes. I took my two collection bowls out of the cupboard.

"I'll go get the eggs and feed the chickens. Do you want me to pick the vegetables now?"

Mrs. Harris sat staring out the window. I wasn't sure if she even heard me, so I decided to go ahead with my usual routine. I tucked the letter in my apron pocket and went outside. When I came back in, she was still sitting at the table. I washed the vegetables, scrubbed the eggs, and got out the dust rags, brooms, and mops I needed to clean the house.

I finished dusting and sweeping and was ready to mop the kitchen floor, but Mrs. Harris was still sitting at the table. She hadn't moved an inch. *This is scary. I wonder if she's all right. People can't die sitting up, can they?*

"Mrs. Harris, are you all right? Can I get you something? More tea?"

She shook herself, and looked at me like she didn't know who I was.

"Mrs. Harris? More tea?"

"What? No, of course not. I don't have time for more tea," she said springing up and knocking her chair over. "Why you standing there? There are chores to do, you know."

"I've done them. I brought in the vegetables and eggs, fed the chickens, dusted and swept the whole house, cleaned the bathroom, and I was going to mop the kitchen floor. I wanted to put the chairs up, but you were sitting on one."

"When did you manage all that?"

"Just now, while you were sitting here. I guess you were daydreaming."

"Don't be ridiculous. I don't daydream. I've no time for such nonsense."

"Yes, Mrs. Harris."

I mopped the floor while she checked to make sure I had really done all the morning chores.

"I'm finished with the floor. May I go to the post office now?"

"And how do you plan on paying for the stamp for your letter, missy?"

"I have some coins we got on the ship."

She scrunched her eyes and glared at me.

"Go ahead," she said. "We'll talk about this money of yours when you get back."

"Thank you, Mrs. Harris. I'll pick up your post, if there's any, while I'm there."

I ran out the door and up the road before she could say another word. *What did she mean – we'll talk about your money? That money's mine and Colin's. She can't take it. Besides, she's already getting paid to take care of us. Not that she really does. I bet the CORB people would be angry if they knew how we were treated here. If I thought we were going to stay, I'd write to them too. But we'll be gone soon, back to England and Mum.*

I posted my letter to Margaret and walked back to the house. A car came speeding up the road, and I had to jump to the side to get out of the way. *Bloody fool. I could've been hit. I wonder where he's going? He's in an awful hurry. I watched as he sped up the road and out of sight. I bet that's the road to Halifax. He wouldn't have to speed to go anyplace in this little village. So now that's two things I've accomplished today. I posted the letter to Margaret and found the road to Halifax.*

"I'm back, Mrs. Harris," I yelled as I walked into

the kitchen.

She sat at the table, staring at the paper she held.

"Mrs. Harris? Are you all right? You look so pale. Can I get you a cup of tea?"

"Sit down, child."

What's going on? She never lets me sit at the table except for our meals during the day.

"I'll make us both a cup of tea," she said.

She's *making* me *a cup of tea? What's happening?*

I sat and watched as she prepared the tea. She even put some biscuits on a plate and set it on the table.

Is she ill? Maybe she's gone barmy.

"Here you are, child. I put some extra sugar in it," she said putting the cup in front of me. "Have a cookie. I... I have some news for you."

I reached for a cookie, took a bite, and a sip of my tea.

"While you were gone, this came."

She held up the paper she was staring at when I came in.

"It's a telegram."

My stomach jumped. At home, telegrams never brought good news. When the telegraph boy bicycled down the street, everyone held their breaths until he passed their house. A telegram meant someone's husband or son had been hit or killed by Jerry. I don't have anyone fighting in the war. Does Mrs. Harris? Do they have a son? They never said anything about a son.

"I'm afraid it's terrible news. Here, you can read it for yourself." She handed me the telegram.

YOUR MUM AND GRANNIE KILLED IN AIR RAID STOP WILL WRITE LETTER EXPLAINING ALL TODAY STOP AUNTIE MAE STOP

I read the message, then read it again.

"This can't be. They can't be dead. How could they be dead? Where did you get this? It's not true. It can't be true. Why did you give me this paper? You made it up, didn't you? You hate me and want me to feel bad, so you made this up, didn't you?"

I was screaming and crying and, right then, I wanted to hurt Mrs. Harris the way she was hurting me. *How can she be so mean? How can she tell me lies like this? It's not true. I know it's not. It can't be. Mum wouldn't leave us alone like that. She wouldn't die. She just wouldn't.*

"I'm sorry, child. I know this is a great shock, but it's true. You probably saw the telegraph man drive away on your way home. He came down from Halifax with the news. I think you should go lie down for a while. You've had a terrible shock. You have to rest up so you can tell your brother the news when he gets home."

Colin! How can I tell Colin? No, no, this can't be happening. Mum dead? Grannie dead? No, I don't believe it. I can't believe it.

I realized Mrs. Harris was putting a blanket over me and tucking it in. *How did I get here? I was in the kitchen a minute ago, now I'm in bed.*

"There. You rest for a while. If you need me, I'll be right outside. Now, close your eyes."

I stared at Mrs. Harris. She smiled at me and tiptoed out of the room.

What's going on? None of this seems real. Mrs. Harris is being so nice.

I closed my eyes. I heard the whine of the bomb falling, and saw my house blown apart when it landed. Bricks and wood flew up into the air. Pieces of furniture burst apart. The chimney fell down in a cloud of dust.

Somewhere in all that rubble lay Mum and Grannie.

I woke up screaming. "No, no, no! Mum! Grannie!"

Mrs. Harris ran in, sat on the bed, and put her arms around me.

"Shhh, shush, child. It will be all right. You'll see. Everything will be all right."

Nothing will be all right ever again. How could things ever be all right? There's nothing left for us, for Colin and me. There's nowhere for us to go. No one to go home to. No home. No Mum. No Grannie. Nothing.

Chapter 47

Colin came home later that day. Mrs. Harris made me stay in bed until she saw Mr. Harris and Colin bringing the boat in. When they came into the kitchen, Mrs. Harris pulled Mr. Harris aside and whispered something to him.

"Damn," he said. The two of them went into the front parlor and left me alone with Colin.

"What's the matter, Lizzie? Your eyes are all red. Have you been crying? Did Mrs. Harris hit you? I'll show her. I'll go right in there and hit her."

"No, Colin, that's not it. Sit down. I need to tell you something."

I took the telegram out of my pocket.

"This came today from Auntie Mae."

"Oh, a letter? It's not very long. What's she say? Auntie Mae's always good for a funny story. Read it to me, Lizzie."

"Colin, it's not a letter, and it's not a funny story. It's a telegram." My voice broke as I handed him the paper.

"A telegram? Why would she send us a telegram? They're only for emergencies or to tell someone when someone else has been killed, or…"

Colin stopped talking and stared at me.

"Was Uncle Francis killed? Or Uncle Joe?"

"No, Colin, they're both fine. Read it."

I waited while Colin read the telegram. His hands shook, and a low moaning sound started.

"No-o-o-o, no-o-o-o, Lizzie, this can't be true, can it? Mum? Grannie? Dead? No, no, no."

Colin pounded his fist on the table. Sobs shook his whole body. I ran to the other side of the table, grabbed him, and held him tight. He yelled, screamed, cried, and beat his fists against me. I rubbed his back and started to cry again. I didn't think I had any tears left, but I did. It seemed like a long time before Colin stopped sobbing. He looked at me with the saddest eyes I've ever seen.

"What do we do now, Lizzie? We can't go home to Mum anymore."

"I don't know, Colin. I just don't know."

Chapter 48

The week dragged on while I waited for letters from Margaret and Auntie Mae. Mr. Harris let Colin stay home with me. As he put it, "he'd probably be more useless than ever." I didn't care what he thought. I was happy to have Colin next to me all day. We did all the chores together, and we talked about where we would go, what we would do.

"Lizzie," Colin said one day when we were feeding the chickens, "do you think we could live with Auntie Mae?"

"I don't know. Remember Mum said she had to take in a boarder."

"I know, but we could work and help out, couldn't we? You're going to be fourteen soon, and I could probably get a job with one of the grocers, or something like that. Could you write to her and ask? Please?"

"All right, but let's wait until we hear from her. Maybe she'll tell us to come home and we won't have to worry about jobs or anything at all."

I don't think that will happen, but I have to try to keep Colin's spirits up. He's so sad. I can't stand to see him looking like that.

Colin finished feeding the chickens, and I took the bowl of eggs inside.

"I'll get the vegetables," he yelled after me.

As I scrubbed the eggs clean, I watched him from the window. I could hear him humming some song he probably learned in school. *Just the idea of going home makes him so happy. I have to figure out how to do that. Where is Margaret's letter? Why hasn't she answered me yet? She must still have some of the writing paper Miss*

Julia gave us. I have to be patient, but it's so hard.

"Lizzie, here are the vegetables," Colin said.

"Huh? Oh, thanks. Guess my mind was off on other things."

"What were you thinking about? Mum and Grannie? I think about them all the time," Colin said, tears starting to spill over onto his cheeks.

I grabbed him and held him tight. "I know. I do too."

"Why didn't they go to the shelter? Why were they home? Maybe they'd both still be alive if they had gone to the shelter."

"Colin, you know how we all hated the shelters. Remember how we begged Mum to let us stay in the house during the air raids? I understand why they stayed home. I just wish they hadn't."

We both cried a little more, then I said, "Come on, we still have chores to do before Mr. Harris comes home."

"That's all right, children, go outside for a while."

Mrs. Harris stood in the doorway watching us.

"I'm sorry, Mrs. Harris," I said. "We'll get back to work."

"No, you go out and enjoy the sun for a while. I'll start supper. Walk up to the lighthouse. You've never been there, have you?"

"No, Mrs. Harris." *Why would she even ask that? She knows we're never allowed out of the house unless we get her permission. And we're never allowed to go out for a walk. She's being so nice to us it's almost creepy.*

"Thanks, Mrs. Harris. Come on, Lizzie. We always wonder what the lighthouse looks like up close."

He grabbed my hand and pulled me out the door.

"I wanted us to leave before she changed her mind.

What's going on? Why is she being nice to us?"

"Maybe because of Mum and Grannie. Tomorrow she'll probably be back to yelling at me about some stupid little thing."

"Do they ever talk about taking us back to Fairview?"

"No, and that's really strange. I'm sure they don't like us any more now than they did before. And Mr. Harris still needs a helper on his boat. Of course, now everyone in the village knows about Mum and Grannie. Maybe they're afraid it will look mean if they take us back now."

We walked through the village towards the lighthouse. Whenever someone saw us, they stopped and told us how sorry they were to hear about our mum. We thanked them and kept walking. *I wish they would all ignore us. Now they really think we're "poor little things." I can't stand the way they look at us. If they really wanted to help, they'd give us a ride back to Halifax. Well, that's a silly thought! Why would they even think we want to go back to Halifax? Margaret better write soon before I go completely barmy.*

"These rocks are massive," Colin said.

We had reached the bottom of the boulders where the lighthouse stood.

"Come on, Lizzie, let's climb up to the lighthouse," Colin said scrambling up the rocks.

Colin looked like the adventurous boy he had always been. *I'm so happy to see him smiling and looking the way he did before we came here.*

"Careful, boy," a voice said.

We both stopped and looked around. An old man sat by the side of the road watching us.

"Many a boy has been swept out to sea from those rocks."

My heart jumped. All I could think of was Peter. *No! I can't lose Colin. I'll die if I lose Colin.*

"I'll be careful," Colin said.

"You'll need to be more than careful," the old man said. "Listen to me, boy. Stay far away from the black rocks or you'll be sleeping in Davy Jones's locker tonight."

"What do you mean?" Colin asked. He walked back down to where the old man sat.

"Didn't you ever hear of Davy Jones's locker before?"

"No, sir."

"Well, the story says that a long time ago, a sailor who was rescued after he fell overboard told his mates he had seen Davy Jones himself while he was underwater. He said he had huge saucer eyes, three rows of teeth, horns and a tail, and blue smoke came out of his nostrils. He's the monster who rules over all the evil spirits in the deep sea. Sailors say they sometimes see him up on the ship's topmost masts just before a hurricane, or shipwreck, or some other disaster at sea. He's a warning to sailors of death. So, when you sleep in his locker, you're a goner, boy."

The old man's story sent a chill up and down my spine.

"That's an old fairy tale," Colin said.

"Maybe so, maybe not, but it's a fact that the black rocks are a real danger."

"Why do you call them black rocks? They look gray to me," Colin said.

"When you climb up to the top, you'll see. The

black rocks never dry. They're the ones that belong to Davy Jones. They're the ones where the ocean comes up, covers them, and Ole Davy grabs your ankle and sweeps anybody on them right back down to his locker and a watery grave."

Colin stood still as the boulders while the old man told the tale.

"Come on, Colin. Let's go back. I don't want to go up there. Remember what happened to Peter?"

"That's not the same thing," Colin said snapping out of his trance. "We'll see the wave coming and we'll be able to run away from it."

"Peter thought that too," I said.

The old man watched us arguing about whether or not we should climb up to the lighthouse.

"Seems this young man won't be satisfied until he's climbed up there to see for himself."

He pulled out a pipe, filled it, lit it, and took a puff.

"And since I'd hate to see a fine young man spending time with Ole Davy, I'll take both of you up there. I know where we can stand and watch the sea without worrying. And you can see the lighthouse too. I'll take you on a tour."

"Really? Lizzie, isn't this wonderful? A tour. Let's go."

"Wait a minute. We don't even know you. How do we know you're allowed to take us inside the lighthouse?"

I heard Colin moan, but I didn't care. *Maybe this old man's barmy. Maybe everyone in this village is barmy.*

"Fair enough, little lady. My name's Albert Massey. I'm the lighthouse keeper. If you don't believe me, you can march right back to the general store and ask."

"I believe you, Mr. Massey," Colin said. "Don't pay any attention to my sister. She worries about everything. Can we go now, Lizzie?"

Oh, Mum, what would you do? Colin is so excited. I guess it's all right. Mr. Massey seems nice.

"I guess so, but..." Before I could finish, Colin was headed back up the boulders. *Now I don't have a choice.*

"Come on, little lady. I won't let anything bad happen to either of you," the old man said, following Colin. "Wait up there, young man. I don't climb these rocks as fast as I used to."

We climbed to the lighthouse door. Mr. Massey unlocked it and let us in. There was a spiral staircase that went all the way to the top.

"Can we go up there?" Colin asked.

"We can, but let me go first. I don't want your sister worrying about you being up there all alone."

He turned and winked at me before heading up the stairs. My face felt like it was on fire. *Maybe I am acting like a mother hen, but I don't care. I have to watch out for Colin. I still have to keep my promise to Mum.*

When we reached the top, I couldn't think of a thing to say. It was beautiful.

"Lizzie, look how far you can see. And look at those waves below us. This is the most wonderful place I've ever been."

It was amazing. I felt like I was on top of the world. Mr. Massey smoked his pipe, watched us, and smiled.

He's made Colin so happy. He's as nice as the Colonel.

We walked around the top floor. He showed us how the light worked, and pointed out the buildings in the village – the general store, post office, school, community hall, and the church.

"What's the community hall?" Colin asked.

"That's a special place. That's where everyone gets together for dances, church suppers, and sometimes even a movie."

He named all the different places around the lighthouse.

"Straight ahead is Halibut Rock, over to the left is Dancing Rock."

"Dancing Rock?"

"Sure, that's where people have picnics and dances. Next to that is Pulpit Rock, then the Devil's Corner. If you go there, be very careful. Those cliffs drop off straight down to the water, and when the sea is rough, ocean sprays shoot up high into the air."

He named all the other places around the cove, Five Alley Rock, Simon's Rock, the American Pond, Clam Pond, Sheep Cliff, Black Rock, and Salmon Net Cove.

"You two see all the black rocks down there? Those are the places you should never go. Those are the places where the waves sneak up, grab you, and drag you down to Davy Jones."

Colin rubbed his palms up and down his thighs.

Good, he's nervous. He won't go near those rocks now.

"Thank you for bringing us here, Mr. Massey," I said. "You've been so kind to us, and we haven't even introduced ourselves. I'm sorry. We must seem very rude."

"No, little lady, you're not rude, just have a lot on your mind I imagine."

"I'm Colin and this is my sister, Lizzie. We're staying with Mr. and Mrs. Harris, but they don't want us anymore, and they're going to take us back to Halifax, then we're going to sneak on a ship and go back home, right, Lizzie?"

"Colin!"

"What, Lizzie? It's true, isn't it? What's the matter?"

I could kill you, that's what's the matter. What a blabbermouth.

"I apologize, Mr. Massey. Colin's a little overexcited. Sometimes he gets things wrong when he's like that. Come on, Colin, we should be getting back."

"It's all right, Lizzie," Mr. Massey said. "No need to apologize. I know Tom and Millie. They can be difficult at times."

"Could we come live with you, Mr. Massey?" Colin asked.

"Colin! Honestly Mr. Massey, I don't know what's wrong with Colin today."

I grabbed his arm and pulled him to the stairs. *I'm so mad I could throw him down the stairs.*

"Let's go, Colin. Not another word, do you hear me?"

I glared at him and pinched his arm hard.

"Ow," he yelled, "all right, I'm going. Can we come back again sometime?"

"Anytime you want. If I'm not here, look in at the general store. They always know where I am."

"Thanks, Mr. Massey. This was a swell day."

"You're welcome, Colin. I hope I see both of you again soon."

If I don't kill him before we get home.

Chapter 49

"Why are you so mad, Lizzie?"

"Because you can't go blabbing everything to everybody, that's why. What do you think will happen if Mr. Massey tells everyone what you said? If Mrs. Harris hears it, we'll get the belt for sure. And why did you tell him about sneaking on a ship? I thought we agreed we wouldn't tell anyone."

Colin shoved his hands in his pockets, kept his head down, and kicked the stones in the road.

"Morning, children," a woman called from the post office. "Been to see the lighthouse, and Albert, have you?"

"Yes, ma'am," I said.

"Bet he told you about Davy Jones, didn't he?"

"He did," Colin said. "Is it true? Does Davy Jones really grab your ankle and pull you down to his locker?"

Colin stared at her and swallowed hard.

"Well, that's what the old sailors say. So, you'd better stay away from the black rocks."

Colin rubbed his thighs and looked back to the boulders.

"But you don't have to worry about Ole Davy right now. You're safe enough here. Why don't you two come in and have some ice cream? I might just have some mail for you to take back to Millie."

"Ice cream, oh boy," Colin shouted.

"Thank you, ma'am, but we don't have any money for ice cream. We'll pick up Mrs. Harris's mail though," I said. "How did you know we're staying with Mr. and Mrs. Harris?"

"Everyone in the village knows about you two.

There are only sixty of us living here so two new children are big news. Now, how about that ice cream? Let's consider it a welcome to Peggy's Cove, okay?"

Colin's face burst into a big grin and he bolted for the door.

"Well, he's ready for some. How about you?"

"Thank you. Yes, Mrs., um, Mrs., um..."

"Mrs. Crooks, and you must be Lizzie. As I said, everyone knows everyone else's business in this village. And your little brother is Colin, isn't he?"

"Yes, Mrs. Crooks."

"We'd better get inside before Colin eats all the ice cream and doesn't save any for us."

She put her arm around my shoulder and led me inside. The only time I had been to the post office was to mail my letter to Margaret. That day, I rushed in, posted it, and ran out. I was afraid if I took too much time, Mrs. Harris would never let me go again. Today, I had a chance to look around. The post office counter was the smallest part of the shop. There were a couple of tables and chairs, a wood stove in the middle of the room, and lots of shelves with groceries, tinned meats, and supplies for fishing. There was another counter with a cash box and that's where Colin stood deciding what flavor ice cream he wanted.

"What do you mean, you've never heard of mint rhubarb? It's delicious, a real gourmet treat."

"Lou, stop teasing him," Mrs. Crooks said. "Colin, we don't have ten different flavors, no matter what Mr. Crooks said. We have vanilla, chocolate, or strawberry."

"Gee, that mint rhubarb sounded pretty good." Colin mumbled, scraping his foot along the floor.

Two men who were playing checkers at one of the

tables roared laughing.

"Lou, you're a card."

"Where do you come up with these things? Mint rhubarb?"

"Pipe down, you two," Mrs. Crooks said, "or you can find another place to waste your afternoons. And to make up for Mr. Crooks' joke, you can have two scoops, syrup, whipped cream, and a cherry, and so can Lizzie."

"Thanks Mrs. Crooks, this is the best afternoon ever," Colin said. "First the lighthouse, and now ice cream. I'm glad everyone's not as mean as –"

Colin clamped his hand over his mouth and stared at me. His face was as red as the cherries sitting on the counter.

"I mean, um, I mean," Colin stammered.

"What flavor did you say?" Mrs. Crooks asked, giving Colin a little hug.

I wish I could disappear. Why can't he keep his mouth shut? Now we'll get the belt for sure.

"And Lizzie, what flavor for you?"

I don't think I can even speak. This is turning into the worst day ever, thanks to you, Colin. Just wait until we get out of here.

"Colin's having chocolate, what would you like?" Mrs. Crooks asked again.

"I'm sorry, Mrs. Crooks. I don't think I'm very hungry."

"You don't have to be hungry to have ice cream. Now, no more nonsense, we are all going to have some aren't we, Lou?"

"Whatever you say, Mary."

"Good, I'll have strawberry, my favorite. Lizzie?"

"I guess I'll have that, too."

"Lou, you heard her. Now get to work and scoop out our ice cream, and don't be stingy with the syrup."

Mr. Crooks rolled his eyes and got three dishes down from the shelf.

"Well, this is very pleasant," said Mrs. Crooks. "What a nice change to have two visitors from England to talk to this afternoon, instead of those grumpy old men over there."

We looked over at the men playing checkers, and one of them made a face and stuck his tongue out at Mrs. Crooks. That made all of us laugh. I think it was the first time I laughed since we came to this village. We sat and talked with Mrs. Crooks while we ate our ice cream. She never called us "poor little things" or looked at us in the funny way some people in the village did.

"Colin, look at the time. We'd better get back. Mrs. Harris will be looking for me to – I mean, she'll wonder where we are."

"Do we have to go, Lizzie? It's so much fun here."

"Yes, Colin, we have to go."

"I almost forgot, there's some mail for Mrs. Harris, and for you too, Lizzie," Mrs. Crooks said.

"For me?"

"Yes, here it is. Oh my, it's from Government House. You must have some very important friends. Imagine, Lou, a letter from Government House."

Mr. Crooks grunted and went through a doorway to the store's back room.

"Government House," Colin yelled jumping up and down in his seat. "It must be from Margaret. She's our friend and she works there, and she's going to –"

I kicked him under the table. He let out a little cry, but at least he stopped talking.

"Thank you, Mrs. Crooks, thanks for everything. Come on, Colin, let's go."

I silently mouthed, "thank you," to him. He stared at me for a minute. I moved my head a little in Mrs. Crooks' direction and he finally got the hint.

"Oh, yes, thank you, Mrs. Crooks. I had a wonderful afternoon."

"You're both very welcome and I want you to come back and visit again, okay?"

"You bet," Colin said. "Come on, Lizzie, let's see what Margaret wrote."

We ran outside and up the road a little way. I stopped and carefully opened the envelope.

Dear Lizzie and Colin,

I was so happy to get your letter. I wondered where you were. I think it's terrible that Mr. Cabot sent you to live with Mr. and Mrs. Harris. They sound like monsters. You have to get away from them. I went to see Patricia on my day off and brought your letter for her to read. She cried when she read how unhappy you are. She's living with the Cabots now. It seems no one wanted to take her, all because of her leg. People are so mean. Anyway, while I was there, I spoke to Miss Burns. Do you remember her? She told me about a place, Brunswick Street United Church City Mission. Since you're going to be 14 soon, maybe they could help you. They find jobs for girls as maids, or other in-service help, and Colin could stay at the Mission all day while you work. They even serve meals and have clothes for anyone who needs them. I'm going to go there on my next day off and get some more information for you. I wish you could come here and work with me, but I asked Mrs. Collingsworth and she said she doesn't need any more help.

I know you want to leave as soon as possible, but no one knows when the ships are going to leave port. I've overheard rumors about the Empress *of Australia leaving soon, but I don't know when. Maybe you should come to Halifax, get a job, and we can work out a plan to get back to England. At least we could talk to each other about it. Letters take so long to get from me to you. Even though it's nice here at Government House, and everybody treats me well, I miss Mum and Dad and really want to go home. So, does Patricia.*

I'll write again after I go to the Mission. I miss both of you a lot.

Your friend,
Margaret

I folded the letter, put it in my pocket, and flopped down on the side of the road. Colin sat next to me, silent tears running down his face. I reached out for his hand and held it tight. *What are we going to do? Now that Mum and Grannie are gone, should we go home? Where would we go? Where would we live? Can I find a place for the two of us? A place where we'll be safe? Can I take care of Colin the way Mum took care of both of us?*

"Lizzie? Are we going to Halifax? To the Mission?"

"I don't know," I said.

Colin reached up and wiped the tears away from my cheeks. I didn't even know I was crying.

"I think we should wait until we get Auntie Mae's letter. Let's see what she says first, and let's see what Margaret writes back about the Mission. Can you wait a little longer?"

"I can if you can. I guess I'll have to go back out on the boat soon. Mr. Harris won't let me stay home with you much longer."

"I know. Is it awfully horrible work?"

"He yells at me a lot, and the work is very hard, but I'm getting better at it, I think. Right now, we're netting fish. I don't know what it will be like when we start lobstering in December."

"*December?* I'm not letting you go out in that stupid little boat in December. We'll be gone by then. And even if we aren't, you'll be in school, not fishing."

"I guess you're right. But he keeps talking about lobstering, and getting the traps ready, and things like that."

"Well, he'll have to find someone else. You have to go to school."

We sat there for a few more minutes, not talking, just thinking.

"We'd better get going," I said. "We don't want Mrs. Harris to come looking for us."

We dragged ourselves back to the house. All the day's fun seemed to disappear. I could hardly remember what the ice cream tasted like.

Chapter 50

Every day I looked for a letter from Auntie Mae. Colin was back working on the boat, and I missed having him around. Mrs. Harris wasn't as mean anymore. She still yelled at me a lot, but she had stopped calling me stupid and useless. Each night, Colin burst through the door and looked at me, but I shook my head in a silent no. He would slump off to our room, put away his gloves, and come back out to sit on the floor and wait for supper.

We listened to the news every night. Nothing seemed to change. London and Liverpool were bombed over and over. *Will there be anything left when we get back?* After the news, we went to bed. The nights were getting cold now. *Tomorrow, I'll ask Mrs. Harris for a blanket. Colin's shivering in his sleep. If he wasn't so tired every night, he'd probably never fall asleep.* I pulled him close and tried to keep him warm.

The next morning, I collected my eggs as usual. *As soon as I'm finished, I'll ask Mrs. Harris for a blanket.* I felt around one last time for any stray eggs and headed for the house. When I walked into the kitchen, I heard voices. *Guess that's Mrs. Robinson. All she does is come here and gossip, and treat me like I'm not worth anything.*

"But, Mrs. Harris, they have to go to school."

Wait a minute, that's not Mrs. Robinson. Who is it? She's talking about us, and school. I tiptoed over to the hallway so I could hear everything.

"The girl doesn't, I'm sure," Mrs. Harris said. "She's probably too old for school. I'm not sure, but I can look for the paperwork that came with her and check."

She makes me sound like something she bought that came with instructions, like the Anderson shelter.

"Would you please? I'm trying to put my roster together for the school year and I really have to know how many students I should have this year. You know school started on Tuesday, September 3rd. You should have registered your two evacuees already, but since you've made no effort to do so, I'm here to do it now. I would have come sooner, but I was only informed about them today, thanks to Mrs. Crooks."

"Mrs. Crooks should mind her own business. I see no reason why I should be responsible for their education, Miss Scott."

"When you agreed to take these children in, you also agreed to see to their education and general welfare. That includes school. Now, if you would please get their papers for me. I have a number of other families I have to see today."

I can't believe she's talking to Mrs. Harris like that. She's almost yelling at her. Wait 'til I tell Colin.

"Wait here, Miss Scott," Mrs. Harris said. I hurried back to the sink to scrub the eggs.

"When did you come in?" Mrs. Harris asked.

"A minute ago. The hens really hid the eggs today. It took me a while to make sure I got all of them."

"Humph, well don't forget the vegetables. We won't have fresh ones much longer, I'm afraid. It's getting colder already."

"Yes, ma'am, it is. Do you think we could have a blanket for our bed? It's pretty cold in there at night."

"Remind me later. Right now, I have to get your papers. Where do you keep them?"

"Why do you need them?"

"You don't need to know that, just get them."

"I think she has every right to know why," said a voice from the hall that made Mrs. Harris jump.

"Miss Scott, please go back into the parlor, I'll handle this."

"You must be Lizzie. I'm Miss Scott, the schoolteacher." She said walking into the kitchen. "Mrs. Crooks told me about you and your brother, Colin, isn't it?"

"Yes, ma'am."

"Well, Lizzie, I'm here to see about the two of you coming to school. Where's Colin? I'd like to meet him today, too."

"He's out working on the boat with Mr. Harris," I said.

"He's where? How old is he?"

"Nine."

"Mrs. Harris, I don't believe a nine-year-old is legally allowed to work, much less be on a fishing boat. We all know how dangerous that work is."

"Dangerous?" I asked. *I knew he shouldn't be out there. I knew it.*

"Miss Scott, he's not working," Mrs. Harris said. "He goes out with Mr. Harris every day for something to do. He enjoys fishing, and he gets to spend the day out on the water enjoying the fresh air and sunshine."

"That's not true," I shouted. "You know it's not, Mrs. Harris. Colin comes home so tired every night he can hardly eat his supper." *I'll get the belt for sure, but I don't care. I have to get Colin off that boat. It's not safe for him to be out there.*

"You mind your mouth, missy. I've spoken to you before about talking out of turn."

"I would very much like to hear what was she has to

say," Miss Scott said. "Maybe I'll get some straight answers. Lizzie, you and I are going for a little walk. Mrs. Harris, Lizzie can get her papers for me when we come back. Let's go, Lizzie."

Miss Scott walked over and held the back door open. I looked at her, then at Mrs. Harris. *I don't know what to do. Should I go with her? Mrs. Harris is so angry already, I'm scared. What will she do if I go? But I have to protect Colin.*

"Lizzie, I'm waiting," Miss Scott said.

"I guess you don't mind your teacher any more than you mind me," Mrs. Harris said. "Go."

I dried off my hands and ran out the door.

Chapter 51

When we got back, I could tell Mrs. Harris was still angry. *I don't care if I get the belt. We're leaving as soon as we can.*

"Lizzie, go get those papers for me," Miss Scott said.

"Yes, Miss Scott." I went to our room and dug through our bags to find our passports and birth certificates.

"Here they are, Miss Scott." I said as I walked into the kitchen. Miss Scott and Mrs. Harris stood glaring at each other. *If they were two men on the docks back home, a fight would start any minute.*

Miss Scott looked them over, pulled out a chair, sat down, and began writing in her notebook.

"Mrs. Harris," she said, "I expect to see these two children in school on Monday. If they aren't there, I'll report you to the Halifax Regional School Board. I also expect them to attend our annual picnic on Saturday, the 14th. You and Mr. Harris may also come if you choose, but the children *will* be there.

"You and Colin will enjoy it, Lizzie," she said, turning to face me. "We have a real lobster bake with corn on the cob, and ice cream. And all sorts of games. It will give you a chance to get to know the boys and girls who live here. There aren't many, of course, but maybe you'll make some friends. Well, I think that's all for now," she said closing her notebook and handing our papers back to me. "I'll expect to see you and Colin on Monday. Good day, Mrs. Harris."

Mrs. Harris didn't say anything. She just stood there like a stone.

"I said, 'good day,' Mrs. Harris," Miss Scott said.

"Good day," Mrs. Harris snarled through gritted teeth.

I wish I could disappear. I've never seen Mrs. Harris look so angry. I'll sneak into our room and put our papers away.

"Where are you going?" Mrs. Harris's voice exploded in the silent kitchen.

"I want to put our papers away."

"Be quick about it. There's work to be done around here. I've been too easy on you, letting you mope around for days. That ends *now*. And since it seems you'll be going to school next week, you'll have to get up earlier to get all your chores done before you leave. And I'll expect you back here right after school to get supper started. Is that understood?"

"Yes, ma'am."

She stormed out the door and up the road. *I guess she's going to Mrs. Robinson's to complain. Well, let her. I'm so happy were going to school next week. I'll make sure I get the breakfast on, eggs collected, chickens fed, and dishes washed before school. I can't let her keep me home, and I can't let Mr. Harris take Colin back out to sea. I can't wait for Monday.*

Chapter 52

"Ready, Colin? We don't want to be late on our first day," I yelled into our room from the kitchen.

"I'm ready."

The night before, I made Colin wash his hair and scrub off the fish smell. I washed his best shirt and shorts, my best blouse and skirt, and cleaned our shoes. *Mum would be proud of the way we look. We both look "shiny as a new shilling" as Grannie always said. I miss them both so much.*

"Lizzie? What's the matter? Aren't we going to school?"

"Of course, I was daydreaming, that's all. Come on, let's go and try not to scuff up your shoes on the way."

"I know, I know, you've told me that a million times."

"Goodbye, Mrs. Harris. We'll be back as soon as school's out. Do you want me to pick up the mail on our way home?"

I waited for her to walk from the parlor to the kitchen. "Mrs. Harris?"

"I'll get the mail," she said from the parlor. "If you go, you'll probably waste time talking to your friend, Mrs. Crooks."

"No, Mrs. Harris, I won't. I promise. I'll get the mail and leave right away."

She walked into the kitchen and glared at me.

"All right, we'll give it a try. Today will be your test. If I find out you were dawdling at the post office, I'll have Mr. Harris show you what happens to people who break their promises. Do you understand?"

"Yes, Mrs. Harris," I said, wondering how I could

get the mail and not be rude to Mrs. Crooks. *I can't worry about that now.*

Colin and I ran out the door and up the road. *School! I never thought I'd be so happy to go to school.*

We saw a few other children headed up the road towards the red schoolhouse.

"Look, Lizzie, there's Pete and Jim. Remember them?"

"Yes, I do, and you are *not* to sit near them and get in trouble the first day."

"Aw, Lizzie, can't I at least say hello?"

"Of course, but no mischief in class. I don't know if I'll see you before the end of the day, but I don't want to get a bad report about your behavior."

"All right, all right, you don't have to be so bossy."

"I'm not being bossy. I'm trying to do what Mum would do, that's all."

I'm sorry I yelled at him. Now he looks like he's about to cry. Why can't I keep my mouth shut?

"I'm sorry, Colin. I know you'll be good. You don't want to get thrown out and have to go back to working on the boat, do you?"

"NO! I'll be the best student ever, Lizzie. You just watch."

I ruffled Colin's hair, gave him a quick kiss on the cheek, grabbed his hand, and we ran the rest of the way to the schoolhouse.

Miss Scott stood at the door greeting all the students. "Hello, Lizzie. This must be Colin. I'm Miss Scott."

"Good morning, Miss Scott," we both said.

"Go right in. I'll be in as soon as everyone arrives."

Even though we had peeked in the windows the other day, I didn't realize we would all be in one room.

There were six-year-olds and teenagers inside. *What kind of school is this? How can we all learn the same things? This certainly isn't like school at home.*

"All right, children, settle down," Miss Scott said when she came into the room. She closed the door and walked to her desk. "Today, we have two new students, Lizzie and Colin. I expect all of you to help them get settled. They've traveled here all the way from England, where the King lives. Who can show me where England is on the map?"

One of the older boys raised his hand and went up to the large map posted on the wall.

"It's this tiny little country right here," he said.

"It's not tiny at all," Colin shouted.

"It is compared to our country," the boy said.

"Thomas, that's quite enough," Miss Scott said. "You're both right. England is not tiny, but it is much smaller than Canada. You may sit down, Thomas. Maybe later today, we'll have Lizzie and Colin tell us about their journey. I imagine it was quite an adventure."

Not the adventure I had hoped it would be.

I looked at Colin. He was nodding his head up and down. *I'm sure he can't wait to tell all about his adventures on the ship. I hope he leaves out the part about the Colonel letting us sample cocktails, but that's probably the first thing he'll talk about.*

The schoolroom was divided into separate areas. The little ones sat at a small table in the front right-hand corner. There was a bookcase filled with picture books, toys, blocks, dolls, crayons, pencils, and paper. Miss Scott told them to copy the letters of the alphabet "in your best handwriting." The other front corner had desks with students around Colin's age. *I hope Colin remem-*

bers to behave. He's sitting right next to Peta. She told them to read some pages from their history book about King George's coronation, and she would come back to quiz them. The back right corner of the room had students my age. There were multiplication and division problems in our textbook that we had to solve. The older teenagers sat in the back left corner. They had to read a story from their textbooks and answer all the questions at the end. *I wish I was in that group. I hate math.*

Miss Scott went from group to group checking work and giving out new assignments. *I thought all of us being in one room would be strange, but it's not. I like being in a little group like this, and I can watch Colin. I'm sure he doesn't like having me so close, but that's too bad. Now he has to behave.*

In the morning, we worked on our math and reading, my favorite subject.

"Lunch, children," Miss Scott said. "I expect you back here at one. I don't want any tardies." Everyone charged for the door. Older children grabbed little one's hands and pulled them along, or carried them.

"What do we do, Lizzie? Mrs. Harris didn't say anything about coming home for lunch."

"I know. Maybe she doesn't know about lunch. There aren't any children on our street, and she doesn't have any, so maybe she never thought about it. We'll go home and see what she says. If she's not there, I'll make lunch for us. She gives me the same thing for lunch every day, so today wouldn't be any different."

We hurried to the house. I wanted to make sure we had time to eat, clean up, and get back by one o'clock.

"Mrs. Harris, we're home for lunch," I said as we walked into the kitchen.

"She's not here," Colin said.

"Maybe she's lying down. Sometimes she does that, so be quiet."

"What's for lunch?"

"A fried egg, toast, and tea."

"That's all?"

"Yes, and don't complain or she won't let you have an egg."

We ate our lunch. I cleaned up and we raced back to school. *I wonder where she was. Maybe she had lunch with Mrs. Robinson. Guess I'll find out after school.*

We were early. Colin ran off to play with some of the boys and I had time to talk to one of the girls in my group, Kathy.

"Where are you living?" she asked.

"With Mr. and Mrs. Harris."

"Do you like it here?"

"I guess. I like it better now that I can go to school."

"You *like* school? I don't. I wish I could stay home and draw all day instead of having to solve arithmetic problems, and read about people who lived a long time ago."

"I don't like math very much either, but I love reading about anything at all. That's one thing I really miss. My mum used to take us to the library every Saturday and I'd get a whole stack of books to read. Is there a library here?"

"Are you kidding? There's nothing here. I can't wait until I'm old enough to leave. I'm going to Halifax, or maybe even Toronto to study art. I want to visit all the museums. Have you ever been to one? I went once on holiday with my aunt. She lives in Halifax. I stayed with her for a whole week and we went to the museum and even saw a play. It was wonderful. I'm going to be an artist, or maybe I'll write a play. I'm not sure yet."

"How exciting. Did you say your aunt lives in Halifax?" *Maybe I could write to her. Maybe she'd let us stay with her until I get a job, or until a ship leaves for England.*

Before Kathy could answer, Miss Scott rang a bell and everyone went inside. In the afternoon, we read about Canadian history and learned facts about Nova Scotia. There was a photograph of The Nova Scotia Museum of Fine Arts.

Kathy poked me, pointed at the picture, and whispered, "That's the museum I visited with my aunt."

"Kathy, read silently, please," Miss Scott said.

Kathy rolled her eyes and made a face. I had to pinch myself so I wouldn't laugh.

It seemed like no time had passed when Miss Scott said, "All right, children, close your books. Check the board to see whose turn it is to collect the books and put them away – *neatly*. All your chores for this week are on the board. Let's get them done quickly so everyone can go home on time."

I looked at the slate in the front of the room. Everyone had something to do: sweep, wash the board, clean erasers, sharpen pencils, wipe desks and tables, straighten bookshelves, empty wastebaskets, clean up outside. *We never had to do this back home. Everything is so different here.*

In a few minutes, all the chores were done and Miss Scott said we could leave. "I'll see you all tomorrow. Have a good night, children."

"Bye, Lizzie, see you tomorrow," Kathy shouted as she ran down the road.

"Come on, Colin, we have to go to the post office, get the mail, and get back to the house. Remember what Mrs. Harris said about breaking promises?"

"I remember. She's so mean. At least on the boat, Mr. Harris yells sometimes, but after the first couple of days, he expected me to know what to do. So now he mostly leaves me alone. Mrs. Harris orders us around all day long."

"I know, but we won't be here much longer. You know that girl, Kathy, who said goodbye at the end of the day? Her aunt lives in Halifax. I'm going to get her address, write to her, and ask if we can stay with her until I get a job, or we sneak on a ship, or we leave to find the Colonel."

"Lizzie, that's a brilliant idea."

Colin started jumping up and down, clapping his hands, and yelling, "Hurrah, hurrah!"

We ran the rest of the way to the post office.

Chapter 53

"Mrs. Harris, today is the school picnic," I said. "Are you and Mr. Harris coming?"

"Mr. Harris is working, and I haven't decided yet. In fact, I have a good mind to keep you home so you can get some work done. You haven't been doing as much as you should around here."

"But Mrs. Harris, I get all my chores done before I go to school, and I do more when I get home. Colin's even been helping in the afternoon."

"The floors haven't been scrubbed in a while, and you're falling behind on the mending."

You *could do something around here.* "I'll scrub the floors tomorrow, I promise. And I'll work on the mending every night. Please let me go to the picnic."

Mrs. Harris took a sip of her tea and stared into the cup. "I suppose if I don't, that Miss Scott will come looking for you. But see that you keep your promise, or this will be the end of picnics, and school, for you."

She can't do that. She can't keep me home from school, can she? I'll ask Miss Scott about that today.

"Thank you, Mrs. Harris. I'll get everything done, I promise."

I ran outside to collect the eggs and feed the chickens. Colin was digging around in the vegetable patch to see if there were still some potatoes or carrots there.

"Lizzie, when can we leave for the picnic?"

"As soon as we finish the chores. Find anything?"

"A few potatoes, but they don't look very good. I think the carrots are done. There doesn't seem to be anything else growing here."

"Well, bring in what you have, and wash them off.

I'll be right in."

"Mrs. Harris, we're all done with the chores," I said a little while later. "Can we leave now?"

"Go ahead. I might walk up there later if I'm not too tired from finishing up your work."

What is she talking about? I finished everything.

"All right, maybe we'll see you later. Come on, Colin."

We ran out the door and up the road.

"Do you think she'll come?" Colin asked.

"I don't know. Maybe she wants to spy on us, or make sure we don't have too much fun."

"Well, she won't stop me. Pete said this is the best day of the whole year. I can't wait."

"Remember, Colin, no trouble. Just because Pete tells you to do something doesn't mean you have to."

"I know, I know."

People from the village crowded the road to the community hall. *I guess the picnic's not only for the students.* I saw Mr. Massey and Mrs. Crooks talking to Miss Scott. All the students were here with their parents. They even brought the babies who were too young for school.

"Lizzie, over here."

I looked and saw Kathy standing with some other girls.

"Come on, we need you on our side for tug-of-war."

I ran over and grabbed hold of the rope right behind Kathy. One of the men from the village had his hand on the flag in the middle of the rope.

"Ready?" he yelled.

The two teams cheered. He blew his whistle, let the flag drop, we started pulling, and everyone started shouting.

"Pull, pull, pull!"

"Come on, girls. Don't let the boys win."

"Boys! Don't let the girls beat you."

"Almost there, a little more."

"Pull harder."

My hands hurt, my arms ached, and my legs trembled trying to tug backwards. Then – whoomph – a pile of girls fell on and around me.

"We won, we won," they shouted. "We beat the boys."

We hugged each other and jumped around in a victory dance. Of course, the boys kept saying we cheated somehow.

"I think everyone could use some cold lemonade after that effort," Mrs. Crooks said.

We ran over to the table and she gave each of us a glass. It had a chunk of ice in it. *I've never had a drink with ice in it before. But no one seems to think it's strange, so I won't say anything.*

"Wow, that's cold," I said as I took a sip.

"Of course it's cold, silly," Kathy said. "There's ice in it. You don't want to drink hot lemonade, do you?"

"No, no, not at all. I'm just not used to having ice in my drinks."

"Don't you have ice in England?"

"I guess we do, but I've never seen it in a drink."

"You're funny, Lizzie. Come on, let's go over there and see what they're doing."

We put our glasses down and ran over to a group playing blind man's bluff. I spent the rest of the day playing games, talking, and getting to know the people who lived in Peggy's Cove. I saw Colin running around with Pete and Jim and some other boys. He looked like he was really having fun. *I'm so happy we came today.* Kathy and I started to walk to the Clam Pond behind the hall when the bell rang.

"Do we have to go into studies?" I asked.

"No, silly," Kathy said. "Miss Scott wants us all to come back to the hall. I bet it's time to eat."

I was having so much fun I had forgotten all about eating. "Now that you mention it, I am a little hungry."

"I'm starving," Kathy said. "Wait 'til you see all the food. This picnic is the best day of the whole year."

We ran back. Everyone was sitting on the ground around the front of the hall.

"I hope you're all having fun today," Miss Scott said.

The whole village cheered.

"I'm so glad," she said. "Since it's starting to get dark, I think it's time to feed everyone."

Another cheer.

"All right, all right," she laughed. "Albert and Fred are over there in the pit taking care of the lobsters, potatoes, and corn on the cob. Bob is at the grill cooking up some wonderful-smelling hot dogs, and Marge and Kate are in charge of the drinks. So, grab a plate and head for your favorite. After we're finished eating, Mary and Lou Crooks will have ice cream for everyone. And of course, Albert will tell us one of his wonderful stories while we roast marshmallows. Enjoy!"

Another loud cheer went up from the crowd.

I guess all the food is good but I've never heard of some of it. I've never eaten lobster. And what is a hot dog or corn on the cob?

"Come on, Lizzie, let's get some lobster and corn on the cob," Kathy said. "After that we can get a hot dog."

"All right, I guess. I've never eaten some of these foods before, but I'll try them. The Colonel always said it was good to try new things."

"Wait a minute. You've never had lobster?"

"No."

"Or corn on the cob? Or hot dogs?"

"No and no, but I'm ready to try them."

"Oh boy, wait and see, they're the best. I'll show you how to eat them and you can tell me about this Colonel guy."

"Here you are girls, a bit of lobster and an ear of corn each."

"Thank you," I said. *An* ear *of corn?*

We found a spot on the ground, and Kathy helped me with the lobster. It was an awful lot of work to find the meat. *I hope the hot dog is easier to eat and I hope it's not really a dog. I know I could never eat a dog.*

I didn't know what to do with my "ear" of corn so I waited to see what Kathy did.

"Aren't you going to eat your corn?" she asked.

"I don't know how to. I've never had one before."

"Really? Well, it's easy, but messy. Pick up the whole ear and bite off the kernels, like this."

I watched Kathy chomp along the length of the "ear." *That doesn't look so hard.* I picked up my corn and dug in.

"I love it," I said after gulping down a massive mouthful of corn. "This may be one of the best things I've ever eaten."

"I can't believe you've never had this before, but I'm glad you like it. Now tell me about the Colonel."

I told Kathy all about him and our time on the ship.

"He sounds swell. Are you going to see him again?"

"I'd like to, but I'm not sure. It depends on how long I'll be here in Canada." *I can't tell her our plans. I don't want anyone to know them.*

"Come on, let's get a hot dog," Kathy said, "before they're all gone."

Two men were cooking over a big grill. The smoke from the fire almost made them invisible.

"Two dogs, please," Kathy said.

"Two just for you?" one of the men asked.

Kathy giggled, "No, one for me and one for Lizzie. She's never had one before, so I figured I'd order for her."

"Never had one! Well, little lady, Kathy here can show you exactly the right way to eat one, can't you?"

"I sure can. Thanks, Mr. Pierce," Kathy said balancing the two on her plate.

"Okay, here's yours," she said. She handed me a long roll. Inside was a sausage.

"I put mustard on mine. Do you want some?"

"I guess so, but where's the dog?"

Kathy looked at me and started laughing so hard she almost dropped her food.

"It's not a real dog, silly. This is called a hot dog. You really never had one?"

"No, it looks like a sausage."

"I guess it's kind of like a sausage, but it tastes different. Here, put some mustard on it."

I did what she said. She took a bite and so did I. "I love it. I don't know if I like this or the corn better."

"I'm stuffed," Kathy said when she finished her dog.

"Me too. I don't think I could eat another thing."

"Ice cream, everyone come get your ice cream before it melts," Mrs. Crooks yelled.

"Oh boy, maybe I could fit in a little more," Kathy said. "What about you?"

"I guess I could manage another spoonful or two."

We both laughed and ran over to the table where Mrs. Crooks was scooping ice cream into little bowls.

"Having fun, girls?" she asked.

"I'm having a brilliant time," I said. "This is the best day I've had since I came to Canada."

"Glad to hear it," she said.

Some of the grown-ups took the ice cream inside, but we stayed outside. It was starting to get a little chilly, but I didn't mind.

"I wish they would get the fire started," Kathy said. "It's getting cold."

"What fire?" I asked.

"The men start a big bonfire over there," she said pointing to an area behind the hall. "Once that's started, we'll roast marshmallows and Mr. Massey will tell us a story."

Guess I'll wait and see what roasted marshmallows are.

Kathy lay down and patted her stomach. "Now I'm really stuffed."

"Maybe I should look for Colin," I said. "I haven't seen him for hours. I hope he's staying out of trouble."

"I'm sure he's fine. There are too many adults around for any problems. Everyone who lives here acts like they're your mom or dad. If they see you doing something wrong, they'll stop you. Then you have to listen to them *forever*. It's easier to be good than go through that."

"It was the same way back home. All the mums yelled at us like we belonged to them."

"I guess all moms are the same, no matter where

you live."

"I guess."

I didn't want to think about mums anymore. I wanted to keep having fun and forget about why I was in Peggy's Cove and not Liverpool.

"I think they're starting to build the bonfire," I said. Kathy sat up and looked where I was pointing.

"You're right. Let's go see if we can help."

We ran over and the men said we could help bring wood from the pile behind the hall to the clearing. All the children ran back and forth with armloads of wood. I saw Colin and Pete. They were struggling with a log bigger than either of them and laughing. *I'm glad to see he's having a good time. This is a great day.*

Before long, there was a circle of wood big enough for everyone to sit around. It wasn't tall like the Guy Fawkes Day bonfires back home, but it was twice as big around.

"Everybody, grab a stick," a woman shouted. "Once you find a seat, we'll come around with the marshmallows."

"Make sure you get a stick that's pretty straight and long," Kathy said. "You don't want to get burned."

I still didn't know what she was talking about, but I followed her to a pile of twigs. Kathy picked one up, examined it, and threw it down. "Too short." One after another, she inspected the twigs and rejected them. They were too curvy, too heavy, too thick, or had something else wrong with them. I went through the pile and showed my picks to her, but she kept shaking her head no. We finally came up with two that Kathy said would be perfect. *I wish I knew what they'd be perfect for.*

"Okay, let's find a spot near Mr. Massey's stool so

you can hear his story," Kathy said.

A couple of boys were spread out in the perfect spot.

"Come on, push together," Kathy said. "You're taking up too much room. That's not fair."

The boys grumbled but moved a little. Kathy squeezed in and leaned on them until they moved some more and made room for me too.

"This is perfect," she said.

I was a little embarrassed by how we got these "perfect" seats, but it didn't bother Kathy at all. The boys stopped grumbling, so I don't think they minded that much.

"Here you are, dear," a woman said, handing me a marshmallow.

I thanked her, took the candy, and watched to see what Kathy did with hers. She pushed it onto the end of the twig.

"This is the hard part – waiting until the fire burns down enough to roast them."

"I've never done this before, either," I said.

"Really? Wow, don't worry, I'll show you what to do. The only thing you don't want to do is burn your marshmallow. They taste terrible then."

The fire was roaring now, and I was nice and warm. *I'd like to stay right here and never go back to the Harrises.*

Mr. Massey sat on a stool set at the edge of the circle, lit his pipe, and looked up at the stars. "It was a beautiful clear night, like this one, when the boy decided to go back and get the bone-handled flatware his mother loved so much, but had to leave in Scotland. His mother had described the knives, forks, and spoons a hundred times during the first year they lived in Nova Scotia. This would be his birthday present for her."

Mr. Massey told us how every night, stormy or not, the boy would leave the house and come back in the morning with one more piece – a knife, a fork, or a spoon. Finally, the set was complete. No one in the village could understand how he did this. Many people said he found a secret passage in the stars that let him travel through time and space to bring his mother a gift she loved.

When Mr. Massey finished, I looked up at the stars. No one said a word. *I wish I could find that secret passage.*

Someone started clapping, and everyone joined in.

"Doesn't he tell great stories?" Kathy asked.

"He does. He told us about Davy Jones the day we met him, and he took us on a tour of the lighthouse."

"Lucky you, he doesn't often do that."

"Looks like the fire's about perfect for roasting your marshmallows," Mr. Massey said. "Everyone ready?"

A loud cheer went up all around the bonfire. Kathy showed me how to hold my twig a little away from the fire.

"Keep turning it so it doesn't burn," she said. "I always burn my first one. I like them so much I can't wait for it to be done."

I tried to be very careful and toast mine perfectly. I saw a few of them catch fire. Some people burned one side black while the other side stayed pure white. The grown-ups had more problems than we did.

"Yours looks great," Kathy said. "Now pull it away from the fire. It'll be very hot so be careful. I usually blow on it and try to pull it off before I eat it, but some people eat it right from the stick."

I touched it and it was hot. I began to pull it off but it collapsed in my hand and a sticky white mess covered my fingers. *I've ruined it!*

"That's fine," Kathy said laughing at my shocked expression. "Lick it off your fingers. It's as good that way."

I licked my fingers and the stick. "This is delicious. It's so sweet and gooey. I love it."

By now, Kathy's fingers were also covered in a white sticky mess and she was busy licking up every last little patch.

"Ready for another, girls?" a voice behind us asked.

"You bet," Kathy said.

We had a little better luck with the next try, but it didn't really matter. They tasted wonderful whether they were in pieces or not. What a treat!

"That was fun," Kathy said.

"It sure was," I said. "I wish today would never end."

"Me too. Uh oh, here comes my mom. I think my day is going to end right now. Hi Mom, did you meet Lizzie? She's from England."

"Hello, Lizzie. Did you enjoy the picnic?"

"Yes, ma'am. This is the best day I've had since I came here."

"I'm glad, but right now, Kathy, it's time to go home. Bedtime for you and your brother. Where is he anyway? Do you see him?"

"I did, but I don't now. He's probably over there where all those boys are playing tag."

"I'll go find him. Meanwhile, your father is waiting for you at the front of the hall. He'll walk all you kids home."

"Aren't you coming?"

"No, the grown-ups are going to have a dance for a while after you children go home."

"Can't we stay? I love to dance."

"No, you cannot. You've had enough for today. You need to go home and go to bed. Now, go meet your father while I round up your brother."

"I guess that's that," Kathy said.

"I should get home too," I said. "As soon as I find Colin."

"He's probably with my brother and that whole gang over there."

"Colin," I yelled. "Colin, let's go, time to go home."

Moms and dads yelled boys' names from every direction. The girls had all stayed close to the fire, but the boys hadn't. One by one, they appeared out of the darkness into the lights of the hall. Colin and Pete were two of the last.

"There you are," I said. "Didn't you hear me calling you?"

"You're right, Colin," Pete said, "she's mad."

"What? You heard me and didn't answer me?"

"But we were in the middle of the game, and…"

"I don't want to hear it. I've been yelling for you forever."

"Well, you finally showed up," a man said.

"Yes, sir," Pete said.

"I should give you a good beating. I've been waiting *and* calling for you much too long."

"Sorry, sir. I'll go right home, and I'll take the little ones with me."

"That you will. Make sure they go right to bed. You'll have to carry Danny. He's already asleep."

"Yes, sir. See you Monday, Colin. I probably won't be at church tomorrow."

"Okay, Pete. See you."

Pete trudged off behind his dad and Colin and I started for home.

"I had a wonderful day, Lizzie. Did you?"

"Yes, I did. Did you try the corn on the cob and the hot dogs? And how about the roasted marshmallows? What was your favorite?"

"I don't know. I liked everything. Why don't we have that food back home? I'm going to write to Mum tomorrow and tell…"

He stopped talking. We both stopped walking.

"Why did she have to die, Lizzie? Why?"

"I don't know, Colin. But I'm sure she would be happy we had such a good day. Remember, she sent us here so we could be safe and have some adventures. Today was like an adventure, wasn't it?"

"Yes, Lizzie. It was a great adventure."

Chapter 54

Days became weeks and there was still no letter from Auntie Mae. I wondered if she would ever write. One day, on our way home from school, I saw Mrs. Crooks standing outside the post office waving to us.

"Lizzie, Colin, there's a letter for you. From England."

We both ran the rest of the way.

"I've been looking for you," Mrs. Crooks said. "I hope this is the letter you've been waiting for."

She handed me the thin envelope. I recognized Auntie Mae's writing.

"Open it, Lizzie. What does she say? Can we go home? Is she coming to get us? Hurry up, Lizzie."

"Be quiet, Colin. I'm hurrying but I don't want to rip it."

There was a red stamp on the envelope "Released by Censor."

"What does that mean?" Colin asked.

"I don't know," I said.

"It means someone read your letter and blacked out anything the War Office thought might help the enemy," Mrs. Crooks said.

"Why would Auntie Mae want to help Jerry?" I asked.

"No reason, dear, but the War Office is extra careful right now. I'm sure there's nothing to worry about."

I opened the letter. Nothing was blacked out.

My dearest Lizzie and Colin,
My heart aches when I think of the two of you so far away. I hated to send the telegram about your mum and Grannie, but I knew a letter would take too long to reach

you. I think of both of them every day and cry a little, as I'm sure you do.

Grannie became ill and your mum asked for a few days off to care of her. She was staying at Grannie's when the air raid started. Grannie couldn't make it to the shelter, so they both squeezed into the cubby under the stairs. They went there the night before, so I assume that's where they were when the house was hit. I was home because I had come down with the same symptoms as Grannie. Some people say I was lucky, but I don't feel that way. If I was well, I could have brought Grannie here, somehow, and we would all still be alive. But it didn't happen that way and all the wishes in the world won't change it. I feel so sorry for you, for me, for everyone who has lost someone in this terrible war.

Children, I know you must be wondering what will happen to you now. To be honest, I don't know. I can't come to get you, and I don't think your mum would want you to come back until this war is over. Even when the war ends, I'm not sure what will happen. Of course, you're welcome here, but I don't have much room. I've taken in boarders to help with the costs, and I'm sleeping in the parlor. I don't know if all three of us can fit in there, but I guess we could give it a go.

I truly believe you might be better off staying in Canada. Lizzie, you'll be 14 soon, old enough to go to work. Maybe you could find a place for you and Colin. Colin, you'll have to help Lizzie as best you can. I wish it could be different, but everything is changed now.

God bless you both, children.

Much love always,
Auntie Mae

"What does she mean, Lizzie?" Colin asked. "Doesn't she want us? Why does she think we want to stay in Canada?"

"It's not that she doesn't want us, Colin. She has no choice. There's no room for us with her. I... I don't know what to do."

"I'm so sorry," Mrs. Crooks said.

I had forgotten she was there. "It's all right," I said. "We'll figure something out. Won't we, Colin?"

"I guess," he said kicking the gravel.

I took his hand and headed home. My tear-filled eyes blurred the road and turned the village into a distorted mix of colors and shapes. *Well, that's that. As Grannie always told me, "Crying doesn't solve anything." Going back to England seems silly now. There's nothing to go back to, no home, no Mum, no anything. Maybe there's not even a Liverpool anymore.*

I looked at Colin, head down, kicking every stone on the road, "What are you thinking about?" I asked.

"I'm mad, Lizzie. I'm mad at the bloody Nazis, at Auntie Mae, and everyone and everything that sent us here."

"Don't be mad at Auntie Mae. She can't help it. She's doing the best she can. Remember, Uncle Francis is still away fighting, so she's as alone as we are right now."

"I don't care. I hate it here. I don't want to stay in Canada. I want to go home."

"We don't have a home anymore, Colin," I whispered. He stopped and stared at me.

"We're on our own now, just you and me."

Colin nodded his head. "I won't leave you, Lizzie,

I promise."

    I pulled him close. "I won't leave you either, Colin. Never."

Chapter 55

Colin and I went to school every day, did our chores, and listened to the news at night. Colin was back working on the boat on Saturdays. Sunday was the only day we had to ourselves to talk about how we could get away.

"Did you write to Margaret yet?" Colin asked.

"I did. I asked her if she had any more information about that mission. I think that's where we should go. I'll turn fourteen this week, you know, old enough to get a real job. One that pays money, and you and I can get a room somewhere. You can still go to school, I'll work, and we'll be fine."

"Do you really think so? It sounds swell, but are you sure?"

"I think so. We have to start taking care of ourselves. Mrs. Harris isn't as mean as she used to be, but she still yells at me all the time. I'm tired of her telling me I never do things right. I'm not her servant. And you shouldn't have to go out on that boat anymore. It's too dangerous. You should be able to play with Pete and Jim, not work."

"It's all right. I don't mind it that much anymore. I'm getting pretty good at netting, but I am a little worried about lobstering. Mr. Harris says we'll start that soon."

"How long can you fish? The weather's getting cold. You'll freeze out there."

"Mr. Harris says lobstering doesn't start until December, so I guess we'll fish all winter."

"Well, *he* might, but I want to be gone by then. I wish Margaret would write. Maybe I could write to the mission and ask them about a job. What do you think?"

Colin thought about it for a long time. "I don't know," he said. "Mrs. Crooks looks at all the mail. She always knows who sent us a letter, right?"

"I guess."

"If you send a letter to the mission, and they write back, she'll know about it, won't she?"

"I guess."

"And what if she tells Mrs. Harris?" Colin asked. "You know what will happen. She won't let you write any more letters to anyone. Didn't she want to read your letter to Margaret? You know she'd want to know why you're writing to a mission in Halifax."

"I hadn't thought of that. How did you get so smart?"

"Sometimes, the men talk about things when we're bringing in our catch. A lot of them say they don't tell their wives everything they do. They call them 'their little secrets.' So, I guess we better have 'our little secret' about leaving here."

I gave Colin a little hug. "'Our little secret.' I like that, and you're right. We'll wait until we hear from Margaret."

We wandered over toward the lighthouse but on the way, Colin spotted Pete.

"Hey, Pete," he yelled.

"Come on, Colin," Pete yelled back, walking down the boulders to meet us. "Old Man Frasier is already barking his nets for the season. Wanna help?"

"Barking? What's that?"

"It's great fun. You fill up a huge iron pot with water, bark from a spruce tree, wood ashes, and cutch, then…"

"What's cutch?" I asked.

"It's a special bark from a tree that grows in India. Then when the water boils and turns brown, you push the nets in and let them cook for a few hours. Then you take them out and hang them to dry on those tall poles that are down by the dock."

"Can I go, Lizzie? Do you mind?"

"No, go ahead. I'll see you back at the house. Don't be late for supper, all right?"

"Let's go, Pete," he said and they raced down the road.

Now what should I do? Maybe I'll stop by Kathy's house and see if she wants to do something.

"Hello, Lizzie," Kathy's mom said.

"Hi, is Kathy home?"

"She's in her room. Go right in. I'll bring you girls some cookies."

"Thank you."

Kathy's room was tiny, but I always felt at home. There was a crocheted afghan on her bed that we wrapped around our shoulders to keep warm. A small bookcase had some of my favorite books in it, and her dolls. Even though we were too old to play with them, sometimes we liked to fix their hair into crazy styles. She also had some games, and cards. Today, a little sister invaded our time. Since they shared the room, we couldn't kick her out. Instead, we spent a couple of hours playing Candy Land and Tiddly Winks with her.

I wanted to talk to Kathy about Auntie Mae's letter, so after our third round of Candy Land, I said, "Want to go for a walk, Kathy?"

"Sure." She jumped up, grabbed her sweater, and raced through the house. "Lizzie and I are going for a walk, Mom. We'll be back later."

Outside, I ran to catch up with her. "Why are we running?"

"So my little sister can't keep up with us. Sometimes I wish she would disappear," Kathy said, slowing down to a trot.

"I got a letter from my Auntie Mae."

Kathy stopped and looked at me. "Is she coming to get you? Did she send you tickets to go back to England?"

"No. She said she doesn't have room for us and thinks we should stay in Canada."

"Oh Lizzie, I'm sorry. I know you hoped she would do something to get you back home. But I'm glad you're staying. I finally have someone to talk to."

"What about the other girls who live here?"

"They're all either younger or older. The younger ones still play with dolls, and the older ones are only interested in boys. All they talk about is getting married."

After we passed the general store, I said, "Kathy, do you think I could write to your aunt in Halifax?"

"Why do you want to do that?"

"Well, since it looks like we'll be staying in Canada, I was thinking about going to Halifax to get a job. I thought maybe I could write to your aunt and ask if we could stay with her for a while. Maybe she could even help me get a job."

Kathy's mouth hung open and she stared at me. "What? You're leaving? You're going to get a job?"

"Shhh, be quiet. I don't want anyone to know. Promise me you won't tell. I have to get Colin and me away from here before lobstering starts. I can't let him go out to sea in the winter. I can't."

"What will I do if you leave? You're my best friend."

"If I'm living with your aunt, you could visit all the time, and we could write to one another."

"I can't go to Halifax 'all the time.' It's too far."

"If I get a job, maybe I could find a place to live.

You could come and live with us and you could go to the museum whenever you wanted. Maybe you could even go to art school."

"Mom will never let me leave home, not while there are still so many little ones to take care of. But she might let me visit. Lizzie, this is so exciting. Imagine, your own place, and a real job. It would be like a dream come true."

It scares me so much, it's more like a nightmare.

"Can I write to your aunt?"

"Sure, let's go home. I'll get her name and address for you. Imagine! Soon you'll be a real working girl. Lucky you."

I tried to smile but a thousand thoughts raced through my head. *A working girl, a place of my own, rent, food to buy, bills. Can I do this? What am I thinking? I'm only fourteen, or will be soon. Am I barmy?*

As we walked back to her house, Kathy said, "When we get home, you distract Mom. I'll have to find her address book to get my aunt's address and phone number, okay?"

I nodded, afraid to speak. The idea of being on my own flooded me with fear. Until now, it was only something I thought about. Now it was becoming real, and it terrified me.

"Okay, we'll go in and find my mom. I'll say I have to get something from my room for you for school."

"Okay," I said. I shoved my hands in my pockets so no one could see them shaking.

"Hi Mom, we're back. I forgot to get something for Lizzie that we need for school. Wait here, I'll be right back."

"Did you girls have a nice walk?" Kathy's mom asked.

"Yes, ma'am." I rocked from foot to foot. The minute hand on the clock clicked loudly. *Why is she taking so long?*

"What's the matter, Lizzie? You seem jumpy."

"Nothing, ma'am. Maybe I'm a little cold."

"Of course, you are. Where's your sweater or your jacket? It's getting too cold to go out without one. That's one thing about Nova Scotia, it gets cold early in the year, not like England I'm sure. Why I wouldn't be surprised if we had snow soon."

"Snow?!" My head snapped around to stare at her.

"Oh, yes, we often have snow in September, so we've been lucky this year. Once the winter starts in earnest around here, we're locked in until Spring."

"What do you mean?"

"Most years, there's too much snow on the roads to go anywhere. We hunker down and wait for it to melt. But don't worry, there's plenty to do. We ice skate on the pond, play hockey, build snowmen. You'll see. You'll have a lot of fun, I'm sure."

"Yes, ma'am." *Oh, no, I never thought about snow. We have to get out of here soon. We can't get stuck here all winter. Colin would have to go out on the boat. I can't let that happen. I have to talk to him today about this. Kathy, hurry up, I have to find Colin.*

"What's keeping that girl?" Mrs. Woods said. "I'll go see if I can help her find whatever it is she's looking for."

"Mrs. Woods," *I have to stall her,* "what's the hockey thing you talked about? I've never heard of it."

"Really? You don't have hockey in England? It's great fun. I bet Colin will want to join the team."

She told me all about hockey, the rules, the sticks,

the puck.

"It sounds exciting," I said.

"It is, and it's very fast. Sometimes I lose sight of the puck entirely."

"Found it!" Kathy said.

"We thought you got lost," Mrs. Woods said. "I was telling Lizzie all about hockey. They don't play it in England."

"You don't? It's fun, you'll see. Come on, I'll walk home with you and explain the assignment."

"Bye, Mrs. Woods," I said.

"Goodbye, dear. Kathy, don't take too long. I need your help with supper."

"I won't. I'll be right back."

When we got outside, Kathy said, "Boy, I thought I'd never find it. Mom had it buried in a kitchen drawer. Anyway, here's her name and address. I wrote down her phone number too. I know you can't call from here, but you can when you get to the city. You know, to let her know you're there."

"Thanks a lot, Kathy. I have to ask you something. Your mom said the roads close down when there's a lot of snow. Is that true?"

"Oh, yeah, it's true, so you'd better plan on leaving soon. We're lucky it hasn't snowed yet, but it'll start soon. The first couple of storms aren't bad, usually; but after that, it keeps snowing every day. The men try to keep the roads shoveled, but they can't shovel all the way to Halifax, so sometimes we're stuck here for a few weeks before they can get through."

"I never thought about snow. I'd better write right away. Remember, you can't tell anyone. It's our secret."

"I promise," Kathy said.

She turned and ran back home. I looked around the yard for Colin. *Maybe he's already inside. I hope so. I have to talk to him* tonight.

"There you are," Mrs. Harris said. "Thought maybe you'd run away."

I froze. "Why would you think that?"

"It's an expression, missy." She turned and looked at me. "Why you're pale as a ghost. What's the matter now? You're not getting sick, are you?"

"No, Mrs. Harris, I'm fine. Is Colin here?"

"No, he's not and he'd better show up soon. You know Mr. Harris won't stand for his supper being late."

"Yes, ma'am. Colin went with Pete to see Mr. Frasier bark his nets."

"Oh, so that's where they all are. Well, I'm sure Mr. Harris is there too, so they'll probably come home together. And you'd better see to the chickens."

"Yes, ma'am." I went outside to collect the eggs and feed the chickens. *Why did Colin have to take off today? I need to talk to him.*

I headed back to the house as Mr. Harris and Colin came into the yard. They were actually talking to each other. *Didn't think I'd ever see Mr. Harris and Colin having a real conversation. Too bad it couldn't have happened sooner. Maybe Colin wouldn't hate everything so much if it had.*

"Lizzie, you should have been there," Colin yelled to me. "It was a lot of work, but it was fun too. Right, Mr. Harris?"

"I guess the first time you bark nets, it's fun. After that it's work," he said as he went into the kitchen.

"Colin, we have to talk – tonight. I found out a few things that might change our plans. After supper, you say you want to show me the nets, or something, all right?"

"Sure, but you're being very mysterious. Is everything all right?"

"I *think* so. I'll tell you tonight."

Chapter 56

That night we walked along the boulders and I told Colin about the snow, the closed roads, and Kathy's aunt.

"Do you think she'll let us stay with her?" he asked.

"I think she might, maybe for a day or two, until we can find a room."

"When do you want to leave?"

"As soon as possible. I'll write to her tonight and tell her we're coming. I think we should leave next Sunday, before it starts to snow. That's the only day we have when we don't have to be somewhere, like school."

"All right, I guess so. I'm a little scared, but it's like Mum said, it will be a great adventure. Won't it?"

"It will be. We'll be fine. I know we will." *I hope we will.*

That week was the same as all the others. *Nothing changes around here. Even supper is the same every night – fish stew. When we get to Halifax, I'm never eating fish stew again.*

On Friday night, Mrs. Harris stood looking out the kitchen window. "Well, it's here, the first good snowfall."

Oh no, it can't be. We can't lose our chance to leave, not when we're so close.

"Looks like a real nor'easter," she said.

"What's that?" I asked.

"Storms that come up from the southwest. They're usually bad ones, lots of wind and heavy wet snow. The kind that closes down whole villages and towns. You should be thankful you have a nice warm home in weather like this. I wouldn't want to be out there tonight."

"Yes, ma'am."

We ate supper in silence. I could barely swallow my food. *Maybe she's wrong, maybe it won't be so bad, maybe the roads will be fine by Sunday.*

After supper, Colin and I were washing the dishes when I heard Mrs. Harris yell, "Are you crazy? You're *not* going out there in this weather, Tom. You know better. Only a fool would do that."

"Millie, *you* don't tell me what to do. You know that. I make the decisions in this house. This weather will stir things up. The catch will be twice as good, and we need that to make our quota. How do you think we're going to get by without our bounty? Answer that for me. You can't because you know I'm right. I've said all I'm going to say on the matter. The boy and I will leave at dawn tomorrow."

Mr. Harris stomped out of the parlor and slammed the bedroom door. Colin and I looked at each other. I put my finger to my lips and we finished the dishes.

"There'll be no radio tonight," Mrs. Harris said coming into the kitchen. "Go to bed. Boy, you and Mr. Harris will go out tomorrow as usual."

"But Mrs. Harris, the storm," I said. "Isn't it too dangerous?"

"No backtalk, missy. Mr. Harris knows what he's doing. If he says it's fine, it's fine."

She turned and walked down the hall to the parlor. We put the last of the dishes away and went to our room.

"Colin, I think we should leave tomorrow before they get up."

"But Lizzie, it'll still be dark, and the roads will be covered with snow. No one's going to shovel in the dark."

"But I don't want you to go out tomorrow. Maybe

you could make believe you're sick."

"That wouldn't work and you know it. Mr. Harris made me go out even when I *was* really sick, remember?"

"Promise me you'll be extra careful."

"I will, don't worry. You'll see, I'll be fine and we'll leave on Sunday, like we planned."

We climbed into bed. Colin fell asleep right away. I lay there staring at the ceiling. *Why did it have to start snowing today? Why couldn't it wait one more week, or even one more day?*

The next morning, breakfast was quieter than usual. Mrs. Harris looked like she hadn't slept at all. Mr. Harris jammed his spoon into his oatmeal so hard I thought he would break the bowl. Not even halfway through, he said, "Ready, boy?"

"Yes, sir," Colin said. He gulped another spoonful and they left.

"No," I yelled. "I'm not going to let Colin go."

"*You*, missy, have nothing to say about this," Mr. Harris said.

He pushed Colin out the door. I started to go after them, but Mrs. Harris grabbed me and held me back.

"Foolhardy man," Mrs. Harris mumbled. "Stubborn as a mule. Never can admit he's wrong. Serve him right if the boat's frozen at the dock."

I was afraid I would scream if I said anything, so I cleared the table, put the dishes in the sink, and started our breakfast.

"I don't want anything to eat, just tea," Mrs. Harris said. She left the kitchen and walked into the parlor.

I'm not hungry either but I'll make our breakfasts and put them in my pocket for our trip tomorrow.

"Here's your tea, Mrs. Harris."

She brushed the tears off her cheeks before she turned to face me. "Put it on the table. This is going to be a long day."

"Mrs. Harris, do you have boots I can wear to go feed the chickens?"

"There should be some in the pantry. Look around, take whatever you need."

I found an old pair of boots that were too big, but I stuffed some rags in the toes and left to get the eggs. I stepped off the porch and sank into two feet of snow. It came up over the top of the boots and filled in all the empty spaces.

"That's cold," I yelled. *How am I going to get the eggs, feed the chickens, and get back to the house before my feet freeze? I'm sure Mr. Harris and Colin will be back any minute. They can't go out in this weather.*

Somehow, I managed to get my chores done, but my feet were numb by the time I got back inside. I pulled off my boots and rubbed my feet. *I've never been this cold before. I can't feel my toes.*

"Tuck your feet under your bottom. That's the best way to warm them up," Mrs. Harris, said coming into the kitchen with her teacup. "Stay there, I'll make you a cup of tea."

"Thank you." *She really must be upset if she's making me a cup of tea.*

In a little while, I could feel my toes again. The hot tea helped warm me. *I guess I won't freeze to death after all.*

The day was cold but sunny. When I looked outside, the sun bounced off the snow and blinded me. I heard children yelling and screaming, having fun in this first snow of winter. But Colin and Mr. Harris didn't come back. They had gone out to sea.

Mrs. Harris paced around the house all morning. Finally, she said she was going to Mrs. Robinson's house and would be back later. I was glad to be left alone. I went to our room and packed our bags. I stuck my lucky shrapnel piece in my pocket. I wanted everything to be ready for the morning. Our plan was to leave for church and on the way, say we needed to use the privy. When we got back to the house, we'd grab our bags. By then, everyone would be inside the church and we could hide our bags behind some bushes. That afternoon, we'd get them and head for Halifax. By the time the Harrises realized we were missing, we'd be long gone. Even if they cared enough to look for us, it would be hours after we left and it would be dark. It was a perfect plan.

"Supper started?" I jumped at the sound. I had been going over our plans in my mind and never heard the door open.

"Yes, Mrs. Harris."

"Good. I imagine Mr. Harris will be hungry when he finally does get home. Fool man."

She fiddled with the pots on the stove then sat at the table. "Guess we could both have a cup of tea while we wait."

"Yes, Mrs. Harris." I made the tea and sat across from her. She picked at the tablecloth and her sweater, got up, walked over to the window, and stood there.

"It's dark already. They should be here any minute now."

I didn't know what to say so I sat quietly, drank my tea, and rubbed my fingers along my lucky shrapnel.

"They should have been home by now."

Her words hit me like someone had punched me in the stomach.

"They should have been home by now," she said again. "I knew he shouldn't have gone out today."

"Mrs. Harris, what are you saying? Do you think something's happened to them?"

"I'm going down to the dock. Maybe someone's seen them."

"I'm going too."

"All right. It's cold. Wear whatever will keep you warm."

I looked around, but I didn't really have winter clothes. We didn't think we'd be here that long.

"Here," Mrs. Harris said. She handed me a heavy sweater, knit hat, mittens, and scarf. I bundled up and we left for the dock. The road had been shoveled so my feet stayed dry.

When we got to the dock, a terrible feeling crept inside me. Once again, I felt like I couldn't breathe. My heart raced. I had never seen the sea look so angry before. I had seen storms in Liverpool when the water washed up over the docks and flooded the streets. I had seen storms in the Atlantic on our trip here. I thought about the storm that snatched Peter. This was even worse than that. The waves crashed upon the rocks one after the other without a minute's break between them. The normally black sea was white with wind blowing it into armies of waves battling each other. And somewhere out there in that tempest was my little brother.

"They're gone, aren't they?" I barely whispered.

"Tom, where are you?" Mrs. Harris screamed into the wind.

I hardly heard her speak. The roar of the water was

the only sound on that dock.

We stood there for hours. I was frozen to the bone, but I didn't care. I'd stay there forever if it would bring Colin back to me.

"Let's go," Mrs. Harris said pulling me from the dock.

"No. I'm staying right here until Colin comes back," I yelled, jerking my arm away.

"That won't do any good. You can't help him by standing here. We'll stop at a few houses and ask the men to get a search party together. They'll go out at first light. That's the best we can do. It won't help anyone if you get swept away. Now, let's go."

I let her tug me along. I knew what she said made sense, but I didn't want to leave. What if they came back and were too exhausted to walk home? What if they were hurt and couldn't tie up the boat?

We trudged along stopping at every house. Each time, the men said they would go out in the morning to look for them. Each time, my hopes drifted further away. Each man's eyes told me what I didn't want to know.

We sat at the kitchen table, drank tea, and waited for morning. As soon as the sun started to lighten the sky, we went back to the dock. I didn't expect to find anything, and I didn't. The sea was a little calmer, so I held onto the hope that they made it through the storm and would be able to sail back today.

One by one, men from the village appeared. They nodded to us and got in their boats. We watched them leave and waited.

Hours went by. One by one, they returned. Each man came over and said the same thing, "I'm sorry, no sign of them or the boat."

We waited until the last boat pulled in. The man tied up his boat and walked over to us.

"I saw this floating on the water, Millie. I'm pretty sure it's Tom's."

He held out a piece of wood that had some letters on it, the boat's name. Mrs. Harris looked at it, took it from him, and held it to her chest.

"Thank you, Frank. You're right. It's Tom's."

"I'm so sorry, Millie, and to you too," he said looking at me. "Your brother was becoming a first-rate fisherman. You should be proud of him."

"Thank you," I mumbled.

Proud of him? Proud of him? He's gone. How can I be proud of that?

Mrs. Harris rubbed her fingers across the wood. We stood there for a while longer.

"Let's go home," she said.

When we got to the house, the kitchen was filled with women, cooking, baking, making tea. They pulled our cold clothes off, wrapped us in warm blankets, and brought us into the parlor. They gave us hot tea with plenty of sugar and warm muffins, rubbed our cold feet, and told us everything would be all right.

"Think there's any possibility they survived?" I overheard one of the women in the kitchen ask.

"Trudy, you know better. They'd die from the cold in minutes. That sea is cruel and unforgiving."

I listened to the women and knew nothing would be all right for me ever again. Colin was gone. The sea swallowed him up, like it had swallowed Peter. I'd never see him again. I'd never hear him laugh again. He'd never grow up.

The rest of the day, somehow, went by. I was numb,

but not from the cold. Someone gave me a bowl of soup, and when they realized I wasn't going to eat it, they fed me like a baby. At last, everyone left to go home to their families and we were all alone. Now I was really alone.

"I think we should both go to bed," Mrs. Harris said. "It's been an exhausting day. I don't know if either of us will sleep, but we need to rest."

"All right," I said. "I'll see you in the morning." I went to my room, our room, and saw our bags all packed and ready to go. *One day, one day has turned my whole life upside down. Oh Colin, what am I going to do without you?* My body exploded. My voice made a sound I had never heard before, a deep sound from the pit of my soul. I cried harder than I ever had before. I threw anything I could grab. I pulled my hair. I fell to the floor, exhausted.

I woke the next morning in my bed. I don't know how I got there, but I did know one thing. I knew that Colin would want me to keep our plans. He would want me to leave here and go to Halifax. He would want me to go on, and live, and find a way to be strong. I knew all this wouldn't happen anytime soon, but I knew he would want me to try.

"Mrs. Harris," I said walking into the kitchen. "I turned fourteen today. I've decided to go to Halifax and get a job. It's something Colin and I planned to do, and I know he would want me to keep those plans."

"I won't stop you," Mrs. Harris said. "Where will you go in Halifax?"

"There's a mission my friend Margaret told me about. I'll go there. Kathy's aunt lives in Halifax too. I'm going to call her and see if she can help."

"Seems you have all your plans in place. So I guess

it really doesn't matter what your letter says after all."

"What letter?"

"This one."

Mrs. Harris opened a drawer, reached in, and pulled out a letter. She held it in her hand and said, "Return address is from Government House. Must be from that little maid you know there. But since you have all your plans made, guess you don't need to know what she has to say."

"What? Give me that letter. When did this come? You had no right to keep it. Mrs. Harris, you are the meanest person I've ever met. Yesterday I felt sorry for you but not anymore."

I grabbed the letter out of her hand and shoved it into my pocket. I didn't want to read it in front of her.

"Take it. I don't care what you do, or where you go. But just out of curiosity, how do you plan on getting to Halifax? Walking? It's pretty far, you know."

"I've already spoken to Mr. Isnor. He said I could ride in his mail cart anytime I wanted to."

"Sneaky, aren't you? When did you have time to talk to him?"

"That doesn't matter. I'm going today. I'll get my bag and leave. I'd be better off sleeping in the streets than I have been here."

"You ungrateful brat."

"No, Mrs. Harris, I have nothing to be grateful for. You never gave me any reason to thank you."

I got my bag, and Colin's. *I won't leave his things here.* I walked up the road to the post office. *I can wait for Mr. Isnor to come with the mail. I still have enough money from the coins people threw at us when we came here to pay him.*

Mr. Crooks had cleared off the bench in front of the store. I sat and reached in my pocket for Margaret's letter. My fingers brushed against the piece of shrapnel.

Dear Lizzie and Colin,

[How will I ever explain what happened to Colin? I don't know if I can.]

I have some news. My roommate's mum has turned very sick. None of us know exactly what's wrong, but Annie had to go home to take care of her. Of course, that's terrible, but now there's an open position here. I asked Mrs. Collingsworth if you could come here to work. I told her about the Harrises. She was very upset when she read your letter. I hope you don't mind that I showed it to her. Anyway, she said yes and told me to write to you straight away. She's even going to find something for Colin. I don't know what that will be, but she's very kind, and I'm sure it will be better than fishing on that old, smelly boat.

[Oh, why couldn't I have gotten this letter sooner! If Mrs. Harris had given it to me right away, Colin would probably still be alive. I'll never forgive her.]

One more thing, the Colonel is coming to Halifax! He's going to be here for a month while the troops get ready to go overseas. I've already told Patricia. She can't wait to meet him.

Lizzie, you have to get here as quickly as you can. I can't wait to see you and Colin and tell you all about what's happened since we were together. Patricia is so

excited about all of us being back together. I'll look for
you every day.

> *Your best friend,*
> *Margaret*

I finished the letter, tears running down my face. I thought about Colin, and could almost hear him say, "It's going to be another adventure, isn't it, Lizzie? This one will be the best of all, I know it."

Yes, Colin, it will be. I've survived bombings, a torpedo attack, and the deaths of the three most important people in the world to me, Mum, Grannie, and you. I will make this the best and biggest adventure of them all. I promise.

Author's Notes and Acknowledgements

A work of historical fiction, such as *Promises,* necessitates myriad hours of research in order to convey both the atmosphere and reality of the time period while creating characters who are believable. Needless to say, this cannot be accomplished without the help of a small army of people, most of whom I have never met. But their stories, presented in books, newspaper articles, interview recordings, and videos allowed me to enter their worlds and extrapolate situations and events which I could incorporate into my story.

While Lizzie and Colin, and most of the other characters in *Promises,* are purely fictional, the ship that carried them to Canada, the S.S. *Oronsay,* was an actual ship used for seavacuee transport. The Children's Overseas Reception Board (CORB) was also quite real. The British governmental agency was established on June 7, 1940. Both before and during World War II, around 14,000 children emigrated from Britain to an overseas location. Presumably, this was a temporary exile; however, for many it became permanent. Prior to CORB's formation, over 11,000 children had been evacuated for their safety by private enterprises. Some of these agencies had been sending children to British colonies since 1869. Most of the children sent abroad prior to 1940 were considered undesirables. They were orphaned and/ or homeless children who populated the industrial cities of England. Many were victims of the Irish Famine of 1845-49 and had traveled to England to seek work. (In the 1800's, it was common for children as young as seven years old to work all day in factories or mills.) As the destitute population grew in England, philanthropists and evangelists set up shelters to accommodate them. However, as their numbers increased, the idea of sending them to Canada and other colonies grew.

Children who had grown up knowing nothing other than city life were shipped to farms in Canada, Australia, New Zealand, South Africa, and other colonies. There the "host family" expected them to assume chores, of which they had no experience or knowledge. This random settlement of the children continued through World War II. The evicted child became known as a "Home Child" in Canada and endured all the stigmas associated with that appellation. Additionally, the children were often subjected to extremely harsh, often cruel, physical and mental treatment, and abuse. While the organizations who supervised these emigrations believed they were offering the children a better life, they did not have the resources to monitor their living conditions after placement.

Another factor that contributed to the continued exile of children prior to World War II was the concept of imperialism. By sending young British citizens to overseas colonies, the theories of nationalism could be re-introduced to the native populations, thereby further cementing Britain's domination. After World War I, there was also a demand for cheap labor in the British colonies. Therefore, the groundwork had been set for a mass emigration of children during the Second World War. Unfortunately, this exportation did not stop with the end of the war. It continued as late as 1967. Altogether, approximately 150,000 children were exiled to British colonies.

Although children were sent to Nova Scotia during World War II, I have not found any records of seavacuees in Peggy's Cove. The selection of that setting was purely fictional on my part. But Peggy's Cove does exist, a place I've visited many times with my family and have warm memories of days spent there. It is a picturesque fishing village, filled with warm and friendly residents, situated outside the more populated areas of Halifax and Lunenburg. I would be remiss if I did not thank the people of the village for all their graciousness and willingness to answer questions and provide information that helped me see the world Lizzie and Colin lived in, for not much has changed in this village of approximately thirty-one year-round residents since the 1940's. I want to extend sincere thanks to the descendant of Lou and Mary Crooks (Peggy's Cove's Postmasters in real life and in *Promises*), Roger Crooks and his wife, Sheila, who invited me into their home and shared newspaper clippings and stories about Lou, and life in Peggy's Cove. I also want to thank Peter Richardson, owner of the Breakwater Inn, and Susan and Stewart, who made my stay so pleasant and introduced me to many of the residents of the village. Susan Casey, the Principal of East St. Margaret's Consolidated School, also spent time telling me about the history of the school and shared artifacts from the original one-room schoolhouse, which still stands in the village, although it is no longer used for that purpose. And lastly, a sincere thank you to the Sou'wester Gift and Restaurant, my go-to place for a great meal.

I also want to thank my beta readers, especially Terry Scaglione and Barb Sinopoli. Your encouragement and belief in the story carried me through the tough years of research, writing, and editing. I couldn't have done it without you. I also want to thank my writing groups in Glastonbury, and Enfield, Connecticut for their critiques and encouragement. Your help was invaluable. As was that of my indefatigable editors at Waldorf Publishing, including Tiffany Maloney-Rames, Debbie Burke, Carol McCrow, Elisabeth Pennella, and Nichole Schack; my designer, Baris Celik; and my publisher, Barbara Terry.

I began this story because of a documentary I saw on PBS, *Lost Children of the Empire*. For about three years, that film haunted me until I finally decided I had to breathe life into Lizzie and Colin, and let her tell you what life was like as a seavacuee to whom some promises were mere words, as she found out.

You can read more about the experiences of these children in *Lost Children of the Empire* by Philip Bean and Joy Melville, *Children of the Doomed Voyage* by Janet Menzies, *Miracles on the Water* by Tom Nagorski, *The Little Immigrants* by Kenneth Bagnell, *New Lives for Old* by Roger Kershaw and Janet Sacks, *See You After the Duration* by Michael Henderson, *The Guest Children* by Geoffrey Bilson, and *Nation Builders* by Gail H. Corbett. Younger readers might also be interested in *The Guests of War Trilogy (The Sky Is Falling, Looking at the Moon, The Lights Go On Again)* by Kit Pearson. This is a partial list of the books I consulted in writing *Promises*. There are many more well-documented accounts of British children's experiences in foreign countries as well as what their lives were like in England in the 1930's and 40's. For this information, I would recommend *Bombs and Bunting* by Sue Wilkinson, and *The War That Saved My Life* by Kimberly Brubaker Bradley for younger readers, and *Liverpool's Children in the Second World War* by Pamela Russell for adults.

Author Bio

Eileen Joyce Donovan grew up in New York City where she worked in advertising as a copy/contact Account Executive. She obtained her MA in English from Northern Arizona University and went on to teach writing in colleges in Arizona, North Carolina, and New Jersey. She currently lives in upstate New York where she is working on an historical novel about three Irish American sisters struggling to find their place amidst their own personal turmoil and changing morals of the 20th Century's Gilded Age in New York City.

CPSIA information can be obtained
at www.ICGtesting.com
Printed in the USA
FSHW020313160719
60018FS